Angel Mountain

Angel Mountain

CHRISTINE SUNDERLAND

RESOURCE *Publications* · Eugene, Oregon

ANGEL MOUNTAIN

All Scriptures are from the King James Version, except for those referenced in the 1928 edition of the Episcopal Book of Common Prayer (New York: Oxford University Press, 1928)

Resource Publications
An Imprint of Wipf and Stock Publishers
199 W. 8th Ave., Suite 3
Eugene, OR 97401

www.wipfandstock.com

PAPERBACK ISBN: 978-1-7252-5980-5
HARDCOVER ISBN: 978-1-7252-5981-2
EBOOK ISBN: 978-1-7252-5982-9

Manufactured in the U.S.A.   04/10/20

In the beginning God created the heaven and the earth.
And the earth was without form, and void; and darkness was upon the face of
the deep. And the Spirit of God moved upon the face of the waters.

—GENESIS 1:1–2

And God shall wipe away all tears from their eyes; and there shall be no more
death, neither sorrow, nor crying, neither shall there be any more pain . . .
Behold, I make all things new . . . I am Alpha and Omega, the beginning and the
end. I will give unto him that is athirst of the fountain of the water of life freely.

—REVELATION 21:4–6

We hold these truths to be self-evident, that all men are created equal, that
they are endowed by their Creator with certain unalienable Rights, that among
these are Life, Liberty and the pursuit of Happiness.

—UNITED STATES DECLARATION OF INDEPENDENCE, JULY 4, 1776

Bless, O Father, these gifts to our use and us to thy service . . .
Give us grateful hearts . . . and make us mindful of the needs of others;
through Jesus Christ our Lord.

—ANGLICAN GRACE BEFORE MEALS,
AMERICAN 1928 *BOOK OF COMMON PRAYER*, 600.

Yes, we'll gather at the river,
The beautiful, the beautiful river;
Gather with the saints at the river
That flows by the throne of God.

—ROBERT LOWRY (1826–1899)

Contents

Acknowledgements

I wish to acknowledge with thanksgiving:

The many friends, family, and clergy who encouraged me in the writing of this work, especially those who worship at Saint Joseph's Collegiate Chapel in Berkeley.

Father Seraphim and his wife, Vicki, who live lives of prayer in the Kentucky hills and who read a late draft, approving my depiction of the hermit Abram and suggesting a few phrase changes for greater accuracy.

The Rev. Dr. Paul Russell, Lecturer in Eschatology and former Dean of Saint Joseph's Seminary, Berkeley, who read a late draft with regards to the theology of Heaven, giving me added confidence that there is truth in my fiction.

The lovely ladies of Curves, Walnut Creek, for their support and friendship as we exercise together, giving me invaluable ideas that found their way into the story of *Angel Mountain*.

Wipf and Stock Publishers, who graciously accepted *Angel Mountain* for publication, written by a relatively unknown author.

Editor Margaret Lucke, who once again has given me invaluable suggestions regarding character and plot, and offered changes in phrasing, punctuation, and grammar.

My dear husband, Harry, who reads my drafts, cheers me on, and provides me safety and sanity, as we travel the path of life and love together, to one day gather at the river that runs by the throne of God.

The saints, angels, and all the glorious company of Heaven, who hearken to my prayers, nudging me daily toward truth, beauty, and joy.

The following authors inspired me to write *Angel Mountain*, and I am greatly in their debt:

On the Holocaust and the Jewish experience in the West:

> Andrew Klavan, *The Great Good Thing: A Secular Jew Comes to Faith in Christ* (2016)

> Melanie Phillips, *The World Turned Upside Down: The Global Battle Over God, Truth, and Power* (2010)

> Yolanda Willis, *A Hidden Child in Greece: Rescue in the Holocaust* (2017)

On creation, evolution, and Intelligent Design; faith and science:

> Francis S. Collins, *The Language of God: A Scientist Presents Evidence for Belief* (2006)

> Phillip E. Johnson, *Darwin on Trial* (1991)

> Eric Metaxis, *Miracles* (2014)

> Steven C. Meyer, *Signature in the Cell: DNA and the Evidence for Intelligent Design* (2009)

On Heaven:

> Francis J. Hall, *Eschatology* (1922)

> E. L. Mascall, *Grace and Glory* (1961)

Prologue

Dawn edged over Angel Mountain in this Year of Our Lord 2018.

It slipped slowly, lighting the darkness.

It landed lightly on grass and leaf and limb, on stone and path and mountaintop, on waters pouring through gullies and over cliffs to pools below.

It gave life, light shining in the darkness.

Birds chattered hesitantly in offering to the light, their whispers gathering and echoing in the crisp air. Starlings soared, two by two, catching currents and chasing away hawks.

Coyotes rustled in the bushes, hunting hares scuttling to hide, hungry for deer grazing on the opposite slope.

A breeze blew over the land, crowning gentle hillsides bowing from the sky, rippling the trees, stirring the waters.

The hermit Abram knew the breeze was the breath of God. And Abram knew that it was good.

SUNDAY

November 11, Veterans Day

Chapter 1

On Sunday, November 11, 2018, Abram Levin, eighty years old, awoke as the Earth shook. The sandstone walls and crevices of his cave on Angel Mountain sent a shower of dust. The old man rose from his rocky bed in the trembling space. He steadied himself and waited for an aftershock; the night had been windy and the smoke from the wildfires in the north had abated, somewhat clearing the air. The night had also been cold, near freezing he guessed, and now the Earth quaked. The natural world was angry. Was it coming to an end?

Earthquakes, he knew, were not uncommon in Northern California, not uncommon in the San Francisco Bay Area or in the hills to the east, not uncommon on Angel Mountain, a.k.a. Mount Diablo. Nor were wildfires. But he had more work to do before the end of the world, and he planned to do it.

As he waited for the next tremor, he recalled his dream, pulling from his memory the images and colors. He had been looking through a wall of windows to canoes paddling to shore. The white boats sailed smoothly over a brilliant blue sea, under a rainbow arcing the heavens. The colors and images reminded Abram of an Impressionist painting, and, like his other dreams, he knew instantly what the vision meant. Man was given free will, the power of choice, and in the choosing would arrive at his final destination, Heaven or Hell. "Yes," he whispered to his Lord God of Heaven and Earth, "I understand."

Abram slapped water from a basin onto his cheeks, smoothed his beard, and donned his white robe. He breathed the early morning air as dawn drifted into the dim cavern. This was the moment, regardless of the haze, that he loved most of all the moments in his day and night. This was the moment that the forty icons on the rock walls began to glow, their gold leaf catching and reflecting the first light. This was the moment when he said his first prayers and sang his first psalms. *This was the moment when the angels of the mountain could be seen.*

Dawn. The light entered the cave and the icons on the walls began their morning song, securely attached to the wooden trellis his sister and her husband had built. Elizabeth was the practical one, the worrier, he thought, grateful for all her worrying. The icons needed a frame against the uneven sandstone. Elizabeth and Samuel had built one.

The icons told the glorious story of redemption and salvation. There were images of not only the saints but also the sacred events of Christ's life and death and life eternal: the Annunciation, the Visitation, the Nativity, the Holy Family, the Crucifixion, the Resurrection, the Ascension, and Pentecost. There was Christ the Creator, Christ the King, and Christ the Good Shepherd. There was the Holy Trinity and the Transfiguration of Christ. It was all glorious, Abram often thought with thanksgiving.

With prayers for his sister, and her husband who passed away two years ago, he began to sing with the saints, and as he chanted he moved through the cloud of witnesses, the host of angels, martyrs, and messengers. They glittered and glimmered, singing with him through centuries of devotion and prayer. They were his friends, a communion of saints. He sang the Our Father, lingering before the Trinity icon.

As Abram began the *Te Deum*, he stepped through the bright doorway and onto the promontory outside his cave.

> We praise thee, O God; we acknowledge thee to be the Lord.
> All the Earth doth worship thee, the Father everlasting.
> To thee all Angels cry aloud; the Heavens, and all the Powers therein;
> To thee Cherubim and Seraphim continually do cry,
> Holy, Holy, Holy, Lord God of Sabaoth;
> Heaven and Earth are full of the Majesty of thy glory.
> The glorious company of the Apostles praise thee.
> The goodly fellowship of the Prophets praise thee.
> The noble army of Martyrs praise thee.
> The holy Church throughout all the world doth acknowledge thee;
> The Father, of an infinite Majesty;
> Thine adorable, true, and only Son;
> Also the Holy Ghost, the Comforter.[1]

The sun was rising behind his mountain, Angel Mountain, and Abram turned to the vast horizon to glimpse the angels hovering between Earth and Heaven. That rim of the planet, yesterday obscured by smoke from the fires in the north, today could be seen, glowing with promise. He looked up to the mountain's peak behind him and down to the valleys below where hamlets of humanity lived their days and nights in homes of stone and stucco. Humanity slept, but soon lights blinked on, as men and women and children prepared for their waking hours of work and play.

> Thou art the King of Glory, O Christ.
> Thou art the everlasting Son of the Father.
> When thou tookest upon thee to deliver man, thou didst humble thyself to be born of a Virgin.
> When thou hadst overcome the sharpness of death, thou didst open the Kingdom of Heaven to all believers.
> Thou sittest on the right hand of God, in the glory of the Father.
> We believe that thou shalt come to be our Judge.
> We therefore pray thee, help thy servants, whom thou hast redeemed with thy precious blood.
> Make them to be numbered with thy Saints, in glory everlasting.

And Abram sang with the saints in the cave and the angels on the horizon who lit up the dark with the light of dawn.

But this time as he sang, he saw movement on the trail below. Three hikers were climbing toward him. The three young men halted, pointing. They were the first, Abram thought. They were the first to come and see.

> O Lord, save thy people, and bless thine heritage.
> Govern them, and lift them up for ever.
> Day by day we magnify thee;
> And we worship thy Name ever, world without end.
> Vouchsafe, O Lord, to keep us this day without sin.
> O Lord, let thy mercy be upon us, as our trust is in thee.
> O Lord, in thee have I trusted; let me never be confounded.

Abram knew the time of his hiding was over, and the time of his revealing had come. He knew that God uses what he hides in, to reveal himself from. As he raised his arms to embrace Heaven and Earth, he felt the sun upon his back. His white robe fluttered. He cried to the angels dancing on the horizon, "What is happiness?"

And the Earth quaked once more.

Chapter 2

Early Sunday morning, Elizabeth Levin Jacobsen, having lived eighty-four years on this good Earth, felt the quake in her house at the foot of Angel Mountain. She was thankful it wasn't worse, especially after the terrible fire engulfing the town of Paradise to the northeast and the smoke that had covered the Bay Area. She steadied herself, gripping the bed and planting her feet firmly on the carpet she had brought from Greece, her birthplace. They had quakes in Greece too, but every shaking rattled her old spine, and she held on until the rolling stopped. Her gratitude journal, with its careful cursive living in its lined pages, fell off the nightstand. She reached for it slowly and returned it to safety.

The quake was a roller, Elizabeth decided, not a jolt. Would there be aftershocks?

Laddie, her orange tabby, wailed, his golden eyes fixed on the rattling windows. He jumped into his cage and curled into a ball on the red cushion, burying his face in his paws and whimpering. She needed to give him his insulin shot before he bolted under the bed, but today she would have to postpone it.

Elizabeth had learned to sit these quakes out, to not rise too soon to check damages, as she had done once and fallen down the stairs. At her age, she couldn't afford another fall. For that matter, she needed someone to live with her, to pick her up if it happened again. She might seriously hurt herself, not be as fortunate as she had been the last time. And who would rescue her, a lone widow in a great, gated property on the edge of town, at the base of Angel Mountain?

Her dear husband Samuel—may he rest in peace—had built this seven-thousand-square-foot house on this three-acre view lot at the base of Angel Mountain with an eye to hiring live-in help one day, the way the wealthy lived, as he said often, or so perceived. He had built the house, far larger

8

than the two of them required, simply because he could. As a young refugee fleeing Hitler's Holocaust, he arrived in America with few possessions. He built his business from nothing, hoping to vanquish forever his memories of poverty and persecution. This house—and its beautiful grounds so lovingly landscaped—was his reward, and he felt justified.

But now, Elizabeth was alone. What if something happened, what would become of Abram on Angel Mountain? Who would look after her little brother? He might well be eighty, but he would always be her little brother. Her suitcase, placed near the front door for a quick escape if need be, included a change of clothes for Abram as well as herself. She slept better knowing it was there, all packed and ready to go. They could leave in an instant, just like in Greece. "Mama, are the bags packed?" Papa would ask regularly. And they were. Always.

Grateful for another day of life, Elizabeth prayed to her God of Abraham to keep her brother safe. Ever since the Holocaust that swept through Greece, she had tried to keep Abram safe. Through the years, after their many hidings and many escapes, she held him close, like a second mother. She and Abram were only children, only six and two, when the invasion turned their cosseted world upside down. They were only children those four haunted, hunted years, hiding in cellars and closets and other dark places. They adopted different names and stories and faiths—how many she had lost count—protected by Christian families in Thessalonica and Athens and Crete. How did they survive? Elizabeth was grateful for those good people of Greece.

And they did survive. They came to America. She met Samuel, wonderful Samuel, a camp survivor, and they built a good life together. Elizabeth turned to a photo of her late husband, dapper in his three-piece suit, silk tie and matching pocket scarf. He was so proud of his success, his becoming a wealthy American, a country club American, after all he had been through, all he had lost in Poland. But he was laid to rest two years ago, leaving Elizabeth a grieving widow, and some days the grief hounded her. It nipped at her heels, biting and scratching, no matter what she did to forget and accept and move on. But she did not want to forget and accept and move on. She did not want closure. Samuel was good and true. He was selfless in his own way. He looked after Abram. He understood that wounds needed tending at times.

But Abram carried his wounds deep within and sometimes she and Samuel had not been able to reach them. The wounds festered. Elizabeth knew she would always need to care for him, find him when he was lost and bring him home, no matter his age. Thoughts of suicide had roamed Abram's mind in the darker times, as they had lived in her own mind as well. She was not sure if they lived in Samuel's mind. He never said.

Abram seemed better, happier, since he found Saint Joseph's Chapel in Berkeley. So if Abram needed to work out his suffering on Angel Mountain as a Christian hermit, so be it. Today, this Veterans Day 2018, she was thankful to know where he was. But what about the earthquake?

Seized with a panic to check on her brother, Elizabeth dressed and descended the grand staircase slowly, grasping the banister. She was on the landing, halfway down, when the second quake hit. She held on tight, bracing herself. This one was more of a jolt, but less intense, and her bones shook with the shaking. As the movement lessened, she looked through the tall picture window on the landing. The sun was rising over Angel Mountain. She felt the great house settle on its moorings like a boat in harbor, and she descended carefully to the main floor.

The books were still on their shelves and still piled in stacks, one title upon another, domiciled on table and chair and counter. A photo of her family after the persecution in Greece had toppled. She righted it. It had been taken when her father, once a successful importer, was reduced to selling honey door to door. Her mother and father had passed on now, but they had lived to middle age in Greece, safe in the knowledge their children were making their way in America, the land of freedom.

Elizabeth entered the kitchen. She checked her quotes, three-by-five cards held by magnets on the refrigerator door. Three had fallen and she reset them:

"Where there is no law, there is no liberty."
Benjamin Rush (1745–1813)
Signer of the Declaration of Independence

"If we are to guard against ignorance and remain free,
it is the responsibility of every American to be informed."
Thomas Jefferson (1743–1826)
Third President of the United States
(Quote probably a paraphrase of Jefferson by Ronald Reagan,
Fortieth President of the United States)

"The general government . . . can never be in danger
of degenerating into a monarchy, an oligarchy, an aristocracy,
or any other despotic or oppressive form,
so long as there shall remain any virtue in the body of the people."
George Washington
First President of the United States
(In a letter to the Marquis de LaFayette, February 7, 1788)

Elizabeth was proud of her quotes scattered around the house, quotes curating ideas, safeguarding them for the next generation. For ideas defined humanity, set man apart from animals. Ideas were important. She loved to collect ideas, ideas that had stood the test of time, been proved by history to be good ones, ideas that had debated other ideas and won, ideas that had survived centuries. And it was ideas, she had found, that unified Americans, not race or creed or class. That was as it should be. Race and creed and class divided. Ideas united. Americans were equal under the law or should be.

There were lists scattered around the house as well, she noted, to-do lists, to-remember lists, books-to-read-next lists, but she kept her lists away from the refrigerator door where her quotes ruled.

Elizabeth rested her hands on the granite counter. Nothing else seemed amiss. Once again she was grateful. She checked again on her books, those libraries of ideas, particularly the random stacks in the family room that adjoined the kitchen. Some had toppled, for after all, like Babel, they were too high. As she righted them, holding each volume and feeling its weight, she was seized with the sense—as she often was—that books were living creatures, carrying and housing precious thoughts of authors living and dead, the language and nuance unique to each writer and uniquely felt by each reader as well. Of course they were mere matter: paper and ink. But in another sense they were the bearers of memory, the memory of a culture, the memory of a person, a family, a way of life, the complexities and challenges of every minute of every day.

Elizabeth knew that her people, the Jewish people, were considered people of the book, for the Torah—the words of Moses, the kings, and the prophets—preserved God's quiet whisperings and vociferous commandments on parchment, linking the People of Israel with their Jehovah, binding the living creation to the living Creator. The Torah was prayer, poetry, and law. It was the great history of the People of Israel. It directed life with the love of God, teaching respect for the individual, the family, and the faith. It was life and not death.

Hitler burned books in raging bonfires, burning ideas rather than vanities as Savonarola had done in Renaissance Italy. Hitler knew the power of words, the power of ideas, the power of books. It was said that the Nazis burned a hundred million books in their twelve years of power. They burned "subversive" books, including, of course, all Jewish books, especially the sacred ones. Bonfires of books were not new. History records this decimation of threatening ideas as a regular occurrence, moments that recognized the power of words and ideas, especially those ideas on pages housed in books.

And so Elizabeth did not live alone in this great house. She lived with books, with memory curated, with thousands of voices that cried to be heard, to freely speak. She lived within the heartbeat of the phrase and the sentence, within the flesh and blood of image and metaphor and story. She lived with all these precious souls, authors forgotten, despised, honored. She lived with her own memory of their voice and what they said, what they taught and what she learned. When she held a book in her hands that she had read—even long ago—she revisited its country, toured its pages and chapters, reliving its salient moments, its pace, its tone, and its voice as if she were a tourist revisiting a favorite site or as if she were stopping by for tea with an author she was fond of and missed. What was the emotional connection with books, Elizabeth wondered. What was the power they held over her? Each one was dear, some more than others just like people. But she had an opinion about them all, for they were her friends. And in some ways, they had molded her into the person she was today.

Language, Elizabeth often thought, was unique to the human species. It was an evolutionary contradiction that Charles Darwin had not addressed. Language—both oral and written—linked us, one to another and one generation to another. Elizabeth gazed upon her tilting stacks and her untidy shelves and saw these stories and these voices as love letters to the next generation, manuals for living.

Having rescued the fallen volumes and settled them once again, holding each one too long, swayed by its siren song, Elizabeth pulled herself away and returned to the kitchen, recalling Abram. She brewed coffee and quickly packed her brother's supplies of snacks, fruit, and drinks, along with the baptism cards detailing the Ten Commandments and other Scriptures, printed matter Abram had requested along with some hand towels that he had asked for. She glanced through a wide window to foothills, where a white cross stood in brown grass. The wind she had heard in the night had blown away the haze and the colors of the Earth had returned, welcomed by the daylight.

"I am coming, Abram, I am coming. Elizabeth is coming to help. Hold on, Abram, hold on. Elizabeth is coming."

Chapter 3

Sunday morning, in the chill of early dawn, Catherine Nelson, still young-ish at thirty-three, awoke with the rumble and rattle of the earthquake, in spite of her exhaustion from the previous evening. She had scrolled online agencies and listings for hours, looking for work that would fulfill her, make her happy. The smoke from the Paradise fire to the north didn't seem as bad this morning, but had they put it out? And now an earthquake. What would be next?

Her ground-floor apartment in north Berkeley, while walking distance to her former job at the UC library, was not up to earthquake standards. Built in the 1950s, the three-story construction rattled, as though the walls were made of plywood. Would it collapse around her? Over her? Would it bury her?

It was still dark or seemed so, and she checked her phone—6:30. She hated November mornings.

She pulled the blankets close against the chill, not wanting to face the day.

But she recalled yesterday all too well. She had been ordered into her manager's office and asked to be careful about her language, what she said and how she said it. "We don't need hate speech here," Ms. Jackson said. "We don't need this kind of trouble. We're inclusive. We welcome diversity. And, Catherine, you have been warned before."

The speech incident to which Ms. Jackson referred had occurred in the breakroom. Her colleagues were discussing a protest on campus, watching as it replayed on a wall monitor. The protesters appeared to be members of antifa, or "anti-fascists", a far-left militant group that terrorized speakers with whom they disagreed; this particular speaker on the screen was defend-ing the right of an unborn child to live, that this life should not be victim to the feelings or whim of the mother. Catherine realized that the speaker's comments would be considered hate speech—denying a woman's right to choose whether or not she should give birth to a baby once conceived. Catherine had blundered into the conversation, saying (stupidly, she knew), in a low voice, that she believed even handicapped children should have the right to live. "Especially babies with Down syndrome," she mouthed, or perhaps hissed, still angry with the father who abandoned them when she was a baby in the womb, thinking she had been diagnosed with Down syndrome, later learned to be a misdiagnosis. "They should be allowed to live, just like you or I, even if they do have an extra chromosome."

She had their attention, and she foolishly continued, her voice rising, strident. "The diagnosis might be wrong. Doctors aren't perfect. They aren't always right. After all, it's murder we're talking about here." Her comments were not well received. She knew better than to challenge her coworkers. Why, oh why, had she done it?

The tension in the room was near breaking point. Catherine could feel her heart constrict and her fingers clutch, as their words bombarded her. In their outrage, they called her a fascist. (Where did fascism come into this? Was she on trial?) She backed out the door and returned to the safety of her desk, biting her lip. She prayed to the God she wasn't sure existed that she wouldn't get into trouble with her boss. But it seemed to Catherine that God didn't hear or God didn't care, and she got into trouble just the same.

Now, lying in bed and waiting for an aftershock, Catherine shivered in the gray dawn. She knew her boss had been under pressure since the books had gone missing from the Classics and European History sections. Her boss had hinted that Catherine stole the books. That was way too much. That was when her boss crossed a line, and Catherine blurted, "I quit. I've had enough of this political correctness."

Why had she done that? How stupid was that? It was as if she had no control, that her mind, heart, and soul were so full of bitterness towards those who misrepresented truth, at least truth as she saw it, and who challenged her reality as though she were the crazy one. Groupthink someone called it. The power of the crowd, the mob. To Catherine this was an adolescent attitude, but it seemed to be everywhere these days. There was great pressure, she realized, to conform. She of all people understood that. Still, she thought the world would be a better place if people could respect one another, no matter what their opinions or beliefs. Respect was important.

But there was one person in the group that sympathized: Annie. Annie Ainsworth wasn't strong enough to side with Catherine publicly, but Catherine met her kindly gaze and was comforted by the friendliness, the concern. Annie was handicapped, a handicap that was to her benefit, and not a handicap at all. Perhaps that was right and an evening of scores, but every time Catherine looked at Annie's missing hand, or rather where her hand should have been, she winced. The stub of her arm today was connected to an artificial hand, and it was remarkable how Annie could function pretty much as anyone could with both hands. Annie was brave to have survived this childhood accident—a propeller on a motorboat—to have made it through public school and into college, and now on the library staff. But she wasn't brave enough to speak out for Catherine, to go against the groupthink.

Now, as she daydreamed herself into full waking mode, a minor aftershock hit, barely noticeable, and Catherine knew she had to face the day. She turned on a space heater and dressed, pulling from her mother's cedar chest (now bureau), jeans, tee, and Cal sweatshirt, making sure not to disturb her mother's tailored jackets she kept since she passed away: the navy, the camel, and the herringbone. They might be useful one day, Catherine thought, but for now, she was glad to have something of her mother close by. She lifted one of them to her face. She could still smell the jasmine scent her mother favored. How Catherine missed her. What would she say if she knew about Catherine resigning from her job?

Catherine braided her auburn hair into a single plait that fell down her back and made tea and toast in the kitchenette. The rapid-transit line ran next door, and the 7:02 BART screeched to a halt.

She returned to scrolling job listings on her laptop while nibbling the toast. There seemed nothing in her field, nothing located in the Berkeley area. Library work was precious. With a month's severance pay, she had some time. She might try retail or even banking. Her mother had worked in a bank in San Francisco as an administrative assistant. But Catherine's postgrad degree was Master of Library Science. She loved books and, in her search for happiness, she was sure this was her field of dreams. How could she do anything else?

She had the right, even the duty, to follow her dream, be passionate about her work and still associate with those who respected her viewpoints. She loved music too, but had no credentials to teach or any marketable skill playing an instrument. No, it would have to be books—either library work or a bookstore. But bookstores were dying and libraries underfunded. Would her supervisor give her a reference for another library job? Catherine thought not. Ms. Jackson might report her to the police. Catherine was innocent of any book theft, but then her life seemed to be unwinding fast and anything was possible.

If her mother were alive, she would know what to do. Her mother would pray and receive an answer, as though God were an obliging grandfather. She would go to Saint Joseph's Chapel around the corner and have a vision or something. She would come home and order all things right for her daughter. She would explain that Jesus had a path for her to walk on and her mother (along with Jesus) would help Catherine find it. Her mother had been her role model, and now she was gone, leaving a great gaping hole in Catherine's heart and soul.

She needed to face reality. Her mother wasn't alive, and dreaming in the dawn wasn't going to bring her back. It was one year since the cancer stole her, Veterans Day 2017, one year of Catherine living alone in their dingy apartment in Berkeley, one year of crying herself to sleep, one year of grieving and grievance. All she wanted was to be happy—why did everyone make it so difficult?

So what if she had made a slip of the tongue in the breakroom? It was just one tiny error in judgment. And it was true that she had nearly been aborted, nearly murdered in the womb, nearly never given a chance. If she hadn't been misdiagnosed, would her father have stayed? Would he have loved her after all? What she had said was true.

Once she found a job she would return to her genetic research and the plan to find her father who abandoned them. She viewed her stack of library books dealing with ancestry and genetics and DNA. They would have to be returned soon, she guessed. Last week, when she still had a job and could afford the fee, she had mailed the Ancestors.com envelope containing her saliva sample. She would see what came back. Who knew what she might find out about her father. It would be a beginning. Who was Catherine Nelson? What was her true identity? Her mother was northern European—Norwegian mostly, she had said. Her ancestors had emigrated to Chicago in the nineteenth century. So Catherine expected that at least fifty percent of her own background would be northern European.

They could do a lot with genetics these days. She had learned at least that much from Dr. Worthington, who had taught her biology class at Cal. He was a quiet, dignified man, she recalled. So soft-spoken, you had to lean forward to hear him. At least she still had his textbook, or did she? She had probably resold it at the student union. Oh, well. Life was not good these days. She needed a job.

She put her plate in the sink and ran water into her cup to soak. She glanced at the laptop.

The sun was rising slowly and a dim light worked its way through the bay fog, brightening the alley but not quite piercing the smudged window. Catherine returned to her online search for a job that would make her happy and fulfill her dreams. She became so absorbed with pointing and clicking and researching companies and firms and agency listings, she barely heard the noon bells of the Campanile, UC's iconic clocktower, or the multiple gunshots that followed.

She assumed the latter were backfires.

Chapter 4

The earthquake shook Sunday's early dawn as Dr. Gregory Worthington, thirty-seven, cleaned his dark glasses with an optical cloth. He was in his car, pondering his life, waiting for Mount Diablo State Park to open. He had slept little the night before and needed to think, and thus had arrived early. He often was early, but not this early. The night had been windy, and he had hoped that the forecast was accurate, that the haze would be cleared away by the winds.

And now the quake. The smoke from the fire raging through the town of Paradise had indeed been cleared away, was far less potent than Friday and Saturday, and the better air quality would allow him to hike a ways up the mountain. He had brought a mask to use if needed. The mountain usually helped him sort things out. But haze was one thing, especially when blown away by the wind, and earthquakes something else altogether.

He got out of the car, zipped his fleece jacket, and slipped on his Broncos cap. He scanned the landscape of wild grass, manzanita, oak, and pine, observing the quake phenomenon as a scientist, standing outside it, pulling relevant facts into the picture. This fault zone often released seismic energy in swarms, rather than with a main shock and aftershock. Yet most folks called the many small tremblers "aftershocks." Regardless, the Earth shook, and the threat to life and property was real.

He had experienced earthquakes before, having lived in the Bay Area since enrolling in UC Berkeley in '99, but had never been outdoors when they hit. This could be interesting, he judged, standing at the foot of Angel Mountain, a.k.a. Mount Diablo. A local story claimed that an old hermit had renamed it, changing it from Devil Mountain to Angel Mountain. The name had stuck. He wondered if the hermit was still around. It was unlikely such a person could stay hidden for long with today's tracking devices and all the hikers that roamed the mountain. Surely the rangers knew about him.

As dawn turned into day, the Earth shifted beneath him once again. Should he skip the hike? On this Veterans Day, he needed to assess his life situation with an eye to making concrete decisions about his future. He thought best when he was hiking, when he was in the natural world and even with haze the sun could pierce the smoke and enliven the old oaks and manzanita. At least he would be able to feel planet Earth beneath his feet. It wasn't the Colorado Rockies, where he had grown up, but the California hills had their own beauty, even today. And these hills were safer, or so he once believed.

The Earth calmed as though nothing had happened. Gregory scanned the brush and grass and patches of soil. He saw no damage, no great cleft opening before him. Would there be more tremors? He was near the Concord and Green Valley faults, not nearly as dangerous as the Hayward fault running under Oakland and Berkeley. He was even farther from the infamous San Andreas fault running under the peninsula, Stanford University (where he had studied medicine), Daly City, then to the west of San Francisco, and into the Pacific Ocean south of Eureka, which caused the 1906 San Francisco earthquake. He had heard about the 6.9 Loma Prieta earthquake of '89, centered in the Santa Cruz Mountains, but he was only eight at the time, living with his Aunt Jane in Denver.

The gates opened and Gregory slipped into the driver's seat. The park was opening slightly later than usual, the rangers assessing damage and danger, and Gregory drove to the trailhead and parked. He headed up the path, focusing on the miracle of night turning to day. The rotation of the Earth as it bowed before the sun filled him with awe. The horizon curved gently to the northwest, dividing Earth and sky, and soon the sun would appear over the eastern ridge of the mountain, light traveling ninety-three million miles to Earth, to fulfill the hopeful forecast of better weather.

It was a propitious and significant day, this Veterans Day 2018, a centennial year celebrating the armistice that ended World War I, beginning at eleven o'clock in the morning, on the eleventh day, in the eleventh month, 1918. He knew this national day honoring those who had served in America's wars might become the turning point of his personal history and career.

One year ago, Veterans Day 2017, Professor Gregory Worthington had stood in one of the larger lecture halls of UC Berkeley, speaking to a packed crowd. His lecture chronicled the wonders of faith and science. He detailed his research with genetics and the stunning elegance of the genome, something that could only have been designed by a master Intelligence, and the impossibility of random selection amidst the billions of genetic choices, in terms of the evolution of species. He referenced the role of Charles Darwin's theory and its nineteenth-century limitations in explaining our world, that it was a nice theory as far as it went. But today they knew so much more about the cell and how it worked. He described the Cambrian explosion, a fossil record with no found links to earlier fossils, a species that simply appeared. How did different species come to be, when there was no traceable evolution from one to the other? He concluded that science points to a Designer and that, at least for him, he had faith that this Designer fit the description of the God of Abraham and the Ten Commandments, an intelligent God who designed an awesome universe.

Dr. Worthington didn't have all the answers, he admitted to the stunned UC audience. There was the question of Young Earth creation and Old Earth creation. Human fossils pointed to life and death occurring as early as 180,000 years ago. If Adam and Eve are dated to ten thousand years ago, as the Young Earth creationists claimed, and their sin of disobeying God caused death, how was this to be reconciled? He could see his listeners wondered at his taking both sides, this esteemed geneticist. He could see they respected him for his honesty. They admired, or perhaps feared, his freedom and courage to speak his mind, to speak out.

But was he too outspoken? The black-clad antifas, the self-labeled "anti-fascists," militant cowards hiding in their anonymity, chanted foul slogans outside the hall, breaking windows in the face of nervous police who stood down. The rioters called his words hate speech; they called him a fascist. Gregory inferred they were threatened by religion in the public square. The University of California was a public square, to be sure, and once God entered the equation, moral parameters shifted like tectonic plates, with seismic commandments that defined marriage and protected the unborn, calling people to love one another. Morality was clearly defined when God entered the public square.

A few months later, the dean had strongly suggested that Dr. Worthington take the sabbatical due him. He could write that book he spoke of.

Veterans Day: the day honoring our fight for freedom, for free speech. The irony was not lost on this Doctor of Medicine, this PhD of Science. And today the doctor proudly carried an American flag, flying from his backpack. Reflecting on the day and the time and the season of his life, he continued up the path, up Angel Mountain toward the summit as the sun streamed over the ridge.

Gregory was of the generation that knew no war—at least no draft— but his Great Aunt Jane, who had raised him in Denver, had known war. Her brother had known war, was scarred by war, by kamikaze in the South Pacific on board the *USS Phoenix*, 1943–44. His old uncle couldn't speak of the terror that rained from the skies, and Gregory wasn't encouraged to ask, but at times in the historic Victorian house with its creaky wood floors, Old

Master paintings and fringed lamps, the young Gregory examined the black-and-white photos of the ship, images preserved in a yellowing scrapbook. The boy asked himself, would he be brave enough to serve his country? To die for what he believed in, for the good, the true, the beautiful? Would he die for freedom? For people he didn't know, for strangers?

Gregory supposed today's free speech battle was his battle, the war of his times. At one time, he had been politically correct as a university atheist. He had embraced the prevailing proud nihilism. He openly scorned belief and self-righteously silenced those who believed, albeit gently, by frown, derision, or scorn. All that was needed, often enough, was a certain look and a roll of the eyes.

Perhaps he was the Saul-turned-Paul on the Damascus road, the unlikely convert who saw God in a most remarkable place, in a genome, in a sterile molecular biology lab. What a time that had been, seeing the intricacy of the cell, how the information was stored in four chemical bases—A, T, C, and G—how each base was attached to a sugar molecule and a phosphate molecule forming a nucleotide. Adding to this design, the arrangement of these long strands formed a double helix, appearing like a twisted ladder. The base pairs formed the rungs and the molecules formed the sides. The complexity and beauty were incredible. He would never be the same; he could not turn back.

He followed the dirt trail through grass and chaparral, pines and manzanita, and rested at a lookout point. The Earth was growing brighter each minute, as light lit the land with its infinitesimal wavelengths. Spectrums colored the foliage, dancing with shadows. All the Earth sang to the glory of God, Gregory thought, shaking his head in wonder. He pulled out his water bottle and sipped. He mopped his forehead with his other hand.

How had he come to this place in his life? To lose it all so easily? All his UC education, Stanford internships, scholarly and laboratory research had been propelled by his heady desire to find a cure for Parkinson's disease. Had he really thrown it all away—his great ambition—for this creed of faith and science, of miracles and matter? Was it that important? His Aunt Jane would have thought so. She had been a believer.

After all, it was her dying of Parkinson's that led him into genetics. It was her generous legacy that funded his study of medicine. He wanted to find a cure, to help people. He wanted to make a difference. As trite as it sounded, it was true.

His boyhood faith was real, he knew, but in university he denied it, buried it in the name of science. He thought back to Saint Mary's Denver, the Victorian church with the Elizabethan liturgy telling a first-century story of salvation. He recalled the sweet smell of incense, the flaming candles, the singing, and the ringing of bells that called attention to holy moments. He had memorized creeds and recited commandments, confessed sins and received absolution. Was he returning to the faith world of Saint Mary's? He wasn't sure.

What he did know was that a powerful force pulled him, just as it pulled him up this trail, up Angel Mountain. He sensed it was a good force, one of joy, of love, of—yes—Intelligence. When he reached the top, as always, he would be more clearheaded and he would better see his path forward. He would see the good land spread before him, this planet Earth that rotated through the galaxy. When he stood at the top of the mountain, he was a man holding onto the rim of the world, a man of reason, of faith, and of science.

These three—reason, faith, and science—must never be separated, he reminded himself again and again. Together, they must inform and define humanity, God's creatures of mind, soul, and body. He would contribute his small part to the conversation, to the informing, to the defining. Perhaps it was just as important as curing Parkinson's. He had a rough draft of a manuscript for that book he was writing. But he had run into writer's block, or writer's doubt, or perhaps simply writer's futility.

A good walk would help him sort it out, increase his circulation, pump oxygen into his brain. He had seen many varieties of birds on his hikes: mourning doves, hummingbirds and woodpeckers, jays and ravens and crows, wrens and thrushes and bluebirds. What would fly above or peek from the trees this early November morning? Their songs would enter the silence of the hour.

He was a good ways up the path, when he heard the rattle. The earthquake might have disturbed some of the natural wildlife, he thought, scanning the brush, not wanting to frighten or challenge it.

He spotted it. It was a Northern Pacific rattler, the only one common to the area. Gregory had seen these before. They were prolific in the nesting months of August through October, but he had never seen one so close up, in his natural habitat. And this fellow seemed oblivious to the human watching him slide across the path. He was several feet long, with diamond dorsal blotches edged with white, lateral darker blotches, and the typical tail rings tipped with black. He had the large triangular head that defined rattlers, distinguishing them from gopher snakes with the smaller heads. Gregory could even see the pale yellow belly, spotted brown, as it slithered into the grass on the opposite side.

Just to be safe, he stepped back farther, knowing the amazing creature could only strike from a coiled position, meaning a distance of four to five feet was sufficient. He kept his eye on the snake as he retreated, cataloging the beauty of movement, the elegance of form and natural camouflage, all clearly the design of an intelligent Creator. But as he stepped back, he slipped on a gravelly patch and began to slide.

Arms outstretched, falling at an awkward angle, he landed and tumbled gently down the terrain. He would have survived this tumble, risen to rejoin the path to chronicle greater glories, but he hit his head on something hard, and his world went dark.

Chapter 5

Malcolm Underhill III looked down upon Sproul Plaza from an open window, high in a library building on a floor closed for renovations. The nearby bell tower would soon chime eleven o'clock. Sundays, he had long ago concluded, provided the best day for a riot for so many reasons. He liked to think that Sunday was a day of prayer. As others prayed he prayed too, only somewhat differently. And today, November 11, 2018, was also Veterans Day. Perfect. His Church of Grievance would convene at the gates of UC Berkeley.

The service would start on time—11 a.m. The petitioners would sing their own hymns and chant their own verses. They would recall Veterans Day, that day when soldiers fought for racism and hate, dying to protect America's great shame. His Church of Grievance would burn a flag or two. They would demand justice and ridicule reason in their litanies. They would pray to the great Lord of Misrule and prey on the privileged. After all, everyone at UC Berkeley was privileged just to be there.

The smoke from the fires in the north was dissipating, and he wondered if one of his acolytes had set the fires. Some had claimed ownership, bragging on social media. Now, as he watched the plaza fill with its unhappy congregation, he considered his victories. Malcolm Underhill III was only thirty-five and had achieved greatness at UC Berkeley and across the country. He often thought he might be a mentor to the world's lost souls.

Malcolm often congratulated himself as he peered over his large dark glasses to tap a number on his phone. A call here, a suggestion there, a money transfer and it was done. These students were so easily led, so hungry for meaning, inspiration, and transcendence. He gave it to them. He was the boss, the puppeteer behind the scenes. He financed the big guns, the professional protestors, those black-clad wielders of sticks, stones, and heavy barricades so useful for breaking windows. And all the while, Malcolm was invisible. At least for now.

Malcolm was the mob maker, the reputation killer, the setter to rights of all that was going wrong in this f-ing country. Stalin could have learned something from his finesse. Mao could have sat at his feet. Marx—and his spokesmen Marcuse and Zinn—would have been proud of his disciple Malcolm.

He encouraged the labels "microaggression" and "safe space" and "trigger." He suggested terms such as "racist," "white supremacist," and "fascist." Language was a powerful tool. He used language in academia the way newspapers used language—ridiculing, name calling, poking fun, selecting or deleting facts to create the proper narrative. It was only recently that the style of the old polemics, the yellow press confined to magazines and newspapers, had entered the gilded halls of higher learning, turning reasoned debate into flame throwing, naturally ending in a bonfire of ideas. Yes, as a conservative recently said, ideas can unify a nation. What he didn't say was that opposing ideas can destroy a nation. The latter was Malcolm's mission. And amidst the ruins, the strong would prevail; the weak would need him. He was strong.

So what if Malcolm *had* been at the bottom of his class. So what if he hadn't graduated, as long as his father naively believed he had done so. In spite of these little lies, Malcolm considered himself a noble knight—good, if not exactly true. He fought for the downtrodden, the underprivileged, the marginalized. He protected the gender-confused and all that the sexual revolution had achieved, enjoying said revolution's benefits immensely. He was both gate guardian for said culture and financial foundation supporting the army of lost boys and girls who formed the rising chorus of protest on college campuses. He did all of this, in spite of his white skin, or maybe because of it.

Malcolm often wished he were of mixed race. While not albino, he hated his whiteness. He hated his blue eyes and blonde hair, his strong jaw, his, well, to be honest, his Adonis-like beauty, although the girls loved him the more for it. But with the large shades, the cap pulled low, his backpack over his hoodie, he blended into the mobs easily enough.

At one time it had bothered him that his friends were disappearing, like water down a drain, but it made no difference now. Being a loner gave him power. He couldn't run such a national network, all from a phone, if he had friends. He couldn't evade his father's occasional probe into his life and operations. He needed that monthly stipend, whether he admitted it or not, and he hated his father for giving it to him and encouraging Malcolm's dependence, like a junkie dependent on a fix. Malcolm didn't need or want friends. He was his own man, accustomed to living in the shadows. The girls came and went. Most didn't know his real name, if he gave them any name at all. He certainly didn't remember theirs.

Malcolm pulled a chair to the window and set his rifle down carefully on a second chair. He might as well get comfortable and enjoy this. It was that golden moment before the curtain went up, or for some, before it came down. It was when he sang his song of blame, a highly satisfying litany, a beautiful art form.

He blamed his father for many things, but most of all his wealth. It wasn't right that a few fascists cornered the banking and finance industries, and propped up their interests in government with political stooges. It wasn't right that his father and grandfather and great-grandfather had homes throughout the world, properties beyond count. It was indecent, shameful. He, Malcolm, would do what he could to rectify the balance and even the score.

Malcolm pulled out a joint and rolled it between his fingers respectfully, lovingly. He lit one end and tossed the match out the window. He inhaled deeply.

Once the old man left the planet, Malcolm could truly exercise his calling. He could fully command the demons of demagoguery and equalize the unequal. The planet would be redeemed, renewed, saved from itself. With equal incomes, equal outcomes, equal housing, equal education, equal everything, there would be no war. His free hospitals would provide free health care. Towns would be clean and controlled, free of poverty, disease, and crime.

Freedom of choice, to be sure, would be of Malcolm's choosing, not the people's, for the people were incapable of such freedom. A few elite, for a time, would need to control the revolution. A few elite would need to rule, to advise and consent and judge and enforce. His chosen people would be welcomed, once chaos (any kind would do) turned into anarchy, and lawlessness demanded martial law to keep the peace. Once he was in power, there would be a cleansing of the unfit, the handicapped, the old, the unborn, and all other enemies of Malcolm's vision, but that would be transitional, temporary. Gene editing would provide the people he desired, the right sort of people, and the right number. The Kingdom of Utopia was near at hand.

Utopia! Some days, as he stood on the edge of student protests and watched his handiwork unfold, he could taste his kingdom coming. Once he rid the world of these fascist pigs, these monsters of white supremacy, all would be right with humanity, with the world, with the planet.

Getting rid of the Western canon was a giant step forward for mankind—and womankind—a needed righting of wrongs. He had noted with approval that Harvard had added a required course for English majors—a study of authors who had been marginalized for historical reasons. Malcolm knew those reasons by heart: racism, patriarchy, and heteronormativity. He was proud to have been a financial supporter of such identity-based curriculum, now taught nationwide. He was proud to support intersectionality, the cult of the victim.

Of course much had been done in the past to prepare his way. In the humanities and social sciences—especially history, English, and political science—modern liberals, i.e., leftists, dominated the faculty, often *were* the faculty. And with teachers feeding and forming such malleable minds, much could be done to secure the future. Critics of these modern programs—those neocons who appeared from time to time—demanded alternate viewpoints, claiming rights to free speech. But why allow such drivel, when it was so harmful to the feelings of the downtrodden, the marginalized? He, Malcolm, was on the right side of history. Such speech must be silenced.

Malcolm could see through the window that the crowd below was growing. A speaker stood on a platform, shouting slogans, like a litany. Malcolm glanced at his watch. Not time yet. He rose and stretched his legs, moving about the construction zone, disgusted with the sanders and paint pails and chipped sills, the thick dust and grime. It would be good when this phase of the revolution was over and he could assume his proper role in his new and great society.

Malcolm had considered an English major, but had switched to art, then sociology, then anthropology. It was true he hadn't finished any of the courses he began (thank God grades were now inviolably private according to state law and his father could not invade his world), but then that gave him, to his thinking, a wider education. He was an eclectic dabbler in the many subjects on offer, a catalog cruiser, a buffet grazer. His mind roved and rambled; his uncommon brilliance could not be roped in. And in the process he had worked with instructors to create marginalization mandates for the curriculum, appealing to their own narrow specialties and hobbyhorses. What could he say, in all modesty? He was a genius, so uniquely gifted! He was building a better, kinder world. He was, well, close to the Second Coming, a true Messiah for today.

And Daddy—Malcolm Underhill Jr.—financed it all. Little did Daddy know how his son had removed several key faculty, quietly, with words whispered here and there. A year ago today, as a matter of fact, the fool Worthington had spoken here on campus in one of the larger halls. With his brazen lecture the religious scientist entered the public square, proclaiming his addled belief that faith and science were reconciled, even mutually supportive.

Malcolm had tapped his phone and hissed into his Bluetooth. Soon his army of protesters appeared, heckling, chanting, and taunting the police who stood by, silently watching. It was easy after that to whisper more words to the right sorts, to greedy junior faculty, and to committee members who owned the dean, who in turn wisely suggested to the good Dr. Worthington for his own health (and safety) that he take a nice long sabbatical. Such finesse, Malcolm thought. Such skill and subtlety. And the Worthington file began a year ago today, Veterans Day 2017. Why, today was an anniversary celebration, the peak of his mission, perhaps the turning point.

Earlier there had been easier prey, history professors whose white supremacy limited the scope of their fields to the Western tradition and classics. They had to go; it was clear they needed to exit the academy. They were the enemy of equality, the enemy of the poor, the enemy of color and gender preference. They were treading dangerous ground. Malcolm merely deepened the danger, shook the ground a bit, toppled them into other careers—waiter, Uber driver, podcast preacher.

There were near failures too, he had to confess. One of his early targets had disappeared completely, a Jew turned Christian (the worst sort), who spoke with an accent. Malcolm sat in his class, his hatred growing daily. The bigot refused to grade Malcolm as he deserved; he finally agreed to give Malcolm an incomplete. The nerve of the sniveling creature! It was said he had become a hermit. What was his name? Lewis? Lexington? *Levin*. It was Levin, of course. Dr. Abram Levin. He was small and hunched, Malcolm recalled, with beady eyes and thick silvery hair. He wore a moth-eaten vest and he would place his tiny hands in his pockets as he paced, reciting his boring lectures.

Malcolm had tried to have the man committed, have his reputation destroyed, so that he would never be a threat to the nation's inclusivity again. But the old man was one of Malcolm's first attempts, not quite as elegant an operation as he would have liked, and in point of fact woefully crude. Malcolm had clearly stumbled. He had nearly been exposed and challenged, but he had learned how to be more effective in the future. It was a tutorial, he thought, as he looked back. He smiled with some satisfaction, running his tongue over perfect white teeth.

Now, through the dirty library window, Malcolm watched the crowd gather and a second speaker rise to the makeshift stage. It was nearing noon, close to time. He loaded his rifle. The protest would not be affected by the earlier earthquake, only propelled by its energy. The fish were swimming into the net, the sheep nearing the fold. His boys in black stood in the shadows, ready to urge the crowd into a frenzy, and later to loot the bourgeoisie who owned shops in the area. It was only just. It was only fitting to follow tradition—this tradition, at least.

The chants began, rising to a fever pitch, then falling. The signs wove through the mist. A few police stood in the porch of the Student Union, rigid, watching, not daring to move. Malcolm wondered if they had orders to stand down or they were just chicken.

The Campanile tolled noon, and the mournful sounds could barely be heard against the shouts and commotion of the crowd.

When the time was right, when the pitch was perfect, when the crowd began to roar, Malcolm trained his viewfinder on his congregation. He sprayed randomly, and the shots were only slightly muted by the damp air. He set down the gun, his heart racing. He wanted to savor the moment, taste the terror. But he knew he could not pause, even in this moment of sweet victory. He laid his army jacket on the floor along with the rifle and the white supremacist propaganda. He descended the back stairs, through the rubble left by Friday's workers, and walked calmly toward College Avenue. He passed by the homeless who littered the sidewalk with their vagrancy and uselessness. He gave them a wide berth, fighting his urge to strike.

Screams echoed in his ears; martyrs were necessary. The script demanded martyrs. The Church of Grievance required sacrifice to populate its calendar. It meant being on the right side of history, *his* history that *he*, *Malcolm Underhill III*, was making.

As sirens wailed, he kicked a sleeping bundle in a chapel porch. He glanced at the crucifix on the outer wall above the silent form and thought of Abram Levin. He would follow the news, check out Angel Mountain. It was time he settled a few scores, cleaned up his own history once and for all.

Chapter 6

Abram felt the aftershock. He gripped the wall of rock along the ledge as it shook, steadying himself. He raised his arms once again, embracing the world, chanting his morning prayers.

> O come, let us sing unto the Lord; let us heartily rejoice in the strength of our salvation.
> Let us come before his presence with thanksgiving; and show ourselves glad in him with psalms.
> For the Lord is a great God; and a great King above all gods.
> In his hand are all the corners of the Earth; and the strength of the hills is his also.
> The sea is his, and he made it; and his hands prepared the dry land.

The three young men worked their way toward him across the meadow to the falls as he sang.

> O come, let us worship and fall down, and kneel before the Lord our Maker.
> For he is the Lord our God; and we are the people of his pasture, and the sheep of his hand.
> O worship the Lord in the beauty of holiness; let the whole Earth stand in awe of him.
> For he cometh, for he cometh to judge the Earth; and with righteousness to judge the world, and the peoples with his truth.[2]

Abram watched the hikers, boys nearing manhood, stop at the pool and the waterfall. A large white cross stood on the opposite bank, a cross used for Easter sunrise services by local congregations. Could the hikers hear him singing? The morning sun broke through the haze and shone in their eyes. They raised their hands to shade their vision. One pointed. Another grinned.

"What is happiness?" Abram called to the hills and the valleys that spread to the far horizon. "Happiness is righteousness!"

Abram saw that they wore jeans and hiking boots. They carried packs on their backs. One wore his cap backwards, a challenge to tradition but useless as a sun visor.

"And righteousness is blessedness," Abram cried, "happiness birthed by joy."

Abram was suddenly tired, and he leaned against a boulder as the boys drew near, staring. Abram continued, raising a hand in peace:

> Blessed are the poor in spirit: for theirs is the kingdom of heaven.
> Blessed are they that mourn: for they shall be comforted.
> Blessed are the meek: for they shall inherit the earth.
> Blessed are they which do hunger and thirst after righteousness:
>   for they shall be filled.

The first stone hit the lower edge of Abram's wide sleeve, but he continued.

> Blessed are the merciful: for they shall obtain mercy.
> Blessed are the pure in heart: for they shall see God.
> Blessed are the peacemakers: for they shall be called the children of
>   God.
> Blessed are they which are persecuted for righteousness' sake: for
>   theirs is the kingdom of heaven.

The second stone missed completely.

> Blessed are ye, when men shall revile you, and persecute you, and
>   shall say all manner of evil against you falsely, for Christ's sake.
> Rejoice, and be exceeding glad: for great is your reward in heaven: for
>   so persecuted they the prophets which were before you.[3]

The third stone hit his chest, knocking out his wind and sending him to the ground.

The boys left, laughing and pointing.

The hermit watched them go. The last one looked back, bowed slightly, and waved. Abram smiled and raised his hand in blessing, for regret lingered in the boy's face.

Abram wasn't sure how long he lay there, leaning against the huge boulder. The sun seemed unmoving. He looked out upon the land, to the white cross, and prayed the Lord's Prayer, asking forgiveness for the boys, asking for more love in his own heart. For Abram understood that to love as Christ loved, he must love the world and everything—everyone—in it. He must pray for those who did not pray. He must ask for mercy for those who did not ask for mercy. To love meant to be one with humanity, one with the creation designed by God, mankind in his image. He, Abram, was responsible for much, for he loved much, and was loved even more by his Creator.

He closed his eyes. Was it time yet to move on? To pierce the veil, to cross by way of the cross, through the cross? He looked forward to his release, to the doors opening, to his Lord welcoming him with open arms.

Toads croaked in the pool below. A red-tailed hawk soared above, catching the wind currents. The waters tumbled down the cliff in the distance, their pouring muted by the breeze rustling the oaks.

Abram listened carefully, for there was another sound, a low cry, perhaps a deer caught by a bobcat. No, it was a human cry. Did the boys meet with danger? Abram listened, his hearing attuned to the slightest whisper of leaves. He heard the cry again, a moan.

He pulled himself up to see better and scanned the hillside sloping into the valley. He spotted something red, something striped.

"Someone is hurt," he said to his God. "I must help."

Abram stepped carefully down a deer path, holding up his robe so as not to trip and watching the uneven earth so as not to stumble. It was the path that led to the pool, the falls, and the white cross, and he knew it well. He padded silently, not disturbing the world in which he moved, like a hunter, watching and listening, singing softly to his Father in Heaven.

> *Great is Thy faithfulness! Great is Thy faithfulness!*
> *Morning by morning new mercies I see.*
> *All I have needed Thy hand hath provided.*
> *Great is thy faithfulness, Lord unto me!*[4]

As Abram rounded a bend he saw a man dusty with dirt, lying unmoving against a stone slab in the grass. Abram judged he was a hiker who had fallen. He appeared unconscious, but the moaning? A large bruise was forming on his forehead, covered in beads of sweat. He had dark brown hair and brows, olive skin, high cheekbones. His Broncos cap had fallen off, and his hair, neatly trimmed, was matted with dirt. Abram examined his forehead, dabbing the moisture with his sleeve. There did not appear to be any bleeding, just the nasty purple welt. Abram placed two fingers on the man's neck and felt a weak pulse.

"Awake!" he whispered. "It is time to wake up."

Abram lowered himself alongside the man and placed his arm around him, lifting his head slightly to help him breathe. He was young, Abram thought, too young to be leaving this Earth—late thirties, he guessed, as he offered a prayer for the young man's recovery.

Chapter 7

Elizabeth pulled on her tweed cardigan and loaded the car with her garden cart and bag of snacks and drinks, including the cards and towels Abram had requested. She tried to respect his sense of divine vocation.

She drove as fast as she dared. She had a terrible premonition something had happened. But then she usually did have just such a premonition every time she carried supplies to Abram and his cave on Angel Mountain. He had been in that cave for over three years now, three years too long. What was he thinking, living like that? Taking such risks? He was fortunate the rangers did not report him and allowed him to use the nearby campground facilities. How long would that last? Would he be arrested? Why could he not live like a normal person—in a house with a roof with running water and plumbing? She knew the answer to that—Greece and the Holocaust. She shook her head, as though the situation was hopeless, and her mourning, as well as the nightmares, would begin all over. She needed to count her blessings and banish the darkness.

She drove through her leafy neighborhood that skirted the mountain. Soon she was at the gates where she stopped and lowered her car window.

Ranger Tony Mitchell peered down at her. "Good morning, Mrs. Jacobsen. It was a mild earthquake—epicenter to the south, magnitude 2.5. All clear now, but take care just the same. Checking on Abram? Glad you are. We haven't had a chance to get there yet." He saluted her, raising his right hand to his brim, his brows pulled together in a friendly way, his eyes crinkly and his smile genuine, reminding Elizabeth of a cowboy from an old Western film. He was probably early forties and well over six feet, a big man, both in spirit and heft, Elizabeth thought. He wore his ranger uniform proudly: a tan long-sleeve shirt with a ranger's star and the word *Ranger* sewn above the right pocket, his name above the left pocket, a circular badge on the upper sleeve, with the image of the California grizzly bear, the state animal, in the gold center with a border of blue and the words "California State Parks" brightly showcasing the state colors of blue and gold. His gun was holstered and a set of keys dangled from one of the waist loops of dark green slacks. A two-way radio hung over one shoulder, attached to a coiled cord.

"Yes, I am checking on Abram. Thank you, Tony."

She headed up switchbacks to a dirt road and parked in a lot near a campground. There did not appear to be many visitors at this early hour, but she guessed there would be more later, this being a Sunday and a long weekend for some.

At the edge of the campground stood massive rock formations. Abram's cave was deep inside the maze of quartz sandstone, soft and porous, said to be forty-five million years old. Elizabeth had read that the rock was cemented with calcium carbonate. When it rained over the years, the water dissolved the calcium carbonate, and the process sculpted caverns and tunnels.

Elizabeth unloaded her bag onto her garden cart and bumped it along the trail until she came to a familiar opening. She lifted the bag from the cart and entered. She had memorized the route. She turned left here, right, right, left and right, weaving in and out. There, hidden behind a broad and dense foothill pine, was Abram's secret entrance, or at least she hoped it was still secret. She glanced around to see if anyone were watching, lowered her head, and stepped inside.

The cavern was dim in spite of the light entering a second doorway opposite, but Elizabeth was relieved to see that there was no obvious damage from the earthquake. Even the icons appeared straight and in place on their trellis.

Abram's icons gazed at her, and she stood for a moment before the Abraham icon, the story of Abraham and Sarah offering refreshments to three visiting angels. Abram called it the Trinity icon and had explained its Christian meaning, but for Elizabeth, it would always be the wonderful story of the angel telling Sarah she would conceive in her old age. Sarah had laughed. But the prophecy came true, and she did conceive and give birth to a son. They named him Isaac, meaning "laughter." Elizabeth recalled that Isaac, son of Abraham, was father to Jacob, renamed Israel, the father of twelve sons, who led the twelve tribes of Israel.[5] And so, the people of Israel were called to follow the Lord God Jehovah. And they did follow him. How Elizabeth loved the litany of her line, her legacy. The names sang like poetry.

But where was Abram? Not here, clearly. She set the bag down, crossed to the sunny doorway, and stepped outside to the stone promontory where he prayed over the land. No Abram. Elizabeth stepped gingerly to the edge of the cliff to view the valley below. Where was he? Had he fallen? She rubbed her hands, scanning the shrubs and trees. What should she do?

Elizabeth felt for the phone in her pocket, but Abram would not like it if she gave away his location. She stepped back from the edge, uncertain. She looked out over the hillside again, scrutinizing the grasses, the pond far below, the white cross on the other side, the waterfall pouring into the pond. All seemed eerily quiet, except for the sound of the water and a hawk soaring above, cawing.

Did he take the deer path leading to the pond? Could she maneuver down this narrow track? It was terribly steep and uneven. Once again, she regretted her slight overweight and poor balance.

She glanced at the sandstone formations behind and above her and headed cautiously down the path, one step at a time.

Chapter 8

Catherine Nelson may not have recognized the gunshots, but she did recognize her entry buzzer. She opened the door a fraction and peeked past the chain guard.

Pat Pearson stood in the hallway, a tiny middle-aged woman, the daughter of Korean immigrants. "Did you forget, Catherine?" Her smile was kind as she entered, but her forehead wrinkled with worry. "And today is the one-year anniversary of your mother's death."

"Of course I didn't forget." Catherine shook her head, surprised that she had forgotten Aunt Pat and her offer to drive her to the Lafayette cemetery. Her mother's best friend and coworker at the bank had been good to Catherine, who had called her Aunt Pat as long for as she could remember.

Aunt Pat fiddled with her car keys. "I miss her. She was like a younger sister."

"I know, Aunt Pat." Catherine closed her computer and pulled her hoodie from the closet. "I'm sorry. I've been a bit distracted. I quit my job."

"Lord have mercy." Aunt Pat rolled her eyes. "We can talk while I drive."

Catherine nodded, locking the door behind them and following the petite form out to her car. Pat reminded Catherine of an antique doll, with her porcelain skin and straight black hair, cut neatly at the nape of her neck and combed to one side. Catherine wondered how old she was. She looked young but she must be early sixties by now. Her mother would be fifty-five if she were alive today.

Sirens wailed as they drove through Berkeley, and Aunt Pat pulled over to the curb, near Saint Joseph's Chapel, where Catherine's mother once attended. They waited for the police and ambulance pass in the direction of the campus. "I'll never get used to sirens," Pat said. "Hope it's not serious." She made the sign of the cross.

Catherine followed her gaze toward the Campanile, its bells tolling, then to the chapel. No windows faced the street, and the plain stucco walls rose to a domed roof, like a fortress. A primitive crucifix hung near a red front door. Catherine recalled her mother saying that the figure on the cross connected the church to the community, a refuge for all the wounded souls of the world. Today, the porch was refuge to a ragged sleeping bag covering a still form, sleeping at the foot of the cross. Nearby, an empty shopping cart held a pair of dangling shoes and odds and ends. A scrawled sign read: "need f'n tobacco."

Aunt Pat smiled, glancing at Catherine. "I met your mother at this chapel. Seems there are still homeless camped on the porch."

"I thought you met at work."

"She found the job for me."

"Really?"

"My brother worked as a janitor for the chapel, and I used to wait for him in the parking lot to drive him home in our family pickup truck. I was nearing forty but had gone back to school part-time to learn accounting so our family could move up in the world. Not UC, but community college—Berkeley City College." She glanced at Catherine and grinned. "The American dream was alive and well in our house!"

"I never heard that story." Catherine listened to each word as though her mother were there, enjoying the telling.

"One day your mother saw me waiting in the truck. She handed me three roses left over from the bouquet she had made for the Lady Altar, in gratitude for my patience, she said. Then she invited me to the service inside. It was lovely and I returned on occasion. And later your mother found me a job in the accounts department in the bank in San Francisco. Your mother was a saint."

The sirens having receded, they drove toward Lafayette, through the Caldecott Tunnel that burrowed through the East Bay Hills. As Catherine explained about quitting her job, Aunt Pat listened quietly, nodding. "I'll keep a look out for you," she said, glancing at Catherine.

"Thanks. It's not going to be easy these days. I should have been more careful."

"It was wrong of them to take offense, and especially wrong of your supervisor to make such an issue over it." Aunt Pat frowned. "What's happening to our world?"

They continued in silence as if in mourning, and Catherine sighed deeply as they exited the tunnel into the world of suburbia, leaving the pressures of city life—its noise and pollution, its fears and anxieties—behind. This eastern side of the tunnel, with its gentle hills populated by old oaks, quiet communities, and more open space, spoke to Catherine of peace. She wondered how accurate that assessment was, or if it was all a mirage. They passed the sleepy village of Orinda, and on the far side of Lafayette, they exited the freeway, taking Pleasant Hill Road toward the cemetery. Catherine recalled that beyond Lafayette was Walnut Creek, a central shopping area, and to the south was leafy Danville with its golf courses and horse ranches. The wild grassy hills, vividly green in winter and spring, turned golden brown in the summer and fall, and temperatures were both colder and warmer than in Berkeley by the bay.

She wasn't sure why her mother had chosen to be buried in a Lafayette cemetery, except that Father Brubaker at Saint Joseph's had approved, since it was a Christian cemetery and well looked after. There may have been a reason Catherine didn't know, for there were many questions she wished she had asked her mother when she was alive, but now it was too late. Would she never see her again? Father Brubaker, a portly priest who seemed to glow with an inner happiness, said they would one day re-unite in Heaven. He was sure of it.

They arrived at Queen of Heaven Cemetery. The gates were wide open, and Aunt Pat steered the car into the parking lot.

They walked through rows of graves nesting in the green grass, and soon stood before a small headstone reading, "Ellen Catherine Nelson, beloved mother and friend, 1963–2017."

They sat on a bench and Aunt Pat pulled her rosary from her purse. She prayed silently, moving small fingers over the beads, her black feathery lashes fluttering.

Catherine stared at the carved headstone, clasping her hands together. Her mother had given her so much, against so many odds, but how little Catherine knew of her. "I'm going to walk around for a bit," Catherine said. "You okay?"

Aunt Pat nodded, returning to her beads. "I'll catch up with you."

Her mother was religious like Aunt Pat, Catherine recalled as she followed the path that circled the grounds. She lit candles and prayed to Our Lady or the crucifix over the altar in the chapel. Catherine often thought that the reason *she* wasn't religious was because her mother *was* religious. Her mother prayed for her, so Catherine didn't have to. But Catherine had liked the chapel. She liked the organ and the singing even if she wouldn't admit it. The beauty filled her with something she couldn't describe, transcending words. It was exciting—but peaceful too—which made no sense at all, as if the far away merged with the here and now, Heaven with Earth, transcendence with imminence. Music did that sometimes, Catherine thought, a kind of miracle.

Aunt Pat appeared at her side and they walked together in silence.

Catherine glanced at the gentle hillsides cradling the cemetery. "My mother liked Saint Joseph's Chapel, so close to home. She took me with her when I was little."

Aunt Pat grinned. "But you don't go on your own, do you?" In the ensuing awkward silence, Pat added hesitantly, "What happened?" She folded her hands and looked into the hills.

"As I grew older, I felt hemmed in by the rules—the many commandments. At Cal my instructors said I should do as I pleased, reach my full potential. They empowered me with grievance and entitlement. They taught me about social justice and consciousness-raising. They said it wasn't fair that some folks had more than others. They said that we should all be equal and the rich owed the poor to make them equally rich. What do you think?"

Aunt Pat shook her head. "I think it's deplorable to be so ungrateful for this country, its freedoms, its opportunities. We are all blessed to be here. I have family in North Korea . . ." Her voice choked.

"I'm sorry. How thoughtless of me." North Korea! Concentration camps. Torture. How could she have been so self-centered, so insensitive?

"It's okay." Pat's voice trembled, the words hanging between the two women like accusations. "Please, go on."

Catherine spoke quietly now, treading carefully. "I learned these lessons from my teachers, and the apartment Mom and I shared seemed to become shabbier and shabbier."

"I can understand that. My siblings have experienced this too. And now? You never returned to the chapel?"

Catherine could feel her love. "I embraced empowerment rather than religion. But I know my mother did her best. I shouldn't complain."

Aunt Pat looked to the hills. "I've found that religion is empowering, maybe even more so than the things you mentioned."

"Maybe for you—I don't know. It doesn't seem to help with the job search."

They walked back in sympathetic silence, arriving at her mother's grave.

"I'm certain of one thing," Aunt Pat said, eyeing the headstone. "Your mother is in Heaven and we'll see her one day."

Catherine nodded. "I'm not so sure, but it sounds good."

Catherine's phone buzzed a local news notification. "There's been a protest on campus again. And a shooter. Not far from the chapel. The police and ambulance must have been heading there."

"I should check on my brother." Aunt Pat pulled out her phone. She tapped a number and left a message. "He was working at the chapel today. He sympathizes with the protests and sometimes goes to watch. Foolish boy. Although he's not a boy—he's turning fifty."

"We better get back."

Chapter 9

Gregory felt a strong arm support his back. He looked up into eyes full of concern, a weathered and wrinkled face, a white beard and bushy eyebrows. Silvery hair pulled back. A muslin robe. "Who are you? Where am I?" Gregory asked.

"It is okay, my son. It is okay."

"What happened?" A searing pain radiated through his skull, and the viselike stabbing increased as he tried to right himself and sit on his own. He needed to assess his damages.

"Careful, son. How do you feel? Chest pain? Leg pain?"

"My head, my head." Gregory pulled away from the man's hold. "I'm all right." He tried to stand, then crumpled to the ground. "Maybe not," he added, holding his head and massaging his temples.

"You need to take it easy, lad."

"Who are you?" Was he dreaming? The man looked like an Old Testament prophet, or at least the Bible pictures he had seen as a boy. "Am I dead? Where am I? Is this Heaven? Are you God?"

The old man rose to his full height. He was not tall, but the billowing robe blown in the wind gave the impression of a giant on this mountainside, his form framed against the sky.

As Gregory gazed at the vision, the old man raised his arms to the heavens. "I am one who comes to prepare the way of the Lord. To preach repentance."

Had he time-traveled? Wasn't that only in fiction? "What year is this?"

The old man, his hood falling from his head, said gently, "It is the year 2018. I am Abram, and this is Angel Mountain. I found you. What is your name?"

"Worthington, sir . . . Gregory. Dr. Worthington."

"Dr. Gregory Worthington, you must have hit your head."

Gregory recalled the snake. He recalled falling. He considered his possible injuries, seeing himself as a doctor would see a patient. He felt his ribs, his legs, his arms. He took his pulse. All seemed good. But the cranial pain screamed through him, from ear to ear. "How did you find me?"

Abram laughed. He raised a small American flag. "Your flag in the grass, and so close to the white cross." He glanced at the cross on the other side of the pond. "Someone was bound to find you, child. But sooner is better than later, on this eleventh day of the eleventh month. Sooner is better in these wilds of coyote and bobcat and rattler and hawk."

"Thank you, sir." Gregory recalled the local stories of a hermit in the foothills. "Are you the hermit . . . they talk about?"

"They talk about me?" Abram asked, sounding worried.

"Stories."

"What kind of stories?"

"A hermit . . . on Mount Diablo . . . changed the name."

"Ha!" He grinned, seeming mollified, and rubbed his beard. "So I did. And high time, too."

Gregory could see he was quite old, with yellowing teeth. His hair, tied in a band at the base of his neck, trailed down his back. Silver brows framed deep blue eyes. His nose was long and crooked, as though once broken. His leathery skin had been burned by sun, parched by wind, spotted by age. He was thin, his shoulders seeming to bend inward as though malformed through genetics or poor nutrition.

"What, what . . . why . . . why . . ." Gregory was growing groggy, and he sensed his speech was slurring. Slowly, he laid his head down on his pack in the grass. "I'm just going to rest for a bit."

As he closed his eyes, he heard the old man whisper, "You rest, but try not to sleep. I shall finish my morning song."

"Just closing my eyes." As he did, the pain in his head lessened, and he struggled to stay awake, listening to the old man sing. He was sure the throbbing in his head would keep him awake, and it did.

And Abram sang:

> O be joyful in the Lord, all ye lands: serve the Lord with gladness, and come before his presence with a song.
> Be ye sure that the Lord he is God; it is he that hath made us, and not we ourselves. we are his people, and the sheep of his pasture.
> O go your way into his gates with thanksgiving, and into his courts with praise; be thankful unto him, and speak good of his Name.
> For the Lord is gracious, his mercy is everlasting; and his truth endureth from generation to generation.[6]

Gregory recognized the Psalm. The hermit sang to the tune of an ancient chant, familiar from his childhood. Perhaps it was Saint Mary's . . .

Chapter 10

Abram looked up and saw his sister Elizabeth struggling down the path, waving her arms, crying, "I am coming, Abram, I am coming!"

She wore jeans and Samuel's cardigan under her down jacket. Her chestnut curls caught the early light, and her large blue eyes were full of concern. He realized he had caused her alarm by being absent from the cave. With the earthquake, he should have known she would come to check on him.

Abram moved toward his sister, smiling gently. "I am okay, Elizabeth, but I found someone who is not okay. He may need medical attention." Abram massaged his chest where the rock had hit. It was probably just a bruise.

Elizabeth looked relieved. Abram embraced her gently, kissing her on each cheek and searching her eyes. "My dear sister, you trouble yourself so."

"But the earthquake?"

"No damage as far as I can see. But there is something you should know—some hikers saw me this morning." He led her to the man lying in the grass. "But that is another story. This fellow seems to have fallen from the trail above. He appears all right except for a headache. His name is Gregory Worthington." His name sounded familiar, but Abram could not place it.

Gregory looked up, tried to stand, but failed, and lay back again. "Pleased to meet you . . . Your brother found me . . . saved me."

"Please, do not get up, Dr. Worthington," Elizabeth said, reaching for his hand with her own. "I am pleased to meet you too. I am Elizabeth Jacobsen, and this is my brother, Abram. We need to take you to a clinic. I will call an ambulance." She pulled out her phone.

"We can manage alone," Abram said hopefully. "It would be best if we could." The young man seemed all right. A bruise was forming above his right eye.

"I can manage," Gregory added, "with a little help." With their support on either side, he was able to stand. "I have a car at the upper trailhead."

"I can bear his weight," Abram said. "He is taller, but slim. Elizabeth, you go ahead." He wrapped one arm around his back.

Elizabeth led the way, carrying Gregory's pack. The three worked their way up the deer path, step by step, to the cave.

"Here we go." Abram was a bit out of breath and a pain shot through his lungs as he gasped for air. "In here with my saints and onto my bed. Bit of a hard bed, but it is all I have." Abram smiled, wishing he could offer Dr. Worthington greater hospitality. He found a cup, filled it with water from a jug, and handed it to him.

"There is your bag of supplies, Abram," Elizabeth said, pointing. "When he is rested a bit, we can help him to his car."

Gregory sat on the edge of the bed. "I mustn't be a burden. Please don't fuss. I'll be okay soon. Feeling better already."

Abram could see he was nervous. Not many would understand why Abram had retreated to this mountain, given up so much to fast and pray and heal. "It is okay, Dr. Worthington. But let this be our secret adventure. It would be best if you not tell anyone about me. Not yet." He tapped his nose and helped Elizabeth unpack the supplies. "Ah, more granola bars, protein drinks, and fresh fruit! Apples, bananas, grapes. And the cards and towels I asked for. Perfect! My dear, you spoil me."

"I wish you would come home."

"Soon," Abram said, thoughtfully stroking his beard and glancing at the icons. "Soon." He turned to Gregory. "Granola bar? Apple?"

"No, thank you." Gregory sipped from the cup.

Abram focused on the Trinity icon. "Tell me, are you an academic doctor or a medical doctor?"

Gregory followed his gaze. "Both."

"Medical?" Abram asked, turning toward Gregory. "What is your specialty?" He loved the stories living inside each person. He wanted to know everything, but had learned that he needed to inquire bit by bit, to not be rude. Still, he wanted it all now. He was greedy for Dr. Worthington's story, all of it.

"Genetics. The genome. Researching cures."

Abram glanced at Elizabeth. Her face had blanched white.

"It is a field fraught with moral questions," Abram said, concerned about his sister's reaction.

"And can be misused so easily by the state." Elizabeth shook her head and turned away toward the doorway and the outside promontory. "I need some air," she said. "I will be out here when he is ready."

Dr. Worthington nodded. "It can be misused. Needs oversight, guidance. I hope to help," he said to Elizabeth's retreating form. "Did I offend her?"

"Let her be." Abram sat next to Gregory.

"But I'd better go." Gregory rose slowly. "If Ms. Jacobsen can help me
to my car."

"She will be happy to do so, not to worry. She did not mean to be rude."
Abram returned his gaze to the Trinity icon.

"Your icons . . . are beautiful."

"They are my friends, my prayer companions, my congregation."

Gregory took another sip. "I'm a believer too, a believer in Jesus Christ."

"Are you?" Abram's curiosity grew. This fact was integral to the man's
story. "How did a believer become interested in genomes? In science at all?
Here, take this walking stick—I have a spare. It will help you to Elizabeth's
car. And do not forget your cap. Elizabeth has your bag." Abram wanted to
continue the conversation, but knew he must let the man go. He needed to
get medical attention, Abram scolded himself. Dr. Worthington needed to
go to a clinic.

Gregory leaned on the stick. "Thank you. And in answer to your question, sir, it was the genome. It led me to God. It changed my life . . . and my
career, it seems." He looked rueful, massaging his head. "The elegance . . .
the complexity . . . the beauty of creation! Clearly an intelligent design. C.S.
Lewis led me to Christ."

Every detail of a story opened another door to more details, more stories, thought Abram. Every person contained a world, a universe, within.
Abram had so many questions. "May you be blessed," Abram said, making
the sign of cross over the young doctor. "I would be pleased to meet with
you again. Visit me soon—when you are better."

Gregory glanced back at the wall of icons, then at Abram. "Thank you.
I hope we meet again. I would like to know . . . why you are in this cave."

Abram nodded. He would give the short answer, the least painful one.
"They say I have run away, but I have, in truth, run towards. Angel Mountain
called me and I came. I found this cavern," he said, looking about his home,
"full of light at night, full of angels. Rainbows descend upon the mountain.
Have you seen them? Angels dance in the prisms, their eyes bright, looking
at me, holding me in their gaze. Can you see them now?"

Gregory's brown eyes had grown large with astonishment, and Abram
feared he had said too much.

"I am not crazy," Abram added, "as some say."

"But visions?"

He nodded, looking at Gregory, then casting his eyes down to his
folded hands. "They say I am a hermit. They say I have renounced the

world, but I have, in truth, great possessions. I forgo much, but receive God back. I abandon time for eternity, for there is no time in my cave on Angel Mountain. There is day and there is night. There is sunlight and there is shadow." Abram now gazed upon the Transfiguration icon. He rested in the transfigured image of Christ, his features full of bright glory, risen in the clouds between Elijah and Moses. The three disciples knelt in awe, not fully understanding what was happening. "They say I am a hermit. They say I have deserted humankind but in truth I lead them. I live in obscurity, but my cave is known to Heaven, as I am known, as you are known."

Gregory stood next to him, his gaze also on the Transfiguration of Christ.

Abram's voice was growing hoarse, but he continued. "They say I am a hermit. They say I am useless, but in truth I keep the world from crumbling, with my prayers to our dear Lord Jesus and my psalms to Almighty God, Father and Creator of us all."

Dr. Worthington touched Abram's arm. "I think I understand." Then he added, "but your sister is waiting."

Elizabeth came in from the outside ledge, and Abram was thankful she seemed to have recovered from the jolt of memory that pulled her back to her childhood, to the terror of Greece and the Holocaust.

"May God be with you," he said to Gregory, making the sign of the cross.

"Until we meet again," Gregory replied.

Abram watched the doctor follow Elizabeth through the doorway to the sandstone passages that led to her car.

"I keep the world from crumbling," Abram whispered to the saints on the wall.

Chapter 11

"Thank you for doing this," Gregory said. "My car is in the upper trailhead lot."

Elizabeth was silent, biting her lip, not wanting to be impolite. Dr. Worthington helped her place the cart and his pack in the back of her van. She opened the passenger door for him, and he lowered himself inside. She took the driver's seat and tapped the ignition button.

"I am sorry," Gregory said, his cap in his hands, "so very sorry to have upset you."

She glanced at his face, his bruised forehead crinkled in worry, his deep brown eyes showing genuine apology. "You did not know," she said. Her voice was harsh, she realized, and she tried once more to be civil as they drove to where his car was parked. "I am Jewish. We are Jewish. We survived the Holocaust. We survived Hitler." That should do it, she thought. End of conversation.

"The Holocaust!" Gregory cried. "How terrible."

"Hitler worked with genes, genetics." How could she explain without going into details?

"I see." He sounded thoughtful as if he were absorbing the full import of what she had said. "Hitler espoused racial eugenics, adopting Darwin's evolutionary theories, to produce the master race."

"That is it," she said. He understood. "Best not talk about it." Elizabeth kept her eyes on the road with a determination honed from decades of survival. "Nightmares," she blurted. "Still have nightmares, after all this time."

"But . . . I want to explain."

"Another time, perhaps." If there is another time, she thought. She hoped not.

They drove in silence to the parking area, where Elizabeth parked alongside Gregory's car.

Gregory turned to her. "Could I trouble you with another question? I'm curious. Why do you think your brother is living up here?"

Elizabeth could see the doctor was trying to change the subject, to end their meeting with some kind of courtesy. "My brother is a Christian," she answered. She faced him and saw his regret, worry, and dismay. "He converted. I did not. It was our host families, I think. We were children. They were Greek Orthodox. He wanted to be like them. He was a baby." She covered her face with her hands. She still sounded rude, abrupt, sharp. "I do not know why he is here. Being here seems to help."

"I think I understand."

"I am sorry. I have been unkind. You are a good man, I am sure. You stumbled into a complicated situation." The poor man fell down the mountain, she reminded herself. He was injured. She wondered at her own hardheartedness.

"I'm bringing back bad memories," he said.

They walked to his sedan, and she handed him his backpack. It seemed the least she could do.

He looked upon her with such compassion, and once again she felt guilty. "Please keep the walking stick," she said. "Abram would want you to have it. You might need it for a time."

"Thank you, Ms. Jacobsen," he said, "for all you have done. Your brother saved me first, and you saved me second. How can I repay you? You saved my life."

"There *is* something you can do. You can promise us something."

"Of course."

"Please do not give away Abram's location. Do not mention you saw him. He will know when the time is right."

"I promise. And I shall repay you somehow." He slid behind the steering wheel and looked up at her through the open door.

"You had better see a doctor," she said, "after hitting your head like that. It is swelling."

"An MRI might be a good idea. Thank you again."

She watched him drive away, then opened her car door. She touched the ignition button and followed the road down the mountain. Turning west toward her home in the foothills, a deep darkness crept over her. How could anyone—anyone—have a career in genetics? And still be human? They must see where it leads—eugenics. She wiped her eyes with the back of her hand. How could these people be so foolhardy, so blind?

Elizabeth Levin Jacobsen did not write in her gratitude journal that evening. Instead, she pulled out her albums to find photos of Samuel. Samuel would banish the ghosts just as he always had. How she missed him.

Chapter 12

Back in her apartment, Catherine heated a can of vegetable soup and toasted whole-grain bread for her supper, thinking about the cemetery visit and her mother. It was dark outside—nearly 7 p.m.—and she shivered as an early fog pressed against the window.

She turned to the local news on her laptop: twelve dead, six wounded, killer at large, shots from the library top floor, looked to be a White supremacist, American flags burned in the central quad for the sins of America. What next? She checked the bolt on her door. Who would have had access to the top floor of the library? It was closed for renovations.

A second news story caught her eye. A hermit had been spotted on Mount Diablo, a.k.a. Angel Mountain. She scanned the article. He hadn't been seen in some time and had reappeared. It was thought that the park rangers left him alone as long as he wasn't a danger to the land or the hikers. But now things might change. Religious hermits—and especially those who preached like Old Testament prophets—weren't popular today. Preachers were objects of ridicule, the reporter continued, since they were enemies of science and reason. And it was, after all, public property, a state park. If nothing else, the hermit was trespassing. He had likely overstayed any camping permit.

Catherine wondered what that was all about, but she remembered how her instructors scorned religious faith, especially Christianity. Other religions were less threatening, not being homegrown, but seeming exotic, she guessed. Christianity, on the other hand, had influenced Western culture for centuries and remained a ghost, one that haunted modernity with objective—not subjective—standards of right and wrong.

She switched websites to the employment listings. There was an antiquarian bookstore that needed a cataloger. A local history museum needed a store manager. No library jobs listed. She would go by the local public libraries sometime this week. She needed to set up interviews for the museum and bookstore, but with the holiday weekend it appeared they were closed.

A text message from Aunt Pat chimed on her phone. Her brother was safe at home—no worries. She would see Catherine at Monday's line dancing class. With that thought, Catherine smiled. The music and the order of the dance, while not exactly making her happy, improved her mood, at least most of the time. It held happiness in the beat and the steps and the sisterhood among the women.

How she missed her mother, she thought as she readied for bed. The BART train whined in the distance. A dog barked. And who was her father? Where was her father? Was he even living? She opened a file on her laptop and began a letter to her father. She had never done so, but she had read that it was good therapy to write down your troubles, so why not write to her phantom father? Maybe it would clear her mind so she could move on with her life.

> Dear Father,
>
> In spite of the fact that you abandoned me, I am still your daughter. Mama said she loved you and you loved her. So what happened?
>
> I may never find your address, but if I do I can send you this. I didn't have Down syndrome, but even if I did it wasn't a reason to kill me off. There—I said it. You wanted me dead. I fully realize this. You wanted a perfect child and that wouldn't be me.
>
> After you left Mama (with me inside), she got a job as an office assistant at a bank in San Francisco. She took rapid transit. She worked eight to five and came home exhausted around seven each night, carrying groceries from the corner market. Somehow she raised me by herself. There never was anyone else for her but you, you dog. You broke her heart. You made her choose between you and me.
>
> Mama liked to go to a chapel near campus. On Sundays, while she was there lighting candles, I hung out with my friends from school. I didn't want to be alone in the apartment. Sometimes we joined other groups and protested righteous causes. Once we joined a pro-choice rally and I recalled how I might have died before even being born, but lived instead, no thanks to you. Something inside winced. But then I heard my teachers' chorus in my head: "A woman should have the right to choose what she does with her own body!" My mother made the right and moral choice.

My grades dropped since I didn't study, and I couldn't fake it any more. Mama got really angry. She rarely was angry since she was praying all the time and was too tired to be angry, but she pulled herself together this once and spoke sternly in a voice that totally scared me.

She sat me down at the scuffed kitchen table—my desk and hers and where we ate. She said that at the end of the year— eighth grade—I was no longer going to public school. She said she had arranged for me to go to Grace Academy, a Christian school. A Christian school! What about my friends? I asked. She said things had to change, and that she had a message from God!

I needed you then to take my side. I didn't speak to her for a week—she called it sulking—but my silence and sulking hurt me more than her, and on Sunday she urged me to go to the chapel with her. She said she just wanted my company. That was kind of sweet, so I went.

Over the summer that year I tried to go to church with her. I guess I felt sorry for her. But in the process, the chapel grew on me, into me sort of. I loved the music. We sat on benches and the sounds boomed high through red barrel vaulting. I liked the preacher and the way he told stories and I could imagine myself in the story, see the setting, hear the words of Jesus. Jesus healed. Jesus made all kinds of wonderful promises, like Santa Claus. Jesus spoke of Heaven as if it were a real place—a man- sion—prepared just for us. In fact lots of things were prepared for us—there was a prayer where we thanked God for giving us good works that are prepared for us to walk in. Mama said the good works were a path through life.

Papa, did you find a path prepared to walk on, a path with- out me?

Your living but not loving daughter,
Catherine

P.S. I wish I knew your name.

Catherine closed her laptop. She did feel better, having written the words down, words that burned like hot coals in her heart. What if she were still involved in protest marches? What if she were in the crowd this morn- ing when the shooter opened fire? What if she had chosen the wrong path to walk on? What if her mother hadn't gotten angry and sent her to a new school, a strict school, away from her gang of friends?

She breathed deeply and pulled out a photo of her mother she kept in her wallet. It was taken at the chapel by the priest. They were in front of the white marble font with the holy water. Her mother held baby Catherine in her arms and Aunt Pat stood next to her. The bishop towered behind them, in his white robe and golden miter, smiling, arms outstretched, encompassing them. Pat and her mother looked happy, but her mother also looked bravely determined. It was Catherine's baptism, and the date was printed neatly on the back, Easter Eve, 1985. She didn't recognize the writing, so she guessed it was the priest's.

Now, without her mother and without employment, Catherine considered a visit to the chapel some Sunday, to hear the music. She hadn't returned since the funeral a year ago. Maybe it was time. Maybe it would help her find the path she was supposed to be walking on.

And tomorrow, Monday, her line dancing class would make her feel better. She was sure that it made all the difference in her depression levels.

Chapter 13

Gregory's head throbbed as he headed to the local hospital. Maneuvering down Angel Mountain was more exhausting than he thought it would be, and he worked to keep his eyes open at each bend in the road. He was relieved to make it through the park gates before closing time, dusk, and to the freeway and Walnut Creek Hospital. At last, safe at the emergency room sliding doors, he handed his car keys to an attendant.

The waiting room was packed and he recalled it was Sunday afternoon, usually a busy time. The registration desk recorded his details and asked him to take a seat. Gregory knew that heart patients came first, but he thought that his head injury might be a close second.

He picked up a magazine and gazed at it, unfocused, his eyes weary.

The last year had been an unstable one, he reflected, rubbing his temples. His life appeared to be continuing in that fashion. He was dumbfounded, and then angry, when he recently received notice that his sabbatical from the university had been extended a second year by the dean who, in a friendly letter, insisted that he take his time with his book and the extensive research required. It was true he was only drawing a partial salary, which wasn't much, but he had Aunt Jane's trust fund. Could this be a crossroads in his life that might be for the better?

Instability, he thought, often resulted in healthy change and a resettling of life. Although painful for the most part, especially for a man with a need for order like himself, still it challenged him to think outside the box. He had discovered that science didn't have all the answers after all and he wanted answers: the truth, nothing but the truth.

Gregory had been awestruck by the elegant magnificence of a genome in a microscope. This led to the genome's creator and belief in God. After reading *Mere Christianity* by C. S. Lewis, he found reasons to believe in the deity of Christ. He had been invited on a stimulating journey of spiritual discovery. He had used the past year not only to work on his book about his conversion experience, a kind of testimony-memoir about the complementarity of faith and science, but also to continue his spiritual quest.

His quest had begun two years ago. He had visited churches to try them out. C. S. Lewis was an Anglican, so Gregory tried the Anglicans first. This meant the modern Episcopalians, then the traditional Episcopalians, who now called themselves Anglicans to set themselves apart. He tried the Catholics and he tried the Presbyterians. He tried the Methodists, the Lutherans, and the Baptists. He even visited the Greek Orthodox church in the Oakland Hills. He finally found he was most comfortable in a student chapel near campus, Saint Joseph's, recommended by his landlord, Father Brubaker, who served there as chaplain. Gregory came to enjoy his mile walk from his home in the hills to the service on a Sunday morning. This was before his speech in the crowded hall about the complementarity of faith and science. This was before the Veterans Day riot of 2017 and his subsequent sabbatical.

Now, in the emergency waiting room, the registration clerk called him back to the counter. "Your address? This hotel in Lafayette? You're no longer in Berkeley?" She looked at him doubtfully, arching her brows. "What happened to the Berkeley post office box?"

"I closed it. I'm a Cal professor on sabbatical and am staying at the hotel for now." He needed to settle on an apartment soon, he thought, but at least the hotel's monthly rate was good. It was a small room, but quiet, in the back with a parking lot view. Once he decided what he was going to do with the rest of his life, he would move into an apartment, along with his books and furniture in storage. But what was he going to do with the rest of his life?

"Okay, then." She smiled. "Just confirming. It won't be long."

He returned to his seat.

He had been exiled from Berkeley by the antifa. After his lecture and the violent reaction to his words, and after the dean recommended a sabbatical, he rethought his own security. He added an alarm system to his cottage in the Berkeley Hills, and Father Brubaker, a man of many talents, helped him install it, since he lived next door. The hate mail and obscene calls, however, disturbed Gregory. He rented a postal box and changed his phone number. He watched for anyone following him and reported a number of false alarms to the police, who gave him tips on increased safety measures. Father Brubaker gave him good advice on how to deal with all of this, but over the summer a window was shattered and obscene graffiti was scrawled on Gregory's front door. Even the pastor appeared shaken. Gregory decided he would do the honorable thing, and protect his kind priest and friend. Gregory knew Father Brubaker would never complain, which made Gregory's decision even more imperative.

Why did they hate him for publicly stating his views as a religious scientist? He had read recently that the chairman of the U.S. Civil Rights Commission had written in 2016 in an official report that "religious liberty and religious freedom remain code words for discrimination, intolerance, racism, sexism, homophobia, Islamophobia, Christian supremacy or any form of intolerance." No wonder some felt they were doing society a favor by shutting down religious speech in the public square.

Gregory shifted in his chair, still holding the magazine, unseeing.

In considering a new location, Gregory recalled his hikes up Angel Mountain, a.k.a. Mount Diablo. He thought, why not go east, find something on the other side of the East Bay Hills, on the other side of the Caldecott Tunnel? It was more rural, and, while not the Rockies, there was space to breathe. And he needed time and space, breathing space, away from the university battles, away from his old life.

He needed to figure out who he was all over again, now that he claimed to be a Christian. What were the good works he was to walk in, the path he was to take, as the chapel liturgy asked him? Who was Dr. Gregory Worthington, geneticist, molecular biologist, professor of science, with advanced degrees from Stanford and UC Berkeley? Who was this thirty-seven-year-old, born in Denver in 1981, orphaned at age four, and raised by a genteel aunt in a century-old mansion? In the last year, he hadn't found many answers.

Thinking of Aunt Jane, he wondered if he should return to research and find that cure for Parkinson's, or practice medicine in a hospital such as this one in which he found himself waiting with a throbbing head? Should he teach the snowflake generation, so prone to meltdowns, try to strengthen those weak minds with truth and logic in a university setting? Was his academic career over for good? He didn't know.

A nurse appeared in a side doorway, holding a clipboard. "Gregory Worthington? This way, please. How are you today?"

MONDAY

Chapter 14

Monday morning Abram gazed upon the icon of the Transfiguration, thinking of his encounter with Gregory Worthington and Gregory's encounter with Christ. The man's face had lit up when he said he was a believer. His face reflected the beauty and light of Christ, like the angels, and like many Christians. Beauty and happiness—how we all yearn for beauty and happiness! Beauty, Dostoevsky wrote, will save the world. A generalization, and one that a Christian would have to qualify, saying Jesus alone can save the world, yet Abram knew what the great Russian novelist was saying. For when the face of righteousness is recognized as beautiful, happiness will follow. Heaven and Earth will be one. Aristotle said something similar; that a life of virtue would lead to happiness. Would mankind ever understand these simple things?

He splashed water on his face and turned to the icon of Saint Michael the Archangel. His dream in the early dawn, the time of his deepest dreaming, had been of Heaven itself. Everyone was active, working and playing, like a Pieter Bruegel painting. But it wasn't simply activity, busyness, he thought, pulling the vision of his night into his day. Abram sensed that each person in his dream was doing what they were meant to do, what they were created for. They were fulfilled by their own being, becoming the unique creature God had designed. And there was music this time, music transcending the spheres, the angels singing in choir, the people singing with them as they worked and played. And there were colors he could not describe, vivid, pleasing, beautiful colors. Holy colors.

"I understand," Abram said to his Lord, "I understand." With the scene, Abram saw why this beauty was so compelling. It was faith in God, hope in Heaven, and charity, love for one another. The cardinal virtues every child once learned—faith, hope, and charity—lead us to Heaven. Heaven now. For, Abram reflected, he never truly knew life until he knew God. Only then did he experience eternal life within this mortal life, knowing that eternity is now, this very moment.

As dawn filled his cave with morning light and his golden icons glimmered, he guessed Eden must have been something like his dream. In Eden, Heaven and Earth were one. Then it all changed. Death entered the garden, and life would need to be recovered, reborn.

Abram sang his morning prayers. With a full heart, he stepped outside and onto his ledge in the early light. The haze from the northern fires had retreated to the horizon. A few more seekers had hiked to his hillside, and they whispered among themselves, in the meadow near the pond and the waterfall. The white cross rose behind them in the long shadow of an oak. The seekers saw him and pointed.

Abram raised his hands in peace, knowing his time had come. He had been born for this hour of revealing, of fulfilling. He needed to empty his heart and soul and mind and let Christ fill him up. He must breathe the name of Jesus, in and out, with each breath, so that the Holy Name would be present among all who found him on this ledge, this hour, this month, this year of 2018 *Anno Domini*. He looked to the heavens and prayed, his emptiness filling up with joy with each word:

"Let the words of my mouth and the meditation of my heart, be acceptable in thy sight, Oh Lord, my strength, and my redeemer."

The gathering was suddenly silent. The seekers—around fifty he judged—were listening.

"What is happiness?" Abram cried. "Happiness is righteousness, following God's law."

A few moved closer, stepping up the deer path.

Abram continued. "Deep within us lies the moral law. We call it conscience. Listen to your conscience, for God has placed it in your soul, uniting your heart and mind." Abram laid his hand on his heart and nodded. "We came from God and will return to God. In the meantime, we must honor and obey God within and without."

Some drew near, sitting on outcrops. Others sat in the grass. Others stood and gazed upon him. Some faces held wonder. Some held disbelief. Some held scorn.

Abram continued. "You want to be happy?"

They nodded.

"Our conscience calls us—our God commands us—to love one another. He calls us to do good, to shun evil, to follow the laws he has given us through time, through the prophets, through his Son, Jesus, God in the flesh, Emmanuel, God with us. Our conscience is our most secret and deepest sanctuary. It is where God's voice echoes, sometimes still and small, as the prophet Elijah described. Listen to God's voice."

"Who are you?" someone shouted.

"You ask who I am? I am one crying in the wilderness. Repent! The Kingdom of Heaven is at hand! All flesh is like the grass, and the glory of man is like the flower. The grass withers and the flower falls away, but the word of the Lord endures forever.[7] This is good news! For this word is written on our hearts. We must learn God's law, trust him, and obey him. And then, my sons and daughters, we shall be happy."

"What is the Kingdom of Heaven?" another cried.

"You ask," Abram answered, "what is the Kingdom of Heaven? The Kingdom of Heaven is like a man who sowed good seed in his field. But an enemy sowed weeds among the good seed. Both the good seed and the weeds grew, but when harvest came, the weeds were burned and the good seed was gathered up.

"The Kingdom of Heaven is like a grain of mustard seed which became a great plant, when fully grown. The least of us become the greatest in this kingdom.

"The Kingdom of Heaven is the tiny bit of leaven that causes the entire loaf to rise. One person can change an entire people.

"The Kingdom of Heaven is a treasure hidden and found. It is a pearl of great price, newly discovered. It is a net that gathers the good and throws out the bad. It is all these things and more.[8]

"My friends! Waste no time! Be baptized today, repent today, change your ways, and enter the Kingdom of Heaven."

Someone shouted from the edge of the crowd that had now formed. "You are a prophet! What happens when we die? How do we know the way to Heaven?"

"Christ is the Way, the Truth, and the Life," Abram replied. "Believe in him. Trust and obey him."

Someone shouted near the pond. "Will we have bodies?"

Abram smiled. "Be baptized and you will be given the seed of your resurrection body. Feed the seed with the Eucharist, the food of immortality, and on the last day your new body will rise from the seed, clothed in glory."

"What will they be like? Our bodies?"

"Saint Paul says they will be incorruptible, immortal, and full of glory and power."

"Will we recognize our loved ones? Will they recognize us?"

"Yes, we will be known by those who knew us before, and we will be happy with the new bodies given to us."

There was a rustle in the crowd. They seemed interested. They were listening.

Abram spoke, and his words buoyed him on a current of image and sound. He had found his rhythm. "We will be perfected in Heaven. Our intelligence will be fully realized. Our sense of beauty will be acute, given the glories we shall experience. We will desire perfection in what we do and what we achieve. We will give to one another and love one another. Each one of us will become all that we were meant to be, unique, and loved."[9]

"How do you know this?"

"Because our dear Lord loves us. God is love. We give ourselves to him so that he can give himself to us. This is the meaning and glory of life."

Abram raised his arms to the skies as though pulling Heaven to Earth. He began to sing one of his favorite psalms, and as he sang, a breeze came up and blew his robes, as though anointing them with the Holy Spirit:

> O praise the Lord from the heavens: praise him in the heights.
> Praise him, all ye angels of his: praise him, all his host.
> Praise him, sun and moon: praise him, all ye stars and light.
> Praise him, all ye heavens, and ye waters that are above the heavens.
> Let them praise the Name of the Lord: for he spake the word, and they
>   were made; he commanded, and they were created.
> He hath made them fast forever and ever: he hast given them a law
>   which shall not be broken.[10]

"Follow God's law, repent, be baptized, and enter the Kingdom of Heaven! And know all happiness and joy!"

Chapter 15

In the dark of early Monday morning, Elizabeth awoke, screaming. Sitting up, she covered her face with her hands, pulling herself out of the nightmare. Laddie moved toward her and placed a paw on her arm as she turned on the light to dispel the demons. It was over. It was over. *Over.* She was safe. Her suitcase was packed and ready. She could run if need be. She was ready.

The nightmare was similar to others.

> *Elizabeth is six and trying to be brave. She is climbing a mountain with her father, sharing a mule, riding some of the time, walking some of the time, in shoes that are too tight. They follow a local tradesman, their rescuer, who rides a white horse.*
>
> *Her mother and baby brother have gone ahead with her grandmother and aunts, carrying supplies. But Elizabeth is with Papa. She is now a big girl, fearless they say. They tramp along a goat path through prickly brush and scattered trees.*
>
> *They are on Crete, a rocky volcanic island off the coast of Greece. It is the morning of May 20, 1941, and the Germans have attacked Maleme, a coastal airbase nearby. In the nightmare, as she climbs, Elizabeth sees the waters of the coast recede as parachutes descend on the beaches. Bombs explode and sirens wail and glass shatters.*
>
> *In the dream she knows that she must run, must escape. She knows her family needs to hide in the chapel at the top of the mountain. In the dream her feet cannot move fast enough as Papa pulls her up the mountain trail.*

Elizabeth turned to Laddie and stroked him. "It is okay, little one. It is okay."

Dawn was moving through the old oak that sheltered this end of the house, the weak light slipping through the curtains. Mice scuttled in the attic above, somewhere in the rafters, or perhaps they were birds sheltering in the eaves, or squirrels running on the roof. Owls sometimes could be heard during the night, but Elizabeth did not mind sharing her home with other survivors.

She slipped into her robe and looked out the window to Angel Mountain. The sun would not appear for another hour, but its promise was in the sky, the promise of light.

Elizabeth knew, as she remained on the gray edges of her nightmare, that the climb up Mount Tilifos on Crete had been preceded by dive-bombers strafing their village of Kastelli on the coast. She and her family lay on the cold floor tiles, covering their heads as windows shattered. The memories were later reinforced by World War II newsreels replayed in an undergraduate history class, videos of the Nazi airborne invasion of Crete with the parachute landings on the beach. The images and sounds and fear merged in her nightmare, as though the fear she would not admit as a child was reborn as an adult, over and over.

Laddie slid around her feet, nuzzling her toes with his head. She reached for him, feeling his weight and warmth and thundering purr, her gaze fixed on the top of the mountain as the sun rose. She would feed him soon, then give him his insulin shot.

They had been so close to escaping. When the Germans invaded Greece in April '41, crossing the Bulgarian border, Elizabeth's father made plans to flee to Egypt. The king of Greece had done so, and many Jews made their way through Crete to Egypt. But Elizabeth and her family were too late.

They had been so close to getting the proper documents to leave the island, but when bombers strafed the town, they joined another family in the trek up the mountain to the Chapel of Our Lady of Mount Tilifos. They made it to the chapel, and Elizabeth slept on the stone floor, beneath the icons. Her grandmother and an aunt slept nearby. Her parents and her baby brother Abram slept outside under the portico, fearing the baby's fever and dysentery were contagious. The family brought goats and chickens and made breakfast in a nearby cave, boiling the goat's milk for the baby and Elizabeth.

Elizabeth now thought how ill-prepared she had been for such a trek, a city girl with city shoes, her feet bleeding. But she adapted. She learned to put garlic under her head to repel snakes. She learned to eat snails for dinner. She learned to be brave and not admit how homesick she was for their home in Larissa, Greece. Her heart clutched even now, seventy-eight years later, as she stroked the tabby, holding him close and forcing her tears away. But it was too long ago to keep crying.

She had not had one of those dark dreams in a while. The nightmare must have been prompted by the young man on the mountain, the geneticist, Gregory Worthington.

Elizabeth buried the dream and spent the morning with her usual routine—making breakfast, tending to Laddie, reading the newspaper. As she wandered through her rooms of books, she was struck once again with the chaos of the shelves, the stacks, the disorder. For over six months she had placed ads, seeking someone to organize her library, but none of the applicants were suitable. One applicant thought she was crazy and another had heard rumors the house was haunted. Most folks in the valley connected her to the hermit on the mountain. It all made for entertaining gossip and news copy for the local media.

The morning had merged into afternoon, when the phone rang. The man's voice was familiar in spite of the muffled effect of the voice box he was speaking into at the top of the drive. Would she allow him to visit? Her finger hovered over the phone pad, nervous about tapping the number that sent the signal to open the gate. She was not sure what to do. But she needed to mind her manners and be more gracious, a little voice told her. She tapped the number.

Elizabeth walked into the entry and waited. She breathed deeply, hoping the visitor would knock and not ring the bell that would scare Laddie.

She heard steps, then silence, then a knock on the door.

She wanted to ignore the knock and fought the urge to turn away.

With deep misgiving, she reached for the doorknob.

Chapter 16

Monday morning, Catherine, in tee and tights, braided her long auburn hair so that it hung nearly to her waist. The braid would swing with the movement. She slipped on her flats, the ones that slid along the flooring best and were the safest, not risking the higher heels that some wore when they line-danced. She didn't want to chance falling. She was a bit awkward, and prone to tripping, with short toes and long legs. She had learned to be careful, to know her strengths and weaknesses, but at the moment she seemed to have more weaknesses than strengths. She would be careful as she walked the few blocks from her dark apartment to the bright studio, to the hall of shiny wood floors and dazzling mirrors.

"Catherine!"

It was Annie, bouncing up to her. "I wanted to say how sorry I am about your job. Our colleagues weren't respectful. You were brave to resign."

"Thanks, Annie." Catherine guessed Annie was multiracial, like most folks in the Bay Area, but what Catherine liked best about Annie was her large dark eyes. Annie was curious about everything, and her eyes stayed wide open as if she didn't want to miss a single thing, a single moment. There was no irony or cynicism about Annie. She was just simply Annie, in-your-face Annie. It seemed she should be skipping instead of walking. Catherine, next to Annie with her curly hair, brown skin, and tightly knit body, made Catherine feel big, clumsy, and a lumbering beast, although they were about the same height. But that was okay, because everyone wanted to be friends with Annie, but no one would admit it. Annie carried her cheer wherever she went and asked if you would like some. She had too much and needed to share.

"Coming to class?" Catherine asked.

"You betcha, Cath! I'm all set to dance up a storm." Her grin was infectious.

Catherine laughed. "Good. Me too." At least now she was ready to dance up a storm, thinking what a strange expression that was, maybe a reference to a tribal rain dance. "Watch that uneven pavement, Annie."

They walked the few blocks together, stepping (or jumping in Annie's case) over cracked pavement and littered gutters. They passed homeless sleeping under soiled blankets alongside shopping carts crammed with belongings.

"So sad," Annie said.

"Yes." Would she, Catherine, end up living on the streets too?

Catherine knew that the homeless had the option to go to a city shelter for a time, for hot showers and food. She also recalled from her sociology class that some preferred living on the streets, prized their freedom, and enjoyed the chaos. Some were mentally ill from substance abuse, from a traumatic past, or genetic malfunction, or all three, and did not desire to get well. Others responded to offers made by well meaning agencies and found employment, housing, and dignity once again.

"They should never have closed those sanitariums," Annie proclaimed.

"You think that's the cause of all this?"

"It's one of them."

Catherine recalled that the closing of the sanitariums in the 1980s freed patients from a locked institution, but in some ways they were given too many choices, too much freedom.

"Family breakdown too," Catherine said, thinking how the breakdown of the family (for multiple reasons) shifted the burden of care and responsibility to the state. An epidemic of homelessness threatened not only Berkeley, but California and the nation as well. Catherine had heard that even affluent Walnut Creek had problems and was looking to churches to provide shelters in their parking lots. And in Berkeley there was a constant battle between shopkeepers and those who slept in the shelter of their porches, discouraging business. "The sanitariums provided shelters, but forced shelters."

"Tough call, that," Annie said. "Freedom and dangerous streets or forced care and public safety. Tough call even today. Panhandling is legal but *aggressive* panhandling is illegal. Where's the line drawn? They get in your face on BART all the time."

"Yes," Catherine said, once again impressed with Annie's succinct summary. She could do that. Boil complex issues into sound bites. Perhaps she should go into reporting the news, or work for a political campaign.

"I'm glad I wasn't put in an institution because of my handicap," she added.

"Me too," Catherine said, smiling at her friend. "Me too, Annie."

It was a brisk walk and a sobering walk, and when they arrived at the dance studio, Catherine knew the music and the movement, for a time, would lift her spirits, especially with Annie alongside.

They entered the bright room with its mirrored walls and gleaming hardwood floor, and Catherine immediately felt better, enjoying the antici-pation of the first beat, the first notes, the first song. They signed in and paid the instructor the three dollars for the class, although Catherine was a little nervous at giving up cash when she had no job. They set their bags against the wall.

They took places in one of three lines of ten dancers and looked about the group for today. They were mostly women. Catherine had come to love the women she had met over the years, women of every age and ability and handicap and race. Some were beginners, and Catherine encouraged them as she had once been encouraged. Some, Catherine thought at first, were semi-professionals who twirled and waved and executed the most compli-cated steps with ease. Catherine didn't mind the mix of talents. She could mentor the newbies and be inspired by the professionals. There was no room for grievance in this dance class, not with the music and the movement.

Annie was in the professional category. She said once she had been dancing since she was three, so that probably explained it. As Catherine waited, primed to move correctly, Annie was limbering up with stretches. That was how they had met. Catherine tried the stretches, and tried too hard to keep up with Annie. She pulled a muscle and had to sit out the dance. Annie bought her a coffee afterwards to soften the loss and they chatted like they were sisters. She was fatherless too, Catherine soon learned, and was raised by two aunts when her mother was imprisoned for dealing drugs. If Annie could be happy, Catherine thought she could too, at least when she was with her friend. When an opening came up at the library for an entry-level shelving position, she recommended Annie. And Annie had in-tersectionality—handicapped and mixed race. She usually described herself as Native American, Jamaican, and Costa Rican.

The songs were mostly pop and country with a good beat. The dancing was fun and it raised Catherine's spirits in some inexplicable, miraculous way. Some days she swam like a fish in a pond, slipping into the dance with the familiar steps she owned unconsciously, her body moving into beauty without her mind directing it. Other days she paid close attention to the leader calling the steps, especially if it was a new dance, and they often learned new dances toward the end of the hour.

Sheila was their leader, a pert, slim woman, maybe mid-forties, with swinging blonde hair that fell straight to her shoulders. Her freckled fea-tures most often reflected intense concentration, seeming to focus acutely on each step pattern and how well her students were learning it: heel toe, tap-tap, heel toe, tap-tap, slide, slide, slide, turn, grapevine right, grapevine left. Catherine could see that Sheila loved the dance, and held these classes out of the goodness of her heart. She and her husband (who signed in folks and sometimes danced too) charged a minimum fee that went to charity.

Catherine waited for the signal to start. She placed her weight on the left foot so that she could step out on the right. She joined the other dancers, moving together with the music, a force both powerful and poignant. They danced, motion expressing music, their bodies reflected in the mirrored walls, their heels and toes tapping the shiny floors.

This Monday, the day after visiting her mother's grave, Catherine wanted to free her mind, to let it roam, and she allowed the rhythm and the leader's commands to rule her steps and muscle memory.

Writing the letter to her phantom father reminded her of the year before she was sent to Grace Academy. The protests she had taken part in had been empowering. Her group's viewpoint was seen as the only correct one. It was the only allowable one. It made them feel good about themselves. If folks disagreed, they were guilty of hate speech. It was like being patted on the back and told you were saving the world. You were sort of a saint.

Catherine spotted Aunt Pat at the door, coming in late. Catherine waved as she stepped into a grapevine right, one of the first steps she learned. Pat found a place nearby.

After that summer of protests and then beginning Grace Academy in the fall, she didn't see those friends too often. They drifted apart. Catherine knew her mother would be terribly hurt if she were rounded up by police during a protest, so she stayed away from those too. Some of her friends were arrested, she had heard, which they thought was grand, as though a badge had been earned. What if that had happened to Catherine? The marches had been exciting, and she missed the supercharged atmosphere of power. The air was tinged with danger and pride and assertiveness. She was never sure what the issues were about—there were no debates. She learned about debates later at Grace Academy.

Catherine slid along the shiny floor. She tapped heel and toe, in patterns of eight beats. She twirled and backed up and stepped forward. One lady stood near the door watching, and Catherine recalled she had done the same thing on her first day over ten years ago. Today the group moved as one, and Catherine belonged to them. She was part of something larger than herself, living in the song with her sisters.

She was glad she had come. Her depression had disappeared, at least for now. Everything seemed to be going her way, on the path that she had chosen. Life wasn't perfect, but that was okay.

Chapter 17

Annie couldn't join Catherine for coffee this time, but Aunt Pat did.

"Look at this," Aunt Pat said, her almond eyes triumphant. She handed Catherine a want ad clipped from a local paper. "I found this in the weekend *Valley Times* this morning. Glad I kept the paper."

They sat across the street from Saint Joseph's Chapel, sipping coffee at an outdoor table at the Durant Cafe, Pat's treat, watching the Open Streets Animal Parade pass by. It was a colorful block of Berkeley, being so close to campus, and included the local post office, a pizza place, a famous hot dog vendor, and street artists who drifted up from Telegraph Avenue. Tall shade trees lined the avenue running east toward the hills. Today, being a holiday, the block was closed to traffic for the pet parade. Dogs, cats, and other pets were dressed similar to their owners, or their owners dressed similar to them, all competing for prizes in three categories: Best-Dressed Pet, Best-Dressed Pet and Owner, Best-Dressed Group Combo. The sun was beginning to pierce the fog, a moment that, to Catherine, seemed slightly miraculous.

Catherine read the ad: "*Librarian wanted for large home collection at Villa Tilifos at the foot of Angel Mountain*—that's where the hermit was sighted." And it might also be the house they say is haunted, she thought.

"Hermit? I didn't hear about that."

"He hasn't been sighted in awhile. White robe, beard, like the Old Testament prophets."

"Is that Mount Diablo? Angel Mountain?" Pat asked.

"Exactly. They say he renamed the mountain."

"I still call it Mount Diablo."

"The name Angel Mountain is kinder, it seems to me," Catherine said. "We had a speaker at the library who gave a short history of the mountain. As I recall he said that Mount Diablo was named by the Spanish. In a skirmish with the Spanish, Chupcan Native Americans disappeared into a thicket, and the Spanish gave the area the name 'Monte del Diablo,' meaning 'thicket of the devil.' The name was misinterpreted by the English as mount or mountain, and the local peak took the name."

Pat nodded. "Interesting history."

Catherine felt encouraged to continue, and tried to recall some of the details mentioned by the speaker. "The mountain was considered to be the sacred point of creation by local tribes. I think the speaker said it is described in Miwok and Ohlone mythologies, and that tribes made ceremonial pilgrimages to the summit." Catherine could visualize the times, and the sense of meaning and purpose these beliefs gave to these early peoples. She wished she had such meaning in her life, a sense of the sacred. Her mother had that sense. Even Aunt Pat had that sense. Was it genetic? Was it nature or nurture?

Pat sipped her coffee and looked to the hills. "I would say that Angel Mountain is definitely more appropriate, especially since the mountain was considered sacred. And now a hermit has been reported. Sounds adventurous to work in a house nearby. What do you think? Are you going to apply? You might hear more about him from the locals. You might see him!"

Catherine shook her head. "Angel Mountain is too far." Her dancing euphoria had worn off. "Nothing seems to work out for me."

"Give it a chance. If you do go for an interview, you could wear one of your mother's tailored jackets. You kept them, didn't you? She let me borrow one for my interview at the bank. It's important to look professional."

The jackets were a nice memory—every day her mother kissed her goodbye and headed for work in one of those jackets. "Mother used to say that looking the part helps to act the part."

"It's true. And you could take rapid transit," Pat offered. "BART stops at Lafayette and Walnut Creek."

"I suppose. I'll think about it." She had no interviews lined up. There might not ever be other interviews. Those jobs she had read about were probably already filled.

"Let's visit the chapel and pray for an answer. Come on. The chapel is so . . . so . . . so transcendent."

Catherine squirmed. "Okay, sure." She didn't want to offend her Aunt Pat after all she had done for her, and Catherine had been planning a visit, but during a service when there would be music.

Pat stood and pointed across the street. "The doors are open in spite of the pet parade."

Catherine followed Pat, weaving between owners and pets, to the relative safety of the opposite sidewalk.

As they approached the open doorway, Catherine heard an organ playing. A sign posted on the rustic red door of the chapel read:

> Experience the rhythm of prayer in the
> ancient tradition of the Western Church
> in the beauty of holiness.
> We witness to Apostolic Christianity,
> offering a holy sanctuary for prayer for
> students and the community.
> We welcome you to worship with us.

Catherine followed Aunt Pat inside. In the narrow entryway, candles
in two basins of sand burned beneath an icon of the Madonna and Child.
Red roses in a tall vase occupied a stand between the votives. To the right
of the icon, an organist practiced. Catherine watched his fingers move over
the keys as his feet worked the pedals, playing "Jesu, Joy of Man's Desiring,"
a lilting piece by Bach.

Aunt Pat lit a candle before the icon of the Madonna and Child and
knelt to pray. Catherine entered the small nave, listening to the sweet melo-
dy soar against the dancing counterpoint.

Catherine remembered past visits, accompanying her mother to the
Sunday liturgy. The space was narrow and vertical, with pale stucco walls—
the color of parchment—rising to a russet barrel-vaulted ceiling. The chapel
interior was pleasing, owning a simple beauty created with simple materials.

Catherine sat on a bench halfway up and gazed at the altar covered
in white linen. Three silver candlesticks holding tall white tapers, unlit
now, stood on either side of a tented tabernacle. In front of the altar, a red
sanctuary lamp burned brightly, suspended from the vaulted ceiling, a sign
that the Blessed Sacrament—hosting the presence of Christ—was in the
tabernacle. Above the altar, light from clerestory windows streamed onto a
primitive crucifix.

Aunt Pat sat alongside Catherine. Catherine recalled she wanted to
pray about Catherine's path to be taken. Pat opened a prayer book she had
picked up at the entrance and began reading the Psalms, glancing at the
crucifix above the altar.

Catherine gazed upon the crucifix. Was Christ the joy of man's desiring? Why? This carved image of Christ crucified was a humble one. He
looked ragged, lost, a defeated figure nailed to rough wooden beams. A
preacher once explained that in that defeat was victory. His death gave life.
A mystery, Catherine supposed, and as the organ notes filled the vaulted
space and her hearing, her heart softened.

Catherine looked at the chapel with different eyes, a year after her mother's death. The polished terracotta floor tiles, in alternating patterns of burnished reds and browns, gleamed, something she didn't recall, but when she had visited before, a congregation filled the space, and the flooring not as easily noticed. Someone polished these tiles often, and with love, she thought. Pat's brother?

To the left of the altar a dove hung suspended in the air, the symbol for the Holy Spirit, the breath of God, the Comforter. Catherine's eye lingered on the dove. She needed that Comforter now, that breath of God, to send her walking on the right path.

As Aunt Pat whispered the Psalms, Catherine asked the God on the cross and the God in the tabernacle, for guidance. It was a simple prayer, the kind she learned at Grace Academy, where they gathered Friday mornings in a plain low-ceilinged worship space and offered prayers spontaneously. That space was called a chapel too, but so unlike this one. Yet they were the same, in that the believers prayed to the same three-person God—God the Father, God the Son, and God the Holy Spirit.

Aunt Pat began to pray, "Our Father, who art in heaven . . ." Catherine joined in.

At the close of the prayer, Aunt Pat made the sign of the cross over her head and heart, and Catherine did the same.

As they left the music and the luminous space, Catherine still didn't have a clear answer to her plea. But she felt oddly peaceful, as though whatever happened would be okay. Her glass was, for the moment, half full, not half empty as usual. And Pat was right. Saint Joseph's Chapel was transcendent. It lifted her into its shafts of light.

Chapter 18

Gregory awoke Monday morning in the early dawn, in the dim grayness of reflected sun, as Earth traveled slowly and steadily in offering to the light, bringing in the new day.

He awoke feeling thankful, as he often did in the traditionally furnished hotel. The small single room had high ceilings that added vertical cubes of space. There was room for one armchair and one desk chair, and, at the moment, the armchair was piled with papers and books. The single twin bed occupied half the room, but the headboard was carved with flowers and vines rising to an Impressionist print, one of Monet's Water Lillies paintings. The chairs were upholstered blue and green chintz, matching the colors of the picture and repeated in chintz panels hanging from brass rings on either side of a narrow window. A mirror over the desk was framed in the same maple veneer as the headboard and the desk. Tradition reassured him, perhaps because of the old Victorian house in which he had been raised. He wondered if home would always be Denver. He hadn't found anyplace that felt like home since he left.

He was also grateful for the gift of time, for another day on planet Earth, another day secured by gravity as Earth careened around the sun.

He thought that one day, if he improved his chapel attendance and paid attention to his prayer life, as Father Brubaker recommended again and again, he might memorize some of the morning Psalms in his prayer book. He would begin his day with thanks and end his day with thanks. It seemed only right, as his greedy lungs breathed life in and out each minute of each day, month, and year.

This morning he was thankful for the doctor in the emergency room who told him to get some rest and report any unusual symptoms to his general practitioner. His head injury would look ugly for a time—his left temple had swollen to the size of a golf ball and had turned a ghastly shade of blackish blue—but he would live to hike again. The doctor sent Gregory home with instructions to ice the bruise three times a day.

He shaved, showered, and dressed. He glanced at his desk with its stack of files, piles of books, and laptop. He would rest his eyes and leave his manuscript for another day.

But as he breakfasted on room service coffee and eggs, he opened his laptop to search the internet. He looked up Elizabeth Levin Jacobsen. He looked up Abram Levin. How could he repay them for saving his life? He soon had an address and the name of Elizabeth's husband, Samuel Jacobsen. An obituary stated that Samuel Jacobsen (1924–2015) died from heart failure at the age of ninety-one.

Like his wife, Samuel was a Holocaust survivor. He had been liberated from Auschwitz and had come to America as a young man. Over his lifetime, he was successful in numerous business ventures dealing with landscape architecture. He was known for his philanthropy, especially for his contributions to the Holocaust Museum's Oral History Project. A new wing of the local Animal Rescue Foundation was named after him, honoring his generosity in caring for unwanted animals. He was survived by his wife, Elizabeth Levin Jacobsen.

There was a link to an interview ten years earlier, a piece entitled "Crossing Guard Award." A photo showed Mrs. Jacobsen surrounded by schoolchildren. When she retired from teaching high school history, she became a crossing guard at the local elementary school. She won the award for 2008, and Gregory could see her pride as she beamed toward the camera. The interviewer went on to say how much the children loved Mrs. Jacobsen and didn't want her ever to retire. "They are my children," she explained. "They have given me such joy."

She seemed a different woman from the one who had saved him on the mountain. This woman was full of love, her features open and welcoming. He realized she had reacted to his occupation, his work with genetics, which was so close to eugenics. She had been horrified. Had she too been in a camp?

And what of her brother? Gregory sipped his coffee. He made a cold pack with a washcloth and ice and held it to his head. He considered the woman who saved him, so diffident and cool, almost rude. Gregory returned to his laptop and with his free hand tapped Abram Levin and search. A local news site featured an interview with a young man who claimed to have seen Abram, the phantom hermit of Angel Mountain. He called the old man crazy, that Abram had shouted at him and his friends and flung his arms in the air in a threatening manner. The hermit wore a white robe and had a long beard. He was dangerous, it was reported with alarm: any information regarding the hermit should be supplied to the Danville police.

Somewhat troubled by the report, Gregory turned away from the screen. He decided to work on his book, reading testimonies from scientists who had disavowed the Darwinian theory of natural selection and had become convinced that there must be an intelligent design behind our world and universe. There were many such scientists, he discovered, and he was only beginning to understand that the scientific community was significantly fractured over the challenge of Intelligent Design theory.

But a nagging sensation turned into guilt regarding the events of Sunday. He wanted to offer apologies and receive forgiveness. He wanted to atone with a visit to Mrs. Jacobsen.

Elizabeth Levin Jacobsen lived on several acres in the foothills of Angel Mountain, according to real estate websites Gregory had checked. The gracious estate called Villa Tilifos had three fireplaces, seven bedrooms, and four baths, and had been custom built in 2001.

Gregory followed his GPS to a closed iron gate at the top of a descending driveway. A voice box and keypad stood to the side of the gate. He tapped the keypad as instructed. On the third ring, a woman picked up.

"Hello?"

Gregory spoke into the box. Yes, she remembered him. There was a long silence and Gregory could hear her breathing.

"Could I visit for a moment?" he asked. "I have a small gift for you." He waited for a reply.

Angel Mountain rose behind the house as though guarding the valley. Farther beyond, to the left of the mountain, dark clouds formed in the northwest over the old town of Martinez and the Carquinez Strait. Red-tailed hawks soared high above in the crisp but hazy air, dipping and rising into the broad sky, catching the wind.

Amber elms and orange maples clustered in the valley, reflecting with their brilliant colors the recent drop in temperature. The local autumn color was one of the glories of the season, Gregory thought, appearing later than the golden aspen of Colorado. Gregory marveled at the beauty often taken for granted, the breakdown of chlorophyll that caused the green to disappear and the yellows, oranges, and reds to be seen. It was a tree's way of conserving energy in the cold season and a blessing to those who witnessed the seemingly sudden appearance of russets and golds.

The box was silent. Gregory looked up to the mountain and shivered. Had he misjudged this situation? He worried he had again trespassed upon this good woman's kindness. He would have called, but couldn't find a number.

"I'm sorry," he said into the box. "I'll come back another time if you prefer?" He heard a click and a dial tone.

The gate buzzed and rattled open, startling the silent stillness. Gregory wound slowly down the drive through oaks, oleander, and rosemary to the large house. Two dozen red roses lay on the seat beside him, wrapped in cellophane and tied with a white satin ribbon. They were named "Freedom," appropriate for Veterans Day, he thought.

As Gregory arrived at the two-story house, he appreciated its blend of tradition and modernity. Classical columns framed a highly varnished front door and brick porch. Cyprus pines rose on either side of the pillars. A terracotta fountain and basin, dry, centered a square garden, and formal paths radiated from the fountain, bordered by olive trees and lavender. Box hedges ran in front of the porch, on either side of the steps. Leaded glass panels, beveled and opaque with floral designs, framed the front door, and a bright red-leafed maple stood nearby. The house, with its pale ocher stucco, blended into the golden hills, much as a French chateau or an Italian villa might grace Provence or Tuscany. It was as if the traditional architecture tamed the land rolling to the horizon, domed by the sky, and Angel Mountain reigned over all.

Gregory parked in a graveled area to the side of the drive. Cradling the roses, he walked past the fountain, olive trees, and lavender, and up three steps to the brick porch and gleaming door. As he reached to ring the bell, he saw a small handwritten sign to the side of the button that read, "Please knock. Sick cat, scared of doorbells."

He smiled and knocked, not sure if she would answer.

Chapter 19

Abram stood on the promontory and gazed at his congregation. Others had joined the Monday morning seekers, a fair-sized crowd, for the air had cleared somewhat and the day was a holiday for many. The young men of Sunday must have reported his presence. These good souls this morning were no doubt curious. Some might be genuine pilgrims, looking for the holy, looking for God.

It was nearing noon, and he was tired. He raised his hand in blessing and retreated to the cave.

Falling to his knees before the golden icons, he prayed the *Angelus*, the ancient noon prayers of Christendom. He nibbled a health bar and drank some water. He returned to his precipice, expecting the people to be gone. They were still there, taking photos with their phones. They seemed peaceful. Some had brought lunch, which they shared.

A wind had come up, whipping his robe as he raised his arms in prayer.

And Abram sang, looking to the skies as the sun burned a path to Earth. He looked over the land, to the scene before him, gesturing with his hands, his heart full:

> *Great is Thy faithfulness, O God my Father;*
> *There is no shadow of turning with Thee;*
> *Thou changest not, Thy compassions, they fail not;*
> *As Thou hast been, Thou forever will be.*
>
> *Summer and winter and springtime and harvest,*
> *Sun, moon and stars in their courses above*
> *Join with all nature in manifold witness*
> *To Thy great faithfulness, mercy and love.*
>
> *Pardon for sin and a peace that endureth,*
> *Thine own dear presence to cheer and to guide;*

Strength for today and bright hope for tomorrow,
Blessings all mine, with ten thousand beside![11]

"God has rewarded me with happiness, distilled into joy. He has been faithful to me, because I have been faithful to him, faithful to truth. And I witness to truth.

"But what is happiness? Where do we find it? We find it through righteousness and through grace. We find it through obedience to the law written on our hearts and God's grace freely given."

As he said these words, Abram's heart overflowed with love for these people. They were seekers. Some sought God. Some sought meaning. Some simply wanted to understand their lives and their world. Some suffered terribly, he knew, invisible wounds of the soul only God could heal.

"My dear children, allow me to suggest a simple list that will put you on the path to happiness: inform your conscience; confess your failings; accept forgiveness; be thankful; be kind; be faithful; live out these rules.

"How do we inform our consciences? We look at God's law, given to Moses and the prophets: worship the one true God; do not worship idols— money, sex, pleasure, goods, power; do not curse; do not take God's name in vain; keep Sunday holy; honor your parents and others in authority; do not kill the unborn nor the aged; be faithful to your spouse; do not steal; do not lie; give thanks for your life and all of God's gifts.

"Our Lord Jesus Christ summed up these commandments with two simple ones: love God with all your heart, mind, and soul, and your neighbor as yourself.

"A difficult rule of life? Indeed. For we are imperfect and we need help keeping these rules of happiness. We need God's spirit within us, given in holy baptism to strengthen us. Would you like to be baptized and receive this source of strength that will make you happy?"

Abram gazed upon the pool, where the waters poured from a cliff near a white wooden cross. He returned to the cave and found his cards and towels and slipped them into a satchel, then made his way down the deer path to the pool, to a place of gravel and boulders. The crowd followed, curious. A young man stepped forward. He reminded Abram of his students at Cal, but this boy had clear eyes, with the sense of being ingenuous, honest, and straightforward. He was not aloof or cynical with lowered lids. He had short curly hair, dark brown eyes, was of medium build, and owned a powerful presence in his seeming humility and honesty. He could have been of mixed race, or simply Mediterranean, but Abram did not like to separate individuals by race. It was their soul he was interested in, not their skin.

"I would like to be baptized, sir."

"What is your name?" Abram looked into his eyes.

"Caleb."

Abram led the lad toward the pool. He cupped his hands and poured the cold mountain water over his head. "Caleb, I baptize thee in the name of the Father, the Son, and the Holy Spirit. Amen."

He handed him a small towel to dry his head, and he gave him a card listing the Seven Ways to Happiness. On the back of the card were the Ten Commandments and their summary.

"Go in peace, and may God's blessing be upon you."

Abram, living in the words and waters, did not notice that a line had formed.

"May I help you, Father?" Caleb asked.

"With thanksgiving, my son."

Caleb held the cards and the towels; he guided the line, leading each person to Abram.

The sun traveled across the skies as dusk approached.

"Thank you, Caleb." Abram leaned upon Caleb's arm, and the two worked their way back to the hermit's cave.

"I must go," the boy said.

"Please come again."

"A thought, though. If I might make a suggestion?"

"You may." Abram nodded, listening closely.

"Shouldn't you explain how Jesus saves us from sin and death? That's part of baptism."

Abram considered the boy. "You are right. I'll add that: *Jesus saves us from sin and death*."

Caleb shifted his weight from one foot to the other. "My father was a pastor. That's what he always said, that we needed to accept Jesus Christ as our personal Lord and Savior." He spoke as though arguing with himself.

Abram laughed, returning Caleb's firm handshake with his own. "He is correct. I will add that." Abram blessed him, signing a cross in the air with his hand. "Now go, with a promise to return. It will be dark soon. The park gates are closing."

"Thank you, Father Abram. My father would be pleased I was baptized. I fell away from the faith in school, and you brought me back." He glanced at the trail, then lowered his eyes in thought. "My father died recently in a car accident. He . . . appeared to me last night. He said to visit Angel Mountain. I wasn't sure what he meant, but then I realized it was another name for Mount Diablo. Then he was gone. Did I dream it? Was it real?"

Abram nodded. "The risen in Christ sometimes appear to their loved ones. Your vision sounds real to me."

Caleb grinned. "I knew you would understand. I'll come back tomor-row." He headed down the deer path to the gathering place below.

Abram watched the lights appear in the valley, the people returning from work and play, making supper, preparing for rest. And Abram began to sing, softly this time, his heart full, to the God he loved so,

> *What wondrous love is this, O my soul, O my soul!*
> *What wondrous love is this, O my soul!*
> *What wondrous love is this that caused the Lord of bliss*
> *To bear the dreadful curse for my soul, for my soul*
> *To bear the dreadful curse for my soul.*
>
> *Ye winged seraphs fly, bear the news, bear the news!*
> *Ye winged seraphs fly, bear the news!*
> *Ye winged seraphs fly, like comets through the sky,*
> *Fill vast eternity with the news, with the news!*
> *Fill vast eternity with the news!*
>
> *To God and to the Lamb, I will sing, I will sing;*
> *To God and to the Lamb, I will sing;*
> *To God and to the Lamb Who is the great I Am;*
> *While millions join the theme, I will sing, I will sing;*
> *While millions join the theme, I will sing!*
>
> *And when from death I'm free, I'll sing on, I'll sing on;*
> *And when from death I'm free, I'll sing on!*
> *And when from death I'm free, I'll sing and joyful be;*
> *And through eternity, I'll sing on, I'll sing on;*
> *And through eternity, I'll sing on!*[12]

Chapter 20

Elizabeth opened the front door. Laddie bolted up the stairs to the bedroom to hide in a deep, dark corner under the bed.

Dr. Worthington looked contrite, standing on the porch, one arm holding a bouquet of red roses. "I came to thank you for saving my life and to apologize for any hurt I may have caused you." He raised his brows hopefully. His eyes showed contrition. He wore khakis, a navy blazer, and a white shirt with a polo emblem embroidered on the buttoned-down collar, reminding Elizabeth of Samuel's "preppy" style.

Dr. Worthington shifted his weight nervously, and Elizabeth recalled she had been harsh. His bruise was still a nasty shade of blue, but the swelling had gone down a bit. He was young, she reminded herself, late thirties, of medium height and build. He no doubt meant well. If she had had children, he would be the age of a son or a grandson. He had the olive complexion often seen along the Mediterranean coasts, even Crete. She and Abram had been unusually fair for Greek Jews. Their blue eyes and light brown hair had aided them in their years of hiding.

"Please, come in," she said, managing a half smile. He still clutched the roses, so she didn't reach for them but waited for him to offer.

"Thanks, Ms. Jacobsen."

They paused in the marble-tiled entry. She waited.

He handed her the roses abruptly, awkwardly. "These are for you."

"Thank you. How kind. You really did not need to." She carried the roses into the kitchen. "I will put them in water."

"Yes," he said, following her.

"Please, have a seat." She motioned to the kitchen table.

"Thank you." He pulled out a chair and sat down, looking around the open kitchen and nook, then toward the golden hills through the large window. "Wonderful views! And a lot of books."

"I do have a lot of books." She realized the books had taken over the wall space even here in the nook and saw them suddenly with an outsider's eyes. She needed that librarian. "I hope to get them organized one of these days." She looked out the window. "We love our view here. The hills are still brown, waiting for rain. But we have our fall color." Elizabeth filled a vase half full with water, cut an inch off the stems, and set the roses in the vase. "These are lovely. Thank you so much. I enjoy roses." She turned to him. "Tea?"

He stood quickly. "No thanks, I couldn't possibly impose any further. I just wanted to apologize and bring the roses as a gift of gratitude."

She tried a smile, but feared it looked forced. "Ah, yes."

"You saved my life," he said.

"My brother saved your life."

"But if you hadn't come—"

"I would have come eventually. For Abram. How is your head?"

"I'll live." He turned to the sliding glass doors opening onto the flag-stone patio and garden. "You can see the mountain from here."

"Do you often hike Angel Mountain?"

"When I can. I'm from Denver, and spent much of my childhood out-doors, hiking and camping."

Elizabeth did not want to describe how she spent her childhood. "My husband and I have enjoyed living here. He passed away two years ago. I have kept the house and the land for the time, to be close to my brother."

He nodded. "He said he was preaching repentance, preparing the way of the Lord? Like John the Baptist."

"I am not sure what he is doing. Finding himself. Finding God."

"Are you . . . a . . . believer?"

"I am not a Christian. But Jews share the same God the Father, the God of Abraham. I do not attend synagogue." Samuel preferred golf and she did not want to go alone.

Gregory nodded. "I was converted by the beautiful design of science. Then the claims of Jesus of Nazareth—that he was the Son of God—made sense, so I took the next step and believed in him."

Elizabeth studied him, intrigued in spite of her misgivings. He was young and enthusiastic about his beliefs, refreshing to see. "Faith and sci-ence do not always go together."

"But they do, and they should. They complement and support one another."

"More people of faith—of morality—should be in science."

"I'm doing what I can. Or at least for most of my career I did."

"Oh?"

"I'm on sabbatical from Cal. They didn't appreciate my speaking about faith guiding science or science supporting faith."

"I understand. I taught high school Western Civilization—our Judeo-Christian-classical heritage. The religious aspect of the course became an issue, at least with the district."

"Similar fear, it would seem." Gregory stood and began to move toward the front door.

She followed him, thinking about her classes. "They called my subject humanities for a time, but it too was abandoned. It is no longer a requirement for graduation. Not inclusive enough, they said." It had been nearly twenty years since she retired, but even now she missed the students, the debates, the ideas fencing with one another, honing definitions, giving depth and texture to one's argument. "Abram taught classics at Cal."

"Really?"

"He does not want anyone to know who he is yet. Something about God's timing." Although he claimed three hikers saw him yesterday, and he spoke to them from the ledge. Was God's timing finally Abram's timing? Had they converged?

Dr. Worthington smiled. "God's timing is everything." He waited by the door, looking awkward.

"You are an interesting person. I am sorry I overreacted on the mountain. I misjudged you."

He flashed a smile, white against his olive skin, and for the first time, Elizabeth thought he might be more at ease. She thought *she* was more at ease.

"Thanks. I wish the university administration was of that opinion."

"I would like to hear more of your story someday."

He opened the door. "I don't want to overstay my welcome. Thanks for understanding and letting me visit. You've been more than kind." A brochure lay on the porch, and he handed it to her.

Elizabeth set the glossy trifold on an entry table by the door. "Thank you for the flowers and your interest in my brother. Do you have a card?" Abram might want to see him again.

He gave her his card and they shook hands. His grip was firm, purposeful. She waved goodbye as he walked to his car.

Elizabeth studied the card: *Dr. Gregory Worthington, Professor, Microbiology and Genetics, School of Science, UC Berkeley.*

She turned to the brochure on the table. *Let us help you take the final journey*, it read. As she scanned the text, artfully placed among photos of happy and caring family members, she grew faint. Finaljourney.com was a drug company associated with a local clinic. They wanted to help her die.

It was legal in California to help people die, even to have a business that offered such services.

Elizabeth gripped the banister and lowered herself onto the bottom stair. She shuddered, thinking of Samuel in Auschwitz, her grandparents, aunts, uncles, and cousins in Ravensbruck and Buchenwald. Laddie padded down one step at a time to where she sat. He nuzzled her arm, staring with large golden eyes, whimpering.

Chapter 21

Monday afternoon Catherine returned to her apartment and scrolled job listings.

She considered the job near Angel Mountain and found the news clipping Aunt Pat handed her: "Librarian wanted for large home collection at Villa Tilifos, at the foot of Angel Mountain." There was no name, no phone number, no surface address, only an email address for an interview. Should she give it a try? Aunt Pat thought so.

Catherine typed quickly in the message box: "Hi. I'm interested in your job offer. I have library experience and a Master of Library Science. Could I come for an interview? Sincerely, Catherine Nelson, Berkeley." She breathed deeply and tapped *Send.*

She made a mug of Earl Grey tea, strong, with one sugar and a dollop of milk, and checked her local news apps. The hermit had reappeared, with a sizable gathering. She checked her social media. A number of threads with #HermitOnAngelMountain. She tapped a few of them and saw the news was going viral. Photos had been posted of a man in white robes on a ledge, his hands raised to the skies. Who was he? What did this mean?

Curious, while waiting for a response from Villa Tilifos, she searched the name of the house and learned it belonged to a widow from Greece, who named it after a mountain on the island of Crete. She searched Crete and learned of its role in World War II. Who was this possible employer? Catherine was both intrigued and concerned. What was she getting herself into?

Thinking of her resignation from her library job, twinges of regret stabbed her. What had she done? How could she have cut herself off from her professional lifeline? She had worked for the library long enough to progress to the department she loved, fiction. She had shelved, manned the information desk, checked out books and checked in books, reset tables and chairs, answered phones, updated computer files. She had catalogued and sorted and carried loads on carts up and down aisles. She had done research, organized tours, and even lectured on library work. She had reached a level where she had an assistant! And now she had given it all up. For what? Would she soon be living on the street, hungry and homeless?

She already missed the books, she thought, but that was silly, since it was too soon to be missing books. There was something wonderful about used books, library books, books borrowed with the promise of returning, books that traveled to other homes and sat on other laps and were opened by other readers. Those chapters had entered other lives and shared their most intimate worlds—hopes and fears of authors scribbled secretly in the dark of night or preached openly in the light of day—and returned to Catherine's shelf to await another journey. It was as if the books were her children, each with its own world, its own people populating the pages, its own story of life or death.

Her favorite authors were without doubt from the Victorian world, since they appeared to live and write in an era of commonly accepted rules or behavioral norms. Heroes and villains could battle or defend rights and wrongs that formed an accepted moral code or natural law. The twentieth century with its collapse of structure, particularly in regards to faith and an objective ethical standard, produced unstructured—deconstructed—literature, subjective and despairing. Duty and responsibility no longer demanded obligation.

Catherine's father was a product of the modern chaos that honored no authority but the self. What could she do about the ancestry search while she waited for her DNA report?

She returned to her DNA research, checking the many free genealogy sites on the web, public records that could help her fill in a family tree. She tried again to remember what her mother had said about her father. Very little. It had been clear her mother didn't want Catherine to have anything to do with him.

Catherine decided it was time for another letter to the phantom jerk who abandoned them.

> Dear Father,
>
> I quit my job and I have no other means of support. Mama passed away—did I mention that? It was over a year ago—cancer. So I'm all alone now.
>
> I have friends but I rarely tell them about you. I'm so ashamed that you did what you did, and every time I think about it I get angrier and angrier that you wanted to snuff my tiny life out like that.

But right now it would be helpful to have family to lean on, I have to admit.

I have Aunt Pat, and she is like family, better than family, but she can't pay my rent or organize my life. She has her own challenges making ends meet. She has her siblings and elderly parents and they all need her help.

I have to face life on my own.

So I blame you for my job situation since I spoke without thinking about abortion and Down's in the coffee room. I finally had enough of the political correctness everywhere so I quit. My field is library work, and that is my passion and dream, which I have the right to follow, so I will, even without you.

How many others have you fathered and abandoned? How many mothers have you pressured to abort their babies? How many? How many survived? How many half-brothers and sisters do I have?

Some believe in God's judgment, so you better get ready, if that's true. My mother is a saint in Heaven, that's for sure. She is probably already organizing my guardian angels to protect me and lead me on the path I am to walk on.

Mama was stronger than she seemed, I realize now. She knew what love was. She knew it wasn't some feel-good thing but a kind of action. Love was selfless and kind.

I just want to be happy. I recall a class at Grace Academy where we studied the Greek philosophers. Aristotle said to be happy you had to be virtuous. One of our debates was the question, "What is virtue?" Another question was, "What is the good life?" I remember those in particular, because the questions have arisen from time to time in my own life since then.

I guess you never found happiness, that's for sure, since it's a safe bet you are miles away from virtue.

Your hoping-to-be-virtuous daughter, the one you didn't want,

Catherine

P.S. I'm waiting for my DNA test to come back. Get ready for Armageddon! All I have to do is give the okay to share the info. That's all. Then one day, there will be me knocking on your door.

Catherine's phone chimed, and she checked for messages. Her heart beat faster when she saw the email with the subject line, *Interview*. She tapped to open it.

Chapter 22

Leaving Villa Tilifos, Gregory drove through the foothills with the intention of returning to his room and icing his forehead, but instead followed an unusual hunch to visit Abram. He rarely had hunches, and when he did he tried not to pay attention to them. They were outside the realm of science, living in the forbidden territory of intuition, superstition, and guesses. But he was intrigued with the hermit and wanted to speak with him again.

While the sun would officially set at 5 p.m., civil twilight would last another twenty minutes, that time when the geometric center of the sun reaches six degrees below the horizon. Nautical twilight and astronomical twilight would continue, but for purposes of closing the park, Gregory would need to pay close attention to civil twilight. He had enough of the afternoon left to see Abram, that is if he could remember the way through the sandstone tunnels.

Gregory maneuvered his sedan through the south gates, and, as he approached the sandstone caves, he was surprised to see a crowd gathered in a meadow nearby. His gaze traveled to the white robes on the ledge above. He parked the car and soon was at the edge of the crowd.

The people were respectful, he was grateful to see, unlike his own experience in Berkeley the year previous. They appeared to be straining to hear. There were about a hundred, he guessed, in hiking gear and backpacks, varied ages, couples and families, probably diverted from their intended plan for the holiday. They had heard the stories. They wanted to see for themselves what was happening on Angel Mountain. Park rangers roamed the edges of the gathering.

Social media was most likely buzzing. Was Abram going viral? Gregory didn't have accounts with Facebook, Twitter, or Instagram, but understood how they worked. They were tools, like all technology, and science for that matter, and could be wisely or unwisely used. The stunning internet revolution had produced major changes in society by speeding up—and democratizing—communication. Today anyone with a phone could command an audience exponentially. These were big changes in society on many levels and in many fields, whether folks realized it or not. Mobs could be formed in an instant. But peaceful discussion with noble platforms could also enrich society and culture and not be subject to gatekeepers.

Here, in the meadow below Abram's sandstone cave, Gregory was curious and somewhat concerned as to how things might develop. He scanned faces and body language for signs of malice. He reflected he had acquired a skill he didn't know he had, a skill honed from experience with student snowflakes, those who melted when hearing words that triggered bad feelings, and who overreacted harmfully. Such snowflakes often became targets of professional agitators who took advantage of their innocence and desire to do good, for, Gregory believed, they did intend to do good. The university students and others like them deemed speech with which they disagreed to be hate speech, so they tried to silence the haters. They made an illogical deduction that was destructive of the First Amendment, but they had been so programmed by leftist propaganda they had lost any ability to use simple common sense, let alone conduct serious analysis.

Serious analysis! Many students today—and faculty—didn't seem to own the rudiments of logical thinking, processes that were once part of high school curriculum, not to mention honed in college essay writing, the kind of thing required in Freshman English 1B, Composition. Was the persuasive or argumentative essay no longer taught? Was English composition no longer required? Did they understand inductive reasoning versus deductive reasoning, the orderly route of premises leading to conclusions? Were they exposed to tautologies, antecedents, precedents? If not, how were they to make judgments about the world, *their* world?

Today, as far as Gregory could determine, the hermit was speaking about happiness, how to find it, how to live within it, a peaceful endeavor to be sure. He wasn't preaching in a university hall or student plaza, but on a hillside. It was a state park, and that might be an issue, given the Scriptures quoted, but it was an issue for debate at some future time.

The crowd seemed quiet, for now.

Abram looked tired, as though he had been at this all day. He probably had.

It was while Gregory was analyzing the hermit's posture and stance with a growing medical concern that his gaze roved to a tall man with an athletic bearing. He wore a cap pulled low, a large backpack slung over his hoodie, and military camouflage pants. He was fair skinned, clean shaven, with blond hair escaping the cap. He wore oversize dark glasses. He stood nearby. Gregory quickly looked away.

Gregory watched and waited, touching his phone in his pocket. Something wasn't right with the fellow, although Gregory couldn't say for sure what alerted him.

Abram was calling for baptisms, and it appeared, from Gregory's distance, that a young man had joined him and was helping. A line had formed alongside the pond where the waterfall poured and the white cross stood. One by one, each person approached Abram. One by one they exchanged a few words. One by one they felt the water from Abram's hands fall on their heads. The youth then handed them something—looked like a card—and spoke to them.

The tall man near Gregory appeared to be sneering, cursing under his breath. Gregory observed him discreetly and was glad when he walked to his car and left.

The baptismal line disappeared. As the crowd dispersed quietly, Gregory observed the young man lead Abram away. The hermit leaned on him as they stepped out of sight, into the hills on the narrow path that Gregory recalled.

The sun would soon set and twilight would begin. He would visit Abram another day. He had so much to say to him, so many questions to ask. Perhaps tomorrow, Tuesday.

A deep exhaustion fell upon Gregory as he drove back to his room at the hotel. His head throbbed. He needed ice. He needed rest.

TUESDAY

Chapter 23

Early Tuesday Abram awoke suddenly, trying to capture his dream in the first light.

The colors of his dreams filled him with joy. He did not want to let them go. Their intensity pierced him, as though he were not yet ready for their fullness, their reality. But to wake was to mourn their absence.

The colors of this dream filled prism pillars, as though a rainbow had changed from arc to arrow, shooting from Heaven to Earth in a straight line. The shafts of dazzling color—for shafts they were, like clerestory shafts in a cathedral—were ever present, but mankind could not see them. The canoes reappeared, as in the earlier dream, but instead of seeing them through a window, he and Elizabeth traveled in one, and they entered and moved through the misty prisms of light.

"Lord, I understand. We are bathed in these shafts of light, each one of us, prisms of love, chrisms of joy, rainbows of mercy. We must open our hearts to see, to send up our own prayer prisms of song to meet yours. When they touch one another, when the Creator meets his creation in prayer, one precious person at a time, joy is born. Happiness is lived in every breath."

Abram recalled Jacob's dream of the angels descending and ascending a ladder between Heaven and Earth. Would he see angels in these prisms? So far, the angels danced on the horizon or glimmered in the icons. So far, they had not spoken to him. In moments of doubt, he questioned whether he had seen them at all and took care whom he told.

As he pulled himself out of the dream and into the day, he considered the hours and what they would bring. Would this be his moment, his time to go home to Heaven? He sensed it was soon, but how soon? He decided to trust and obey, and not worry too much. Worries could warp things—make them change shape, wrinkle them. *Lord, teach me to trust and obey. For there is no other way.*

The park was not yet open, and Abram had many prayers to sing. He donned his long muslin robe. He ate some fruit and drank some water. He stepped onto his ledge, his cowl raised over his head for warmth, knowing he had some time before the seekers would arrive. The sun had not yet appeared behind the mountain, but dawn bathed the valley, gently waking the sleepers. He could see lights appearing in the dwellings and his heart beat with love for each soul, each and every child of God. He prayed they would see the colors of Heaven as he had seen them in his dream and still could recall, his grasp reaching, but his memory dimming with each minute.

Abram prayed his morning songs as the light brightened, dispelling the shadows of Earth:

> *This is my Father's world*
> *And to my listening ears*
> *All nature sings and round me rings*
> *The music of the spheres.*
>
> *This is my Father's world*
> *I rest me in the thought*
> *Of rocks and trees, of skies and seas*
> *His hand, the wonders wrought.*
>
> *This is my Father's world*
> *The birds, their carols raise*
> *The morning light, the lily white*
> *Declare their makers praise.*[13]

"Abram!"

Abram heard his name, but it was a human voice, of that he was sure. It was coming from his cave.

"Father Abram!"

He turned toward his cave entrance and saw Ranger Tony Mitchell coming through the doorway, his head lowered to fit through. The ranger removed his hat, holding it with both hands respectfully.

"Just checking on you, Father. Seems we have some interest in your sermons."

Abram looked into the ranger's eyes, so caring. They crinkled with amusement this morning, his brows slightly furrowed. He tilted his head, as though waiting for a report from the holy man as to what happened during the night and what was going to happen today. He gazed out over the valley. He whistled through his teeth. "Quite a view from this ledge. The haze seems to be returning."

"It is good to see you, Tony. Can I offer you some refreshment? Fruit? Granola bar? Have you had breakfast?"

"I've eaten, thanks, Father. The reason I came—hope I didn't startle you, Father—is that we were questioned by the Superintendent of Parks as to what might be going on here . . . the gatherings in the meadow and all. Freddie is an old family friend, but he needs to have a report, so I'm working on one. I think I know what he needs, and if I use the right language, he'll have talking points for his superior."

Abram nodded. "I did not think of this before. I am grateful, Tony."

"We may need to give you a temporary permit or such." Tony rested a broad hand lightly on Abram's shoulder.

"Yes, a permit." Abram looked up to the man's friendly face, praying Tony would not be reprimanded for these gatherings.

"The good news is that we are receiving publicity for the park, and the superintendent is pleased with this. There is no such thing as bad publicity, he says. So that might be my angle."

"Really?"

"Folks will want to come and see, and when they come and see, they will be introduced to Mount Diablo State Park."

"Angel Mountain."

Tony grinned. "Of course, Angel Mountain." He rested his hand on his holster and spoke into his radio. "Seems okay here. Be back at the gate soon."

"I do not want you to be in trouble," Abram said. "You have a family to feed."

"Any idea how long these gatherings might go on? How many days?"

Abram looked over the valley. "Only God knows, Tony. But not too much longer now." Abram sensed the ranger had something else to tell him.

"Father, there's something else, some good news." Tony's face lit up like a boy's on Christmas morning.

"Tell me! What is it, Tony?"

"My family—it's growing, Father." He winked, clearly pleased with his hint.

"Is Jennifer having another child?"

Tony rubbed his hands together. "She sure is. We are tickled to death . . . er . . . I mean we are so happy!"

"I have been praying for this."

"We could only have the one boy, as you know, and, well, we always wanted a big family."

"I know." Abram smiled. "So there you are! How wonderful. God is so very good."

"Thanks, Father." Tony nodded and shifted his weight from foot to foot. "Could I . . . uh . . . could I . . . um . . . have your blessing, Father?" He raised his brows and the squinty eyes opened wide with hope.

"Of course."

The hefty ranger knelt on one knee before the wizened preacher.

With great tenderness and love, Abram laid his palm on the man's head. "Tony, the Lord bless thee, and keep thee. The Lord make his face shine upon thee, and be gracious unto thee. The Lord life up his countenance upon thee, and give thee peace."[14] As Abram made the sign of the cross over Tony, he intoned, "In the name of the Father, the Son, and the Holy Spirit. Amen."

The ranger rose to his full height, looking satisfied. "I'll keep an eye out for you. And the others will too. Don't you fear about anything."

"Thank you, Tony."

Ranger Tony Mitchell saluted and left the way he had come, through the cave, through the sandstone tunnels, and to the gates.

And Abram continued his morning song, adding to his thanksgivings the news from Tony:

> *This is my Father's world*
> *He shines in all that's fair*
> *In the rustling grass I hear Him pass*
> *He speaks to me everywhere.*

> *This is my Father's world*
> *Oh let me ne'er forget*
> *That though the wrong seems oft so strong*
> *God is the ruler yet.*

> *This is my Father's world*
> *Why should my heart be sad?*
> *The Lord is King; let the heavens ring!*
> *God reigns; let the earth be glad!*

With a full heart, Abram waited for his children of God, hoping Gregory Worthington would return (he had not noticed him on Monday), and Caleb would help. He gave thanks for all, and for Tony once again, his family, and the child to be born.

Chapter 24

Tuesday morning Elizabeth awoke to the bright light of day, knowing she had overslept. The clock said ten. Laddie needed his twice-a-day insulin shot, eight and eight. She was two hours late.

She quickly donned her robe. Laddie was sound asleep in his cage with the door open, a habit Elizabeth encouraged, to be ready at a moment's notice to escape for whatever reason. There were times she thought she would never be safe again. The suitcase near the front door helped her sense of security, but even so, she regularly rehearsed the drill she had devised should they need to run. But why should they need to run? She was in America. *She was safe. She was safe.*

She would be ready for evacuation in case of fire as well, she thought. The fires were moving north toward the town of Chico, the last she heard, having devastated the community of Paradise.

At least, she reflected as she found the small bottle of insulin in the bathroom, she did not have nightmares last night. Or did she?

Laddie looked at her with his sleepy eyes, and Elizabeth hoped he would stay put. At first, when she was learning the procedure and Laddie was not sure what she was up to, he ran under the bed. He could run suddenly, just like Elizabeth could. They were two of a kind. They understood one another.

Elizabeth removed a syringe from the drawer and twisted off the plastic caps at the top and the base. She filled the syringe with eight units of insulin and approached Laddie. So far, so good: he remained where he was, watching her. She pulled open the roof door of the carrier. She pinched together Laddie's furry skin between his ears, making a small tent, and inserted the needle, releasing the insulin. Done. Laddie was good for another twelve hours.

Elizabeth walked to the window and gazed out to Angel Mountain. She recalled her nightmare. In many ways, Angel Mountain reminded her of

Mount Tilifos on Crete, although she rarely admitted it. She was in America now. She was safe.

She wrapped her robe around her as the dream surfaced in her memory. How many nights did they sleep in the chapel and the surrounding grounds? Elizabeth was not sure. She was six and trying to be brave as they ran from the Nazis.

> *Elizabeth is woken from a deep sleep and told to keep silent. It is pitch dark. German paratroopers from the coast are climbing up the mountain to their hiding place, coming closer and closer with each minute. If she makes a noise they might be shot by Germans or even by friendly fire, the British or the locals who, in the dark, might mistake them for Nazis.*
>
> *She rushes from the chapel, from their campsite. She desperately reaches for something, someone, to hold on to. Where is her family? Is she with strangers? She stumbles with the others, for there is no trail, and they step silently, parting the brush, slipping on twigs. Her feet hurt from the thorns and the pebbles.*
>
> *She holds on tight to the coat of someone she does not know, for if she lets go she will be lost in the dark. They will abandon her. She tries to keep up, but she is left on the mountain, lost, alone in the dark. They have forgotten her, left her behind.*

Elizabeth pulled herself out of the memory. She was not left behind, she told herself, watching the hazy sky swirl around Angel Mountain. She found her family, or they found her, but fear eclipsed relief in this recurring dream that would never end.

She picked up Laddie and buried her face in the fragrant fur, inhaling the animal's closeness, his comforting warmth. She needed to prepare for today. She needed to pull herself together. She needed to write in her gratitude journal all the blessings she was showered with—her life, her home, her brother, even the beautiful mountain that rose over her own Villa Tilifos. Not to mention her safety. For she *was* in America; she *was* safe.

Today she would interview another librarian. How long would this process take, she wondered, and how long would she have the energy to see it through? Her hips hurt with arthritis and she seemed to be forgetting things, so she made lists. Her lists lay in odd places all over the house, lists of groceries, lists of errands, lists of calls, lists, lists, lists, bits of hotel pads from long-ago trips with Samuel, bits on the backs of receipts, bits on edges of newspapers and junk mail, all thoughts that came into her head and were domiciled on bits of paper. She often forgot where she put the last list, but hoped that the process of making the list would help her memory. Still, the disorder added to her confusion.

She had a hair appointment coming up, she recalled, and she was sure she had put it on a list. Did she add it to her kitchen wall calendar? Apparently not. Was it this week or the following week? She glanced in the entry mirror. No silver roots showing yet. Should she go silvery white all over as many did? It would seem a good deal easier. Samuel liked her hair tinted its natural shade so she tinted it every six weeks. But Samuel was gone. Another day she would consider her hair. Today she was focusing on the librarian coming to see her.

There was also, she recalled, a book club meeting scheduled at the country club. That was the last Wednesday of every month. What was today? Had November gone by already? She returned to the calendar. Today, she was positive, was the week after Veterans Day, so no book club meeting until after Thanksgiving. They were reading a novel by Melanie Phillips, *The Legacy*. She was nearly finished with it, but she wanted to make some notes. She was the leader this time, since she chose the book. She hoped they liked it as much as she did.

Elizabeth carried her coffee to her home office, opposite Samuel's study at the end of the hall. It was already eleven, and she needed to review her emails. She had stayed up late reading and rereading an encouraging thread and its attachments, a reply to her ad for a librarian.

She settled herself in front of her laptop and found the email thread of the day before.

> Mon, Nov 12, 2:12 PM
> Dear Ms. Jacobsen,
> Hi. I'm interested in your job offer. I have library experience and a Master of Library Science. Could I come for an interview?
> Sincerely,
> Catherine Nelson, Berkeley

> Mon, Nov 12, 3:47 PM
> Dear Ms. Nelson,
> Thank you for your interest in the librarian position. I have a large home library and it needs attention, sorting, cataloging, etc. You may come for an interview tomorrow at 2 p.m. if possible. Please reply.
> Best regards,
> Elizabeth Jacobsen

Mon, Nov 12, 3:55 PM
> Dear Ms. Jacobsen,
> That would be fine. I'm attaching my resume and references for your perusal. I don't have a car, but will take BART and Uber.
> Thank you,
> Catherine Nelson
> Attach:3

Mon, Nov 12, 4:10 PM
> Dear Ms. Nelson,
> Thank you for the resume and references. I look forward to seeing you. My address is: 2 Green Hill Lane, Danville. There is a gate. Call through the box and I will let you in.
> Best,
> Elizabeth Jacobsen
> P.S. I will reimburse you for your transportation.

Elizabeth turned to the printed resume and references. Catherine Nelson had worked at the UC library for eight years, after receiving her Master of Library Science, and earlier a Bachelor of Arts in English literature. Before the UC position she had part-time shelving experience while in school. Elizabeth wondered how she would adapt to such a change in environment. And there was the issue of distance, a bit of a commute, especially for someone without a car. All in all, she seemed an unlikely candidate, but Elizabeth was grateful she was coming all this way to the interview, which showed a kind of determination and strength, as well as focus. All three attributes, she had found, were valuable ones for anyone to foster, not least for an employee.

Elizabeth perused the letters of reference. Neither were work references. One was full of praise from a Pat Pearson, a family friend. The second reference was from a clergyman, a Father Albert Brubaker. The name was familiar but she could not place it. Character was important, Elizabeth concluded, perhaps more so than skill sets.

Character, at the end of the day, might be everything.

The grandfather clock in the entry chimed noon, a sweet reminder of Samuel. He had found the antique pendulum clock in a local estate sale. She smiled—Samuel was always looking for deals. She would never forget Samuel; she would always mourn him. Grief was good, Elizabeth decided, for it admitted the reality of suffering in this world. It admitted that to love was to suffer. Most of all, she did not want to forget Samuel. Most of all, she did not want to stop loving.

Chapter 25

Tuesday afternoon Catherine took BART from Berkeley to Walnut Creek. When she handed the Villa Tilifos address to the Uber driver, he shuddered. "They say the place is haunted, you know."

Catherine ignored the comment. Soon, he dropped her off at the top of a gated drive that descended down the hill, curving to a large Italianate house, and sped away. Catherine tried to think of the visit and interview as an adventure. She had read about these crazy places. Now she was living in the stories. With a slightly trembling voice, she spoke into the box and waited for the gates to open.

She walked with some difficulty down the steep drive, paying attention to her balance so as not to trip on the graded pavement. She wore her best skirt, mid-calf length, heather gray, and boots, with her mother's navy blazer. They were neutral shades, business attire, and with her auburn hair pulled into a bun, she thought she had done her best, all things considered.

As she stepped down the drive, her brown tote slung over her shoulder, she sensed she had entered another world, far from Berkeley, a world of immense—intense—quiet. The silence was like a blank canvas showcasing every sound.

City sounds, the discordant background of her life, were absent, and this short walk down the drive was bathed in expectant silence. It was as if the silence emphasized the chirpings, scuttlings, and rustlings from sources unseen in the surrounding landscape. Italian cypresses lined the drive like spires, swaying slightly. A giant oak sheltered a three-door garage to the side of the house. Was that the cooing of doves she heard, deep within the oak's branches? As she stepped down the drive, she looked above the house and beyond to the mountain she assumed was Angel Mountain, a.k.a. Mount Diablo. The mountain rose to a peak, climbing above the golden hills to the sky, and where the hills folded into its flank, old oaks shaded the trails she thought must disappear into dark ravines, paths leading into the heart of the mountain.

Catherine stood on the front porch of Elizabeth Jacobsen's house. The afternoon was hazy, the sun weak, the breeze chilly. In her present nervousness, she recalled her dream that awakened her in the early morning, a vision of her mother standing at the foot of her bed, saying what she usually said in these dreams, that Heaven was real and she was happy and Catherine would see her again. As before, Catherine tried to hold onto the vision, but also as before, her mother disappeared into the cold dawn.

She pulled herself out of the memory, noticing a sign over the gleaming mahogany door, the letters scripted in dark green, reading *Villa Tilifos*. A smaller handwritten note had been taped over the doorbell: *Please knock. Sick cat, afraid of doorbells.*

Catherine knocked.

Footsteps.

The door swung open.

A short, welcoming woman stood in the entry and shook Catherine's hand with both of her own, smiling and nodding. Her gaze was friendly. "You must be Ms. Nelson. I am Elizabeth Jacobsen. Thank you for coming all this way. Please, come in." She spoke with a slight European accent, slowly and carefully, as though conserving energy.

"Thank you." Catherine was a few inches taller than Ms. Jacobsen, but the elderly woman maintained a powerful presence, as though she protected something of great value at the center of her being. Would she have said that Ms. Jacobsen glowed? Not in so many words. But she owned some kind of happiness. She was thickset, with short curly brown hair that framed a pretty heart-shaped face, with wide blue eyes, porcelain skin, and a pink-lipped smile. She wore a tweed cardigan over a cream turtleneck and tan slacks, pale colors, Catherine would learn much later, designed to hide cat hair.

They shook hands, and Catherine hoped her grip was firm but gentle. Ms. Jacobsen's grip was tender, lingering, as though she were reading the girl's palm with her own.

"I hope you had a pleasant journey," she said, studying Catherine.

Catherine nodded. "It was fine, thank you." She looked around the marble entry. Leafy ferns surrounded a grandfather clock to her left. Hallways led from either side of the entry, and a formal staircase with a white spindle bannister ascended to her right. Straight ahead, a polished mahogany table holding stacks of books occupied a dining room. The table ran the length of a large picture window framed by heavy silk drapes cascading to the floor like ball gowns. Beyond the dining room, through the window, Catherine could see a broad terrace and a swimming pool. Golden hills rose beyond.

Books clustered on an entry table reflected in an ornate mirror and peered from a sideboard in the dining room. Ms. Jacobsen owned a great number of books, it would seem. While they most likely weren't library books, Catherine thought they might become friends anyway.

"Please come this way. We can talk in my husband's study."

Chapter 26

Catherine followed Elizabeth to a room at the end of the hall that looked out on the terrace and pool and beyond to the hills and the mountain. Green brocade panels were swooped back by tasseled ties on each side of the window. The walls held books, many books, spines dusty. Some volumes were behind protective glass and some were arranged neatly, artistically. They appeared to be hardbacks with no jackets, books treasured in the past as well as the present, Catherine imagined.

Elizabeth sat behind a desk of inlayed wood in the center of the room. A pen, a notepad, and a silver framed photo were the only objects on the desk, except for what appeared to be Catherine's resume. "Please, have a seat," Elizabeth said, pointing to a green settee opposite, upholstered in fabric matching the draperies.

Catherine felt as though she were in an English country house, something belonging to a lord or lady of a manor, something described by Austen or Trollope. She looked about the room. "Are these some of the books you need organized?"

Elizabeth smiled. "No. These are fine the way they are. This was my late husband's study. Samuel died two years ago. It has been difficult. I miss him." She turned the photo in its tarnished silver frame toward Catherine.

The gentleman's image seemed both serious and restless. His eyes gave him away, Catherine decided, as though he had never really found the happiness he sought. He leaned forward awkwardly, his arm around Elizabeth, who leaned into him. The photo was taken in the backyard, and the mountain loomed behind them. He wore a V-neck sweater over a plaid shirt. He was a tall, slim man—a full head taller than his wife.

Elizabeth held the photo, gazing at it wistfully. "Samuel. He was my life."

Catherine felt she had intruded on the woman's grief. She waited silently.

Elizabeth turned to her guest, as though forcing the spell to be broken. "He collected special books, shopped the antiquarian fairs." She glanced at the cabinets housing their precious residents. "He had first editions, late editions, and books he simply loved, mainly from the classical period—the Greeks, the Romans, some early medieval scholars. No, I need someone to help with the rest of the house, *my* books. I am not quite as organized as dear Samuel was." She glanced at the resume. "I see you are an experienced librarian with an advanced degree in library science."

Catherine nodded. "Yes."

"You might be disappointed working here. It is quiet. Isolated."

Catherine raised her brows and tilted her head. "It would be different for me, that's true. I'm used to the city. But I need a change from all that, if you're interested in hiring me."

"You worked for the UC library?"

"I was—"

"Might I ask why you left?" Elizabeth glanced at the resume. "You do not explain why you left."

Catherine breathed in deeply. "I resigned."

"Any reason I should know?"

"Only that I didn't get along with some of the staff."

"There would not be that problem here, since there is no staff to speak of. No library staff anyway."

"There was a disagreement about one of the UC protests, and I should not have said what I said, since it was deemed to be hate speech. My colleagues—and my supervisor—were angry with me."

Elizabeth eyed her closely. "Really?"

"I said that the unborn had a right to live even if they weren't wanted." There, she said it. Might as well get it out there and face the repercussions now rather than later.

Elizabeth nodded and looked away, then at Samuel, her features shadowed by thoughts, or memories, or some deep darkness. Her eyes were moist, nearly tearing.

"I'm sorry," Catherine said. "I've said something to upset you."

Elizabeth shook her head. "It is okay. No, more than okay. I am glad to hear you were so brave. We have more in common than I had thought. I am pro-life too. I escaped the Holocaust in Greece many years ago. Life—all life—is precious."

"I understand." Catherine considered the tragic history of the woman who faced her across the gleaming desk. Concentration camps and the Nazi experiments on women and children were far worse than anything Catherine had experienced. She would never forget the images shown in a

Western Civilization class at Grace Academy. Old newsreels had recorded the Allied armies liberating the camps, filming what they found. The scenes were branded in her memory. In a softer voice, she added, "But I should guard my tongue, as my mother often warned me. I tend to be blunt when I feel strongly about something. And this issue was personal."

"But enough," Elizabeth said to herself forcefully, as if to ban the ghosts. "You may have the job if you like. I can pay you forty dollars an hour, six hours a day, five days a week until the cataloging and arrangement is complete. Then we could review where we go next. See how you like it here."

"That sounds reasonable."

"You may have heard rumors about this house?"

"I have. Hauntings?"

"Pay no attention. There are no ghosts."

"I don't believe in ghosts." Although, Catherine recalled, her mother appeared to her. Was she a ghost or simply a dream? How was one to know?

"Could you start tomorrow? I can take you on a tour of the areas that need attention."

Catherine decided to ignore any misgivings and choose this path to walk on. She liked the elderly woman. She found her intriguing and touching. Anyone with so many books—and such a tragic history—must not be too dangerous or spooky. "I can start tomorrow."

"Excellent." Elizabeth led Catherine across the hall. "But I had better show you *my* books before you make a final decision. I am used to the chaos, so I tend to forget its extent."

The room they entered mirrored the size of Samuel's study, but not the order. Books were stacked randomly, on the carpet, on a maple rolltop near French doors opening onto a small patio. Two mahogany desks formed an L-shape in the center of the room. Two wing chairs sat in an alcove where a bay window, shuttered in white, looked out to the front garden of grass, fountain, and olive trees. The remaining walls held books spilling from built-in bookcases.

"This is where you can begin," Elizabeth said. "You see how disorganized it is. Books have filled my life, my real life, here in America. Mainly history, especially Western civilization, but novels too, and poetry. And I keep adding to the number." She chuckled lightly, glancing at Catherine with twinkling eyes. "I am an addict, I fear. I cannot resist a book review and then I have to have the book. Ah, well. I do read most of them, and give many away, and I rationalize the extravagance by the thought of supporting some writer somewhere on planet Earth. And my brother's books are mixed in too. He taught classics and religion."

Catherine walked to a shelf and glanced at some of the authors' names. Paul Johnson. Winston Churchill. Russell Kirk. T. S. Eliot. Gertrude Himmelfarb. Irving Kristol. Will and Ariel Durant. Barbara Tuchman. James Q. Wilson. Steven Spender. W. H. Auden. Dante. Richard Pipes. Roger Scruton. She recognized a few but most were beyond her experience.

"Western civilization," Elizabeth announced, as though the phrase explained everything. "I taught Western Civilization at the high school level until they phased it out. I wanted to understand our world, what was good and what was bad, to encourage the good and discourage the bad."

Elizabeth's gaze drifted to the garden and Catherine watched her enter a place in her mind as though it too were a garden, a place to wander amidst the growth, both wild and tamed, that bordered formal paths. A silence settled over them, for the elderly woman seemed far away.

Catherine knew the joy of such wandering. To her, entering a book—walking into the forests of words and mountains of pages, allowing the many hues, people, ideas, to clothe her imagination—was a miraculous journey, as she traveled through time and space with characters, real and imagined, who became her friends. Some of the journeys were short; some were long; some challenged her to struggle and commit; some invited her to believe. Books were like that: worlds born into words on a page, orderly progressions through chapters, with beginnings and endings, and middles linking the two. As Catherine watched Elizabeth, she guessed Elizabeth was in the middle of her meandering thoughts; she guessed Elizabeth was, at that moment, content.

Elizabeth turned to Catherine. "Forgive me, my mind wanders at times. You can see the reason I need you to put this all in order. We can talk about the strategy tomorrow. I have a few ideas. And I have a lot of lists," she added. "If you could gather them into one place, that would be helpful."

"I'll look forward to beginning," Catherine said, "to making a start."

"Good. Samuel collected special editions, and books he loved, especially the Greek classics—Aristotle, Plato, Socrates. But he was a businessman first, and building his business was more important than building his library or his intellect for that matter. Collecting was a hobby. I am not sure how many he read, but he did appreciate their beauty and their own personal history, not to mention their rarity."

"I understand. What was his business?"

"Landscape architecture. He designed and built and maintained gardens, home and commercial. He had a large company. He did pretty well, having come from nothing."

"And you taught history?"

"I was and am keenly interested in the Enlightenment and the rise of democracies and the principles of freedom. How did the Western tradition birth a maniac like Hitler? How did the most civilized of countries, the nation of Beethoven, Bach, and Handel, produce a mass murderer? Genocide on such a scale? These were the questions I wanted to answer. These are the questions I wanted my students to ask—so that we would never forget what happened and never allow it to happen again."

"Did you find answers?" Catherine considered this a rhetorical question. How could there be answers to such questions? She was surprised by Elizabeth's reply.

"Pretty much. Our decline in the West is a result of a decline in the Judeo-Christian ethic that is the foundation of a democratic and free society. The Judeo-Christian tradition provides the moral imperatives for a political order that ensures respect for the dignity of all people. We need these codes to ensure meaningful lives, to lead us to the good, the true, the beautiful, right and wrong. One could also include the classical world with its interest in the virtuous life, the good life. Some have said Western civilization is the partnering of Athens—reason—and Jerusalem—revelation."

"What about the Enlightenment?" Catherine recalled that this period was often referenced today, but there seemed to be many definitions of what the term actually meant.

"It is the miracle of the religious Enlightenment, suborned by the secular Enlightenment of progressives, that must be reclaimed."

Catherine absorbed her words, hoping to understand one day. "I want the good, the true, and the beautiful too."

"And that is an excellent beginning," Elizabeth said. "But enough philosophy. One day you will understand what I am saying. One day you will see how civilized civilization hangs by a thread, and we must weave a stronger thread, a more trustworthy fabric, to survive not only natural disasters but human horrors as well, such as tyranny and genocide."

She led Catherine to the front door. "Can you return by ten in the morning? Here is something for the trip today." She handed Catherine a twenty-dollar bill and a card with her name and phone number. "Maria, my housekeeper and driver, can take you to the BART station. When you arrive at the station tomorrow, call, and she can pick you up." She spoke into her phone.

Soon a heavyset woman with an energetic air appeared. She dangled her keys and nodded at Catherine. "I am Maria. I'll bring the car out of the garage."

Elizabeth opened her palms. "Until tomorrow, then."

"Until tomorrow," Catherine said and waited on the porch for the lively Maria.

Chapter 27

Tuesday morning Gregory awoke at sunrise, 6:47 a.m., full of a terrible dread, as though condemned to everlasting darkness.

Unable to shake the feeling, he soon headed for Angel Mountain. He had slept little, debating what he should do.

How could he help Abram? How could he protect him?

The dread grew, metastasizing. The contemptuous man on the edge of the crowd appeared and reappeared in his thoughts as Gregory breakfasted in the early dawn, and as he drove to the southern gates of Angel Mountain. The man's arrogant bearing was eerily familiar. He had seen him or his like before, perhaps at that lecture when the antifa roused the crowd against him. The rabble-rousers, dressed in black, were hooded and masked. They were cowards, every one of them, afraid of the light, afraid of discovery.

Should he warn Elizabeth? Should he bring in the authorities? Was he paranoid, influenced by his own experience? He had nothing to report. The eerie man had been peaceful. The crowd had been well behaved. Nevertheless, he listed in his phone the numbers of the local police and the gate guards for quick contact and made sure the device was fully charged.

He drove to the parking lot closest to the gathering place of yesterday, the meadow below the sandstone caves. Others were arriving: vans and families; hikers, scooters, bicycles; people of every age, gender, and race; the curious; the seekers. The rangers had returned, as well as news vans.

Gregory locked the car and swung his pack over his shoulder, joining the crowd heading to the meadow. The haze was dissipating, or was it? The air seemed clearer here beneath the mountain, even fresh, yet the horizon was hazy with either smoke or fog or pollution, or all three. He watched for the tall man with the backpack, but there were many tall men with backpacks on this chilly November morning.

At 9 a.m. Abram appeared on the ledge and beckoned the crowd closer with welcoming arms. He sang psalms and preached repentance, baptism, faith in Christ, as a way to happiness. It was old-school, traditional Christianity, Gregory observed. Abram preached the moral law, the civilized code passed down through generations in Christendom and other faith traditions as well: love your enemies; do good to those who persecute you.

Several young men circulated with cards detailing the Ten Commandments and how to find happiness. They led some in the crowd to the pool under the falls, to be baptized.

All the while, in the chill air of the November morning, Angel Mountain woke up. Gregory took photos—the soaring hawks, the light touching the trees, the faces of the people. Some were gawkers and didn't stay long. Others edged forward to hear better. The mountaintop, outlined against the hazy winter sky, seemed to hold its own secrets.

Gregory moved closer to the pool and the waterfall where a line had formed. Mothers handed children to Abram to be blessed. Couples held hands, asking for blessings. Others braved the pond's cold water and were baptized.

Gregory saw that Abram recognized him. The hermit smiled, nodding. He motioned to his assistants to tell the crowd he would return in an hour. He approached Gregory.

"Dr. Worthington, so good to see you. Come. I have something for you."

Gregory held the old man's hand briefly, comforted by his sure grip. He followed him up the deer path to the cave.

They entered the luminous space, and Gregory could not determine where the light came from. To be sure the golden icons glimmered, but even gilt needed reflected light to glimmer. There was not enough light coming through the two entrances for that to happen. Had he noticed the light when he was here on Sunday? He didn't recall, but he was dizzy and woozy and not observant.

Abram handed Gregory his American flag. "You forgot this. You might need it."

Gregory laughed. "It saved me."

"It did indeed."

"Thank you."

"Could you join me for some lunch? I have fruit and health bars."

"And I have roast beef sandwiches and coffee . . . and chocolate.

Abram's eyes lit up. "Really?"

"Really."

They set out their offerings on a low table and sat cross-legged on woven matting.

"Now, I want to hear all about you, young man. Tell me again how you found our Lord, our dear Lord Jesus Christ."

"Bless the food first, Father." Gregory's fears seemed to have disappeared in the presence of this holy hermit. He had completely forgotten the sinister man with the backpack.

Gregory handed a chocolate bar to Abram and poured him a cup of coffee from his thermos. They had finished the sandwiches and were ready for dessert.

"Thank you," Abram said, clearly delighted. "But do not tell Elizabeth."

"I promise."

"So you were converted to theism by seeing the intelligent design of the universe, from the tiniest cell to the cosmos."

"I had read about the Genome Research Institute and the mapping of the genome, well underway during my undergraduate years in biochemistry in the late 1990s."

Abram nodded. "A big project, as I recall."

"1993 to 2003: ten years under two presidents—President Clinton and President Bush."

"And that led you into genetics?"

Gregory sipped his coffee. "More than that. I saw the elegance and complexity of creation and became convinced it could only have been designed by a great Intelligence. The sheer magnitude of numbers and the odds of a good selection given the billions of possibilities, numbers only recently understood, make natural selection essentially impossible on any significant scale. Slight mutations within a species, but no more than that."

"Darwinian evolution has been accepted science for nearly two centuries," Abram said, "and taught in grade school for decades. They say we are descended from apes, and before that dinosaurs." Abram examined his square of chocolate and bit into the corner, as though to thoroughly savor it.

Gregory nodded. "Many skeptics saw it was a only a theory but knew they risked their professional lives to argue against it. All the funding was for Darwinian evolution, in both academia and research. Even scientists have to eat and pay rent. After World War II, big government began funding research institutions with huge grants. A scientist had to be brave to criticize or debate Darwinian theory, to question and go against such power. Some say scientists spend 90 percent of their time writing proposals for grants."

Gregory shook his head in disbelief and reached for a chocolate square, popping it into his mouth. "Crazy."

Abram looked thoughtful. "Darwin's theory of random selection answered some of the questions people have, especially those who do not believe in the Judeo-Christian story of creation. Even Christians accepted it, separating their faith from their reason."

"It's taken a few brave souls to challenge the orthodoxy. More are coming on board, respected names. Science needs to progress beyond Darwin of the mid-nineteenth century and face his challengers of the twenty-first century. Darwin didn't have the knowledge that we have today: our study of DNA and the nature of the cell and how it works."

"And your faith in Christ? How did that happen?" Abram leaned forward as if hungry for every word.

Gregory smiled. "That's the best part. During my Stanford residency I was deeply touched by the faith many patients showed in the face of death, and I began reading accounts of scientists becoming Christians."

"This was when you were training to become a physician?"

"Right. One of the conversion accounts I read recommended *Mere Christianity* by C. S. Lewis, the Oxford scholar. The logic made sense, and I eventually became a believer in Jesus Christ."

Abram nodded. "Lewis presented the moral law argument."

"The idea that we all have a sense of fairness and justice that comes from an outside source. Darwinian evolution, survival of the fittest, doesn't account for man's altruism, when he acts for others and not in his own interest, when he acts out of sacrificial love. Also, science cannot answer *why* the universe came into being, nor explain the meaning of human existence or what happens when we die."

"And Christ?"

"Lewis looks at the claims of Christ, saying he had to be either a lunatic, a liar, or the Lord God he claimed to be, the God of Israel, the God of the Jews."

"But what about the argument that the Gospel accounts were merely the authors' opinions, or even wishful thinking? What does he say about that?"

Gregory sensed that Abram knew the answers to these questions, but he wanted to hear another person's description of the argument. "Lewis looks at the style of the Gospels, and he concludes they were written as history, not allegory. Allegory was the style of other myth-making in those times."

"History?"

Gregory divided the rest of the coffee and offered Abram more chocolate. "Lewis was a classics scholar. He knew the Greek-Roman world that
Jesus of Nazareth was born into. He understood that the Gospels, written as
eyewitness accounts, were meant to be just that, simple testimonies of what
happened."

"So it was Lewis's conversion that helped with yours," Abram said,
nodding and clearly savoring the chocolate once again, raising his eyes to
the heavens. "This dark chocolate is wonderful. Go on."

"My training was scientific. I was looking for rational belief. I came
to see that this God is a theist God, one who desires a relationship with his
creation. Deism is ruled out—a Creator who walks away from his creation. I
agreed with Lewis, having seen the beauty of the world and the sense of love
in the created order. Poetry and music were part of this God. The music of
the spheres reflected this kind of God. The nature of mankind—a creature
with self-awareness, can imagine the future, and who develops language—
points to a God of love. Add the sense of righteousness, the moral law, and
we have described the God of Abraham found in the Scriptures of Judaism,
Islam, and Christianity."

"Beauty and righteousness, reflections of a God of love."

"In some respects," Gregory added, "beauty is a universal language.
Our spirits respond to beauty, goodness, love, yet we cannot scientifically
quantify these qualities or our responses. One could also say forms of
righteousness, as Lewis claimed, are valued by every culture. Mystery and
miracle and majesty abound."

Abram leaned forward, speaking quietly and firmly. "I found mystery in Saint Joseph's Chapel in Berkeley. I found beauty there too . . . and
righteousness."

"You know the chapel?" Gregory asked. "The one on Durant?"

"Father Brubaker introduced me to Christ, and the rest came naturally."

"Father Brubaker? A good man. He's still there."

"I am glad," Abram said, raising his brows and sounding relieved. "I
might need to see him about a few things."

Abram rose and moved to the Trinity icon. Gregory joined him.

"Did you know the bishop who oversaw Saint Joseph's?" Abram asked.

"No, I didn't. He was before my time. But Father Brubaker quoted him
often. He must have been a man of great stature and wisdom."

Abram nodded, his features mapped with memory. "And great love.
Great stature both physically and spiritually. He passed into eternity a number of years ago. He was a blessing to us all. He loved this Trinity icon and
the story behind it. He often said that the mystery of the Holy Trinity is the
mystery of love. The love between the Father and the Son is the Holy Spirit."

The image showed three angelic visitors standing around a table. The central angel pointed to the lamb in a dish. Gregory assumed the central one was Christ, and the other two were God the Father and God the Holy Spirit. This Trinity icon had additional figures to the sides, drawn smaller in scale.

Abram pointed to the icon. "One of my host families in Greece gave me this when we were liberated by the Allies. I was only six years old at the time. They were Orthodox Christians. Mama Katrina said I would understand this one the best, since it includes Abraham and Sarah. And of course my name is the same. He was called Abram at the time of the visitation. God changed it to Abraham later."

"They were good people, caring people, the Greeks that took care of you."

Abram glanced at Gregory. "They were my family. I was two to six years old. I learned their prayers, their ways. I welcomed their faith, as they welcomed me. The Jewish ways were foreign to me. I fear I was unkind to my biological mother and father when liberation occurred. I thought home was with my Christian family in Athens and I wanted to return."

Gregory could see his remorse. Tears streamed down his cheeks.

"One day I shall see my birth parents and make it up to them. I will give them the love they deserve. One day in Heaven."

WEDNESDAY

Chapter 28

Wednesday morning Abram stood on the promontory ledge and watched the restless crowd. Some faces looked expectant. Some looked bored. Some looked angry. There seemed to be, on the fringe of his congregation, figures in black. A helicopter twirled and droned overhead, bearing a news channel logo. Cameras flashed from below, and a group carrying video equipment was setting up to the side, near the pool, the waterfall, and the cross.

The air was still and cold, but the morning sun was melting the night's frost. The temperatures had dropped to freezing and Abram appreciated the down sleeping bag that Elizabeth had provided. A thin film of ice covered the surface of the water in his pitcher. He had spent two winters in this cave, so this was no surprise. He was still here. But the kindness of the park rangers and his dear sister made all the difference. In the end, that was the secret of the cross, the miracle of Christ: love. Love one another. Love God as he loves you.

The smoke from the fires in the north had dissipated and the colors of the Earth sang, the sunlight awakening the hills and valleys, the waterfalls and ponds, the oaks and manzanita. Color. The joy of the colors prompted memory of his dream in the early dawn. Was it a dream or a vision?

An angel had appeared to him. This was a first visit and Abram nearly wept for joy. While his other dreams had been about journeys, this dream was about Heaven. The angel was all light and movement, like a cool flame shifting shape, as if dancing to music Abram could not yet hear. The shape would not be still, and the rhythmic motion of the image, as it wrestled with Earth's gravity and spatial dimensions, so transfixed Abram that he found he was not listening to the angel's words.

"Do not be afraid!" the angel repeated. "I am Michael, come to proclaim the Lord Jesus Christ, the Alpha and Omega, who will save you from yourself, from your sins, from your death, so that you will know your *true* self. Each soul is a prism of color, a song, when each soul is fully realized. Listen! Remember!"

"Yes, good Michael, lead me, oh lead me, never leave me," Abram replied, but his own words sounded as if they were spoken by someone else.

The angel sang with a lilting voice that soared, perfect in the harmonic ratios of poetry and music, words and phrases pulled into man's world, carried over and through the great void, past the stars of the cosmos, between the planets, pulled from Heaven to Earth: "The Kingdom of Heaven is like . . . the music of the spheres, the music of the heart, the music of beauty, and the beauty of music. There is the Lamb and the throne and the martyrs in white robes. There are the four beasts—who gave witness in their Gospels— and there is the woman giving birth and the snake she grinds underfoot. It is all revealed in John of Patmos's vision. It is all revealed. I only repeat what you know and have read and have seen."

Now, recalling the remarkable dream, Abram surveyed his congregation gathered in the meadow. Some waved large placards. He could not read the words from this distance, but he guessed what they said. It was time, he thought. The end was beginning, and in his end was his beginning. He raised his arms in peace and prayer. He prayed the Lord's Prayer, and as he prayed, the screamers fell silent. The crowd rustled, as though settling in, and Abram spoke into the cold air the words that soared from his heart and soul.

"The Kingdom of Heaven is like . . . "

As he preached, he saw a familiar figure coming up the deer path. It was young Caleb, and Caleb brought a young friend. God is so good, Abram thought, so faithful. He followed Caleb down to the pond, to these seekers after God.

"This is Steven," Caleb said. "My brother."

"It is good to meet you, Steven," Abram replied, nodding to him. "Thank you for coming here."

"It is for me to thank you," Steven said. "You were in my dream last night. I think that maybe . . . I have been sent to help."

Caleb and Steven assisted Abram with the line of penitents leading to the pond of baptism. Abram could see that the brothers watched the crowd for any sign of trouble. He could see, as a brisk breeze freshened the air, that the crowd was growing restless again. Nearby, the TV team filmed, and a reporter spoke into a microphone.

Abram saw all of this as the hour approached noon. He trusted his new friends, Caleb and Steven, to be vigilant. He knew he must focus on Christ alone and the baptisms, the Good Shepherd and the sheep, the chosen ones who had chosen Christ. As Abram cupped the cold water in his hands and poured it over each soul, he prayed to his Lord for each person—for Glenn, Susan, Sarah, Linda, Carol, Naomi, Nancy, Edward, Frank—praying that God's Holy Spirit would fill each one, cleanse them, rebirth them with the waters of baptism. For now, they owned the promises of Christ. A new covenant with Heaven had been made in each heart. The promise of eternal life was assured. The hope of eternal joy was born. Life—and death—would never be the same. Fear was banished; happiness took root. With watering and feeding, through sacraments, prayer, and praise, happiness would grow and blossom into a field of flowers, a crown of life.

All would be clear, all colors would be seen, all melodies heard. The haze would be blown away by the wind of the Holy Spirit, and the fires in the north would be snuffed by the breath of God. Once again, Earth would sing to God's glory.

Chapter 29

Elizabeth awoke early on Wednesday, moaning loudly and trying to speak, but no words sounded.

Laddie squealed and jumped off the bed.

The nightmare clung to her as she tried to recall and face it, hoping the facing would erase the memory, a distorted memory of what happened on Crete. For they made it to safety; they made it to the boat; they made it off the island. And here she was, safe in America, she repeated. Safe in America.

> She is hiding in a cave with her mother and aunt and baby brother. They have descended Mount Tilifos to the foothills. Soon they are hidden by a family in the coastal village of Kastelli where they pretend to be Christians, visiting the chapel across the square from Gestapo headquarters. They make the sign of the cross as they enter and as they leave. They need to pretend or they will be imprisoned or killed. She feels her mother's fear and her father's determination to survive, to outwit the Nazis.
>
> But they need travel permits to leave the island, now German occupied. Her papa obtains the permits and they board a fishing boat headed for Greece.
>
> They are sailing home on the open sea, but a German patrol forces them to shore. No, Elizabeth cries inside, we are going home! The commander tells them not to be afraid. He does not know they are Jews.
>
> He tells them that the Germans respect the Greeks, that the Germans respect classical learning and tradition, and want to liberate the Greeks by bringing back the glory of ancient Greece. He tells them that the Jews caused everyone's troubles. Do not fear, the German commander says, for you are Greeks.
>
> But we need to go home! Elizabeth cries inside.

They made it to Athens, she told herself, gazing at the white cross on Angel Mountain in the dim November dawn. And they were able to hide throughout the war in Greece, moving from family to family until liberation. But after liberation, the communists took power. They too hated the Jews. They too were tyrannical. Even so, her brave papa found ways for the family to survive. And finally she, Elizabeth, was sent to college in America, along with Abram.

She reminded herself again that she was in America now, and *she was safe.*

She had met Samuel, another survivor, in her undergraduate years, and he made her even safer. How she missed him! Why had the nightmares returned? Was this because of the scientist she met on Angel Mountain? Was she still that fragile?

The nightmare of escaping to Athens and the fear of being caught lingered as she gave Laddie his morning insulin shot. She hoped she had the right dosage, with her mind so far from her sweet cat. She lifted the neck fur to make the pocket as she had been instructed. She discharged the insulin into the pocket. Did the needle go in? She could not feel it puncture his skin. She withdrew the needle and shook her head. She needed more faith.

Elizabeth needed more faith in regards to Abram as well. She worried about him, for she had seen on social media that crowds were coming to hear him preach. But what could she do? Her brother was stubborn. He would not leave his mission—or whatever it was. He would not listen to sense. He said he was part of something greater, and he had signed on for this when he was baptized, and re-enlisted when he was ordained.

She made breakfast as the morning news reported in dire tones about the northern fires. She opened her back door a crack, smelled the smoke, and closed it securely. Surely the sooty haze would keep the crowds away. Surely they would not risk breathing it in. The air quality was not healthy. And yet the news reports claimed that the area where Abram preached was clear, a strange atmospheric phenomenon that sometimes happened. How could that be? The hermit was baptizing, they said. Did he think he was the second coming of John the Baptist?

Elizabeth did not see herself as religious, although she believed in God. She did not attend synagogue or observe holy days. Samuel wanted to merge into their Christian (mainly Protestant) business world without actually converting, so being a secular Jew was best; he did not want to be a Jew at all; he wanted to be a part of the country club set, to melt into American culture with all of its promises and rewards. He was a businessman first and a lover of success—even excess—an ambitious although immensely kind and courteous man of means. In fact Laddie was the last of many cats they had brought home from a shelter that they had supported generously over the years. Samuel had left a significant bequest to the shelter foundation, in addition to a long list of other charities.

So Elizabeth and Samuel had no religion, and Abram had too much. Or so she believed.

As she toasted a muffin and brewed her double espresso, she looked forward to seeing her new librarian. Catherine Nelson would be a breath of fresh air in this stale house of books. Elizabeth hoped Catherine was not deterred by the stories of Villa Tilifos, the hauntings. Of course there were no hauntings—even on Halloween when the local boys threw toilet paper on her olive trees in the front yard. Of course there were no hauntings. The spirits in her dreams could not be seen by others. The spirits belonged to her and no one else.

When Elizabeth opened the front door, she saw that Catherine was frightened. Maria bustled in ahead of her, proclaiming that whoever did such a thing should be arrested and put away for a very long time.

"What is it?" Elizabeth asked.

Catherine motioned to the outer wall near the door.

Elizabeth gasped. A swastika had been scrawled on the stucco.

Maria had already returned with cleaning fluid and a towel. "This should remove it," she said, immediately going to work on it.

"Please, come in, Catherine. I am glad to see you." Elizabeth inhaled deeply, a technique she had learned to calm her heart when it beat too fast.

Catherine stepped inside. She touched Elizabeth's shoulder in sympathy. "Are you calling the police? Do you want me to?"

Elizabeth's heart pounded. She breathed in. She breathed out. "I am not sure." Who could have done this? "They might be on Angel Mountain. There is trouble . . . and the rangers . . . may need help."

"I saw something about that on the news," Catherine said. "Does a hermit really live up there? They say he has been seen by some hikers."

Elizabeth nodded. "More than seen. He is preaching to a crowd." And risking everything, she thought.

"Do you know him?"

Elizabeth hesitated, then led Catherine to her home office. They entered, and as Catherine's glance rested on the books, Elizabeth replied, "He is my brother, my baby brother."

Surprise, then sympathy, mapped Catherine's features. "You must worry about him out there."

Elizabeth moved the books on the armchairs and sat down, motioning to Catherine to join her. "I do worry. We survived the Holocaust. We were children. I was six and he was two when Hitler invaded Greece, and we went into hiding. Abram never knew Judaism in his early years. He became a Christian because of his host families, and he remained a Christian."

"Even after coming here?"

Elizabeth nodded. "He became more religious after coming to America, as though one door opened to another." She was not sure why she trusted Catherine, but she seemed vulnerable in her own way, as though having suffered as well, and it was good to have someone to talk to. "He attended a Greek Orthodox Church from time to time and then a student chapel near the university. He retired from Cal in 2003 and eventually studied theology. He became a deacon, then a priest. He came to live with Samuel and me. We had no children, so we had plenty of room. Three years ago Abram found the sandstone caves on the mountainside and has been living there, praying for the world, he says."

"I think that student chapel might be Father Brubaker's chapel."

"Brubaker! I thought the name was familiar. Abram mentioned him often. Says he saved his life. Abram liked the bishop there too, although I believe he has passed on now. Father Brubaker gave you a glowing reference."

"It was kind of him. The chapel is beautiful."

"Are you religious?"

"Not really. I visit the chapel from time to time. It's a good place to think. It's quiet."

"You should meet Abram."

"I'd like that. You said he taught at Cal?"

"Classics. Do you remember him? Dr. Levin?"

"I'm afraid I don't recall him, but I didn't take anything in classics."

"It used to be a part of the required Western Civilization core curriculum, but no more."

"I was an English major. I took some art history and women's studies. And then my library science grad degree. It would be interesting to meet Abram."

"And good for him to meet you." Set his feet back on Earth, in the real world, Elizabeth thought. "Perhaps with all the fuss out there, he will come home." As Elizabeth said this, she knew it would not happen, but still, she wanted to believe it. Today, crowds, even friendly crowds, could turn into unfriendly mobs in the blink of an eye.

Maria peered through the doorway. "I think I was able to scrub the markings off the wall, Mrs. Jacobsen. A terrible thing!"

"What would I do without you, Maria? Thank you."

"You really should report it," Catherine urged.

"I will, later." Elizabeth was not sure what to do, with Abram taking such risks on the mountain. But clearly he was no longer in hiding. "I will do it now. Oh, the books! I have a list somewhere of how I wanted it all done. Where is that list?"

Elizabeth searched the room, picking up several lists from various locations. "I do not know what I did with it." She found a stack of papers and leafed through them. "I cannot find it. Let us begin by sorting them into fiction and nonfiction. Then we will go from there. History and modern culture. Fiction by author. Oh, and a classics section with Abram's books. What do you think?"

"Sounds good." Catherine smiled tentatively, and rose to begin her sorting. "Stacked or shelved?"

"Start with fiction shelved and the rest stacked. I may need more shelves. Maria's husband can build shelves. He is so talented."

Elizabeth stood in the doorway for a moment and watched Catherine work, recalling the young woman's frightening arrival and the hated Nazi swastika to the side of the door, the twisted cross that became a symbol of death for her people and those who protected them. She knew that anti-Semitism had been around far longer than the Nazis, and yet the Holocaust intensified it, distilled and weaponized it, making it a killing machine.

Was the hate returning, even here in America, the last hope of the world for freedom and the rule of law? The shooting at the Pittsburgh synagogue last month was evidence of such a resurgence. There were reports of European incidents. The United Nations seemed more friendly to Palestine than to Israel, claiming Israel was the aggressor and Palestine the victim. And yet, Elizabeth knew, as she returned to the entry, how deeply some Arabs hated the Jews. The radicalized Muslims were raised to hate. They were indoctrinated in their families and their schools. In London, she had read, anti-Semitism was on the rise, encouraged by mainstream politicians. Elizabeth shivered, suddenly cold, and she wrapped Samuel's sweater snugly about her.

She opened the front door and examined the stucco that had been defaced. The hated symbol was gone, leaving a trace that was apparent only to those who knew it had been there. And yet the trace reminded her of the fragility of freedom. It reminded her of the importance of the past, so necessary to understand the present. There would always be darkness, and it could always be redeemed by light, by love, by respect for all races, classes, genders, ages. But it was vital to recognize the demonic shapes hovering in the dark in order to shine light upon them and reveal their true faces.

She could hear Maria bustling in the kitchen. She too had a painful history. Most immigrants, Elizabeth judged, had suffered in their past, and it was heartening to Elizabeth that all Americans were immigrants or descended from immigrants. That was why they came to America. They came for a better life, greater opportunities, and freedom from tyranny. They came because of America's laws, her liberties, her great melting pot, or vegetable stew as some said.

In Mexico, Maria's family had known the horrors of a violent drug culture protected by government elites. Maria immigrated legally to America with her family, waiting in line like so many others, receiving her work visa, and finally, after studying at night and learning English, she was granted the great prize: American citizenship. How happy she was on that day, Elizabeth recalled. Maria could not stop smiling and gazing to the hills, as though she were reborn. And since that glorious citizenship day, she gazed to the hills often, and Elizabeth noted it was toward the white cross on Angel Mountain that she most often directed her focus.

America was indeed a haven of freedom protected by legislated, democratic law. But corruption was everywhere and needed to be faced. She recalled something Abram once said: "We need to face our human nature. Only then can we make changes and rebuild our world." Perhaps he was right. He often spoke of Moses and the Ten Commandments, saying if everyone kept the Mosaic Law, wrote it on their hearts, there would be no war, no poverty, no hate.

The secret, Elizabeth knew, was keeping the commandments—easy to say and difficult to do. She would settle for respect among all peoples, races, genders, beliefs.

Who had scrawled this sign of hate? Was it connected to Abram and his preaching?

Entering the kitchen, she smiled. "What is for lunch, Maria?" Elizabeth was so very thankful for her home and her housekeeper, and now for Catherine. She would add these to her gratitude journal for today, Wednesday, November 14, 2018.

Chapter 30

As Catherine reached for a volume, opened it, checked the jacket and front matter, determining each book's category, Elizabeth's words returned to her. Did Elizabeth's parents survive the Holocaust? Was she orphaned? Did she grow up as Catherine had grown up, full of loss? Catherine had felt cheated in not having a father, but what if she had not had a mother as well?

For a brief moment Catherine felt shame that she could be unhappy with all that she had been given. She had never hidden from the Gestapo. She had never felt that kind of fear, especially as a child. She had never had to emigrate. She had been born here. How lucky was that? Elizabeth had been through a lot. She had acquired a lot too, in the course of time—the house and land, security of sorts, work she valued. And she found Samuel, her late husband, whom she clearly loved and now mourned.

The house settled about Catherine like a garland: the oil paintings, the high ceilings, the moldings, the airiness of the rooms and hallways, the large picture windows looking out to more beauty—to the golden hills, to the garden of olive trees and formal pathways that radiated from a fountain. From time to time the soft gong of the grandfather clock in the entry reminded her of the steady and relentless passing of time. Still, it was a quiet and genteel sound, comforting in some inexplicable way, as if the hours were honored as they slipped away. She was glad she had dressed professionally once again—camel jacket and black slacks—for somehow the house encouraged her to be her best, just as her mother had done. She would wear her mother's herringbone on Thursday.

She didn't want to go back to Berkeley, to her small, dingy apartment.

Elizabeth peeked in. "All going well? Any questions?"

Catherine stood and smiled, eyeing her stacks of books. "You have an interesting collection," she said. "Would you like a separate stack for biographies? Types of history? European, American, British?"

Elizabeth sat in one of the wing chairs. She appeared tired. "You decide. Then I will simply use your system. It is too overwhelming for me now."

She crossed the room to the doorway, then looked back. "Maria is making soup for lunch. If you like, you are welcome to join us. I can let you know when it is ready."

"That would be lovely."

Catherine watched her go and returned to the books. *Eliot and His Age* by Russell Kirk. There was something else here by Kirk. She found it: *The Conservative Mind, from Burke to Eliot.* Who were they? And why hadn't she heard of them? As she continued reaching and opening and wondering, it became tempting to scan the first page, just to sample the style. She came across a copy of T. S. Eliot's *Four Quartets* and considered the elegance of the title, a combining of music and poetry. She opened it and read a page slowly, as poetry was meant to be read. It was difficult, but the cadence pulled her into its world, the images flooded her with power and beauty, and again, she wondered what it was all about. The Kirk biography of Eliot used the phrase "permanent things" on the jacket summary. Perhaps this was a theme of Eliot, ideas that never went out of fashion, a kind of deep and abiding human truth, that which made humanity human. When she knew Elizabeth better, she might ask.

Footsteps could be heard in the hallway. Had she been reading all this time?

She looked up. Elizabeth.

"Time for lunch. If you would like to freshen up, there is a powder room between the two offices." She smiled. "Mmm . . . Eliot. Difficult, but profound and lately controversial . . . come join us when you are ready."

"Mrs. Jacobsen, the soup is delicious." Catherine could taste cumin and coriander. Hispanic flavors laced a vegetable soup.

"Please call me Elizabeth," the older woman said. "And thank you. I have Maria use ordinary soups and add different spices. This is a take on the Southwestern tortilla soup. Would you like sour cream?"

"Thank you." Catherine helped herself to a square of cornbread and a dollop of sour cream.

Maria had joined them. "It is very much like the soup I remember as a child."

Elizabeth eyed Maria with admiration. "Maria is a great cook, but I do not want her to work too hard. She has enough work with this huge house. Her father and her eldest son look after the grounds and pool. I sometimes wonder if I should downsize."

"But the house is close to your brother," Catherine said, and Maria nodded in agreement. Catherine judged that Maria and her family enjoyed working here. What would happen to them if Elizabeth moved away?

"He does need looking after," Elizabeth said, "and I hope he will come home, especially after his collapse and the hiker's fall on Sunday—"

"He collapsed? Someone fell?" Catherine asked. "How awful."

Maria frowned. "These hikers take such risks. What are they thinking, standing too close to the edge of the mountain?"

"It was not like that, Maria," Elizabeth explained.

"But he fell and Signor Abram found him. Then you found them both."

Catherine watched the two review the events. They were friends, she could see. Almost mother and daughter, or aunt and niece. Maria looked to be about forty-five, but she had the confidence of someone older.

Elizabeth turned to Catherine. "A hiker lost his footing and fell down from an upper trail. He is all right as far as I know. Abram found him. He hit his head on a rock and there was a nasty bruise, but I was able to take him to his car. Earlier Abram had been preaching." Elizabeth grew pale as she revisited the events of Sunday. "The hiker we rescued visited on Monday and brought me these flowers as a gift of thanks."

The roses occupied the center of the table. Their long green stems could be seen through the tall crystal vase. Their red buds were half opened, reaching high amidst abundant green leaves.

"They're beautiful," Catherine said truthfully, then added, "I heard about Abram's preaching. It was on the news. It sounded as if he had a message for the world, almost an urgent warning, like a prophet."

Catherine tried to imagine what the hermit was like. Living in books and their stories, fiction or nonfiction, she found she craved the threads that wove together to create character. Here was Abram, a hermit. How many hermits had she met? None. Would she ever have a chance like this again? Unlikely.

Catherine asked, "So that's good that he's preaching, right?"

In the following silence, Catherine tried to soften the question. "But you must worry about him. It must be difficult, not knowing for sure what he's doing out there, and if he's safe."

Elizabeth nodded, sitting back and twisting her napkin in her fingers, her brows pulled together. "I do worry. We been through so much. I have always looked after him except for the time when he disappeared—and we found him at People's Park in Berkeley. But now he seems to be beyond my reach once again, beyond my ability to care for him."

Catherine recalled Elizabeth's words earlier. "You said Abram collapsed?"

Elizabeth breathed deeply as though pacing herself. "He prays from a high ledge outside his cave. On Sunday three young men saw him on the ledge and threw rocks at him, knocking out his wind. A little later Abram found the hiker who had fallen, not far from the waterfall and pond."

As Maria cleared the dishes, she added sympathetically, "But your brother Abram did a great and good thing, Elizabeth. He saved Dr. Worthington, an important scientist. And you did a good thing too. You saved them both." She fingered a cross around her neck.

"Dr. Worthington?" Catherine recognized the name, but was he the same Worthington who had been her instructor? "A scientist?"

"He taught at Cal and is on sabbatical," Elizabeth replied. "You went to Cal, Catherine. Do you remember the name?"

"A Gregory Worthington taught one of my undergraduate sections in biology."

"He went on to receive a medical degree," Elizabeth said nervously.

"But he decided to teach, not practice medicine?"

Elizabeth looked uncomfortable. "He went into research, genetics."

"He spoke of genetics in the class."

"The subject is difficult for me, coming out of the Holocaust."

Catherine wasn't sure how they were related, but didn't feel right asking. She needed to resist her temptation to speak bluntly. It generally was not a good plan. Think before speaking, she told herself. She waited in the uncomfortable silence.

Elizabeth murmured, "Microbiology, biochemistry . . . today so noble, but so frightening."

Maria was rinsing bowls and placing them in the dishwasher. The sound of the running tap and her melodious humming couldn't completely ease the tension, but was welcome to Catherine. She recalled how her mother hummed as she worked as well.

"Isn't genetic research a good thing?" Catherine finally asked, unable to control her curiosity.

Elizabeth eyed Catherine with a gentleness that must have come from her years of patiently teaching high school.

Suddenly the sound of birds squawking and gobbling came from the front yard. Maria turned, dried her hands on a towel, and walked briskly to the entry and out the front door, crying, "Go, go, go, away, away, away, away with you, you messy turkeys!"

She looked back from the doorway. "Such a mess they make on the lawns. Such a mess." She disappeared outside to the front yard.

"Wild turkeys," Elizabeth explained. "Have you seen them? Probably not in Berkeley. But they roam these hills—entire flocks, or are they gaggles?" She stood and beckoned Catherine to follow her. "Maria is a woman of many talents. Come and see."

They walked into the entry and onto the porch, and saw a large flock of turkeys flee from Maria, trotting and half-flying down the hillside behind the house.

Elizabeth smiled. "They migrate through the neighborhoods, sensing they are protected. And so close to Thanksgiving, too."

Catherine's thoughts had remained with Dr. Worthington and genetics. Could he find her father?

"I am sorry," Elizabeth said. "You asked about genetics and its connection to the Holocaust. Hitler was the product of many historical events and trends. Darwin wrote of the survival of the fittest and natural selection—evolution, an evolving of life. The eugenics movement of the early twentieth century was based on this idea, seeking to eliminate so-called undesirable traits—and undesirable persons and peoples."

Maria re-entered the house, murmuring to herself and shaking her head. Elizabeth and Catherine remained on the porch as Elizabeth told the unthinkable history, the story of eugenics.

"Simply put," she said, opening her palms as though releasing words into the air, "Hitler sought to create a master race of the fittest, to speed up evolution, as it were, to kill off those he did not see as fit as the German, Aryan race, his northern *folk* or *volk*." She eyed Catherine with an intensity meant to brand the facts on her heart and mind.

Catherine held her gaze, absorbing her words.

"He planned to eliminate the ill, the handicapped, the old, the gypsies, and the Jews. Christians were next, along with anyone who did not support his program. He was the ultimate racist. The Holocaust was a direct result of the eugenics movement, which took hold in the U.S. as well. Ideas have consequences. Never forget. Words and stories are important, for they communicate ideas."

"And Dr. Worthington?" Catherine heard a loud gobble and clucking coming from the hillside.

They paused, watching the turkeys return to the yard. "These birds are so stubborn. They leave and then come right back." She glanced at Catherine. "Dr. Worthington claims that genetics is a noble calling, that he wanted to find a cure for Parkinson's disease, and that he thought he could bring moral oversight to the field. But I did not learn how he planned to accomplish moral oversight. I am not sure it is possible."

"I'm interested in genetics." Was she too blunt? But she wanted to be honest with Elizabeth. The elderly woman deserved to know, since she had been so forthright herself.

"How so?"

The turkeys were now feeding on the lawn, gobbling loudly as if at a convention. "I never knew my father. He abandoned us. I'd like to find out who he is or was, to know who I am, I guess."

Elizabeth rested her hand on Catherine's shoulder. "I understand. We all want to know ourselves. And the genetics genie is out of the bottle, as they say. We cannot go back. I suppose the challenge—and today's urgency—is to use genetics for good, not ill. Prospective parents will soon have the right to abort a child because he or she is the wrong gender or has the wrong coloring or carries traits they do not desire. Abortion on demand, meaning if the mother does not want the baby for any reason, is legal in many states, even in the last trimester."

"It's like ordering designer babies," Catherine said. "Just doesn't seem right, doesn't respect human life, all human life." Catherine followed Elizabeth back into the house. They paused in the entry. "I was misdiagnosed as a Down's baby, and that's why my father left. He wanted me aborted, and my mother refused." Catherine surprised herself, that she revealed this to someone she had known for so short a time. But she trusted Elizabeth. "I hope I haven't disturbed you."

"I am disturbed to hear of your father's actions. How terrible," Elizabeth replied. "Our world is scary. It is painful to face what we do to one another, especially to the innocent, the unborn."

"It *is* painful." Catherine, for the first time, questioned if she really wanted to know her father, all things considered. Her lip trembled as she added, "But I had better get back to the books."

"I will check on you after a bit," Elizabeth said.

Catherine stepped down the hall and entered the room full of books that desired her acquaintance, piled in their assigned stacks or waiting to be sorted. She would try to stay focused and not be lured into reading them, but they had become her friends already.

She considered Dr. Worthington. She would like to meet him, but she wouldn't ask that of Elizabeth, not yet.

Chapter 31

On Wednesday morning, Gregory Worthington smelled smoke. He checked the air quality alerts on his phone. It was a spare-the-air day with breathing alerts for the elderly. He looked to the gray skies, but didn't see ash raining upon the Earth.

He decided to visit Abram anyway, drove to Angel Mountain, and made his way to the meadow, the falls, and the cross.

The sun had risen at 6:48 a.m., its fiery ball diminished by the smoky haze. But when Gregory reached the meadow the air was far clearer, the skies merely appearing overcast and hiding the sun. He didn't smell smoke, at least not here in the meadow—Abram's meadow—beneath the sandstone caves.

Gregory watched the crowd, scanning for the ominous man he had seen Monday. Buses were parked in the lot nearby. The TV news van, reporter, and cameraman did not worry him, except he knew the crowd would increase as the news spread. Large numbers could soon turn a peaceful gathering into a violent one.

A helicopter circled. Gregory drew closer to Abram to offer his help. Should Gregory contact Father Brubaker? While middle-aged, he was a burly fellow, and understood people. He had a military background and was experienced with crowd control, with the recent riots on campus.

Gregory hadn't been back to the chapel in a while. Perhaps it was time. He quickly tapped the pastor's number and left a message. As he spoke into the phone, he spotted a group of black-clad protesters on the edge of the crowd.

He recognized the suspicious fellow from Monday, who now approached one of the protesters. He could see they knew one another, as they pulled away from the others. Money, it appeared, was exchanged, as the protester nodded and returned to his group, carrying a stack of signs.

Soon the signs were held high and words were chanted that Gregory couldn't make out, grunts launched into the atmosphere like missiles. The signs decried pedophile priests, white supremacy, and fascism.

Others in the crowd joined in the antifa shouts and propaganda slogans, leaves taken from the communist playbook, words full of outrage for its own sake. Nasty and violent language was housed in childish rhyme, turning verbal assaults into righteous incantations: "Racist, sexist, anti-gay, fascist bigots go away." There were other rhymes without reason or truth behind them.

Gregory could see that many in the gathering could not hear Abram, for his words were drowned by the protestors' screams. Slowly, the crowd fell under the spell of the antifa propaganda wielded by professional rioters using historic brainwashing tools. Urged into a frenzy, the crowd waved their arms, calling Abram's words hate speech, simply because he was a man of God, a prophet robed in white. They couldn't hear his words of love.

A police van arrived, and officers entered the crowd at the periphery where the commotion brewed. They carried only nightsticks, no guns, Gregory observed, and he hoped they had body cameras to protect them from any later charges against them. They raised their hands in peace, urging the screamers to quiet down, to allow the man his freedom to speak. But the hooded and masked men—they seemed to be mostly men but it was difficult to tell—now leading a mob, pushed the officers back, forcing them into their van.

As the bullies made their way through the crowd toward Abram, the first bolt of lightning struck, crackling through the leaden skies. The crowd looked up, some hoping for rain on the parched earth, some fearing fiery retribution for their disrespect of the old man on the mountain. Gregory waited for the rolling thunder to follow, for while they occurred simultaneously, he knew that light travels faster than sound.

Abram raised his walking stick, which appeared like a shepherd's staff, and looked to the heavens, reminding Gregory of Moses descending Mount Sinai with the Ten Commandments or Aaron turning the Nile River into blood.

Thunder rumbled and the skies parted.

Abram opened his arms, welcoming the rain falling in fat drops and splashing the dry grass.

A second bolt of lightning crackled, lighting up the mountain and the meadow, the falls, and the cross.

Gregory pulled his hood over his head. The black-clad protesters had vanished and their acolytes had dispersed, disappointed if not fearful. Their leader had gone as well. They had disturbed the Earth enough for one day, and the heavens were angry. The crowd moved quickly to the shelter of their cars and buses, as rain poured over the land. It was as if angels had opened floodgates.

Gregory found Abram on the deer path and saw that two young men had covered him with a blanket. He followed them into the protection of the sandstone caves.

They dried off as best as they could, and Gregory turned to Abram. "You're in danger. The crowd is full of professional rioters—antifa. You cannot be heard. There is no point in this anymore."

Abram smiled at Gregory as if humoring a child. "It is all right, my friend. It is all right. God is in charge of this."

"But Elizabeth wants you to come home." He would try a different tack.

Abram sipped some water and nodded. "I know. But this is all as it should be. Not to worry, all is grace."

Caleb handed Abram a health bar, and Abram held it, gazing unseeing. He turned to his icons, as though asking them for directions.

"I must rest now. It is nearly finished." Abram returned the bar to Caleb with a nod of thanks. He reclined on his hard bed of stone and closed his eyes.

The boys covered him with a blanket and stood watch.

Abram reached out to Gregory with his hand. "My son, never you mind, it will turn out well. All is well, all is well. Go to Elizabeth and comfort her. And thank you for being a friend to this old man."

Gregory took Abram's hand and held it between his own. It was cold, so cold, and Gregory tried to warm it by gently rubbing his hands over Abram's, but to no avail. "I will do as you ask, Father." He turned to Caleb and Steven. "Call if you need me," he whispered. They exchanged numbers and Gregory returned the way he had come, down the deer path and through the meadow to his car.

He looked back to the sandstone caves, the falls, the pond and the cross. The white cross, soaked with rain, gleamed against the brown grass, and a ray of sun settled upon it, the pond, and the meadow, forming a holy light that Gregory would never forget.

Gregory drove down Angel Mountain. He did not want to leave Abram—he wasn't sure why—and his heart ached.

The rain stopped as suddenly as it started. But dark clouds hovered over the mountain, and Gregory guessed there would be another storm. Rain was welcome in California, especially with the infernos raging in the north, and he could not complain. But lightning lit fires even as rain quenched them. Nature was like that, oblivious to man's desires, incantations, or dances.

Yet man was drawn into that natural world like a moth to a flame, as though the beauty, the breathtaking drama of the forests, lakes, and seas, could and would save him. In the end, man retreated to shelter for protection from the elements of wind and weather. In the end, he stored provisions in the good times to see him through the bad, those times of famine either of harvest or income. He stored water in the wet seasons to see him through the dry seasons. Man needed to outwit nature and tame the wilderness, subdue its wildness.

Gregory drove through the quiet neighborhoods at the base of the mountain, returning to his room for a bite to eat and a few hours' work. He would check on Elizabeth in the afternoon. He wanted to research the news sites for information about antifa or any other group that might harbor hate toward Abram. It made no sense to accuse the gentle prophet of hate speech. It made no sense at all.

Why had the antifa gone after Abram? Gregory believed they were antifa, or at least they were modeling themselves on antifa's riots nationwide, not just in Berkeley. Perhaps they were the viral children of antifa.

Gregory recalled his earlier conversation with Abram. In his memory, it appeared that Gregory did most of the telling, that Abram did most of the listening. But Gregory had learned that Abram had taught classics at Cal. Abram's years had overlapped with Gregory's time as an undergraduate student and then as a teaching assistant. Gregory hadn't taken courses in the classics department, and Western Civilization was no longer required. He took various history courses, cherry-picking things that looked interesting.

Now he wished he had been better advised, that he had supplemented science with liberal arts, now called humanities. He wished he had taken more history, especially of the Western world—Europe and America—to have a better understanding of what made the free world free and those institutions that supported freedom and democracy. But would he have listened to such advice? He had focused on a science major and that was that. He had been narrow-minded and no one had pointed out his errors, his foolish choices. They should have.

Abram was Jewish. Was this threatening group an anti-Semitic outburst? The recent shooting at the Pittsburgh synagogue was one more incident on a growing list of anti-Semitic terror.

And then there was Gregory's manuscript, his slow progress on the book he was supposedly writing. He could not deny that all of this Angel Mountain business had diverted him from his purpose. He should revisit his memoir of conversion. He should at least try to work on it. His sabbatical couldn't last forever, even if the university wanted it to.

He also needed to look at his photos from the other day, the people in the crowd, and to follow up with Father Brubaker from the chapel.

And he promised to comfort Elizabeth.

Chapter 32

When Gregory arrived at Villa Tilifos Wednesday afternoon, he spoke into the box at the gate. Elizabeth buzzed the gates open. It took a few minutes before anyone answered his knock at the front door. Had she forgotten him? Gregory considered ringing the bell in spite of the sign about the cat.

The door opened, and Elizabeth stood there beaming. "Dr. Worthington! Welcome. We were just talking about you."

Gregory sidestepped the curious announcement, focusing on warning Elizabeth about Abram. "Mrs. Jacobsen, could I have a word with you? It's important. Something I think you should know."

"Of course, come in. How is your head?" She eyed his bruise.

"I'll live. I was fortunate. And so grateful to you." He touched his forehead, still tender, as he followed her into a parlor where armchairs angled toward a fieldstone fireplace.

"Just let me check on something," she said. "Please, have a seat. Would you like tea? We were just finishing tea."

Gregory took a seat. "No, thank you, I won't be long. I don't want to intrude. It's about your brother." He had not forgotten her reaction to his career as a geneticist, and he didn't want that to come up again. He could see she was a different person when she was happy. Today she was happy.

He heard her speaking excitedly to someone in the kitchen, and there was a quiet, measured reply by a woman, he guessed, a woman with a low husky voice.

Elizabeth returned, accompanied by a young woman. Gregory stood as they entered the room.

"Catherine Nelson, I'd like you to meet Dr. Gregory Worthington, a recent acquaintance. I believe you might recall him from my tale of the mountain." She eyed Gregory as if to explain she had already introduced him with his own adventure.

He offered his hand. The young woman—he guessed early thirties—held herself together tightly, as though trying to project a confidence she didn't have. She glanced at him and took his hand, smiling and nodding briefly. Her fingers were pale and delicate and long, her handshake cool and soft and gentle, and reserved.

Her auburn hair was braided into a coil on top of her head and she wore pearl earrings, white tee, camel jacket, and black slacks. It was as if she were covering a fragility with a tailored costume that announced proficiency in all enterprises in which she took part. She wore little makeup, her fair skin marked by a tiny mole on her upper cheekbone. Her green eyes, framed by dark brows, locked on his, betraying curiosity. She was slim, about five foot six, he thought, slightly shorter than his five foot ten.

"I'm pleased to meet you," she said.

"My pleasure, to be sure," he replied. "Yes, indeed, my pleasure, to be sure . . ." Was he stuttering? He felt as if he were. "Oh, I said that didn't I?" He grinned—sheepishly, he feared—looking to Mrs. Jacobsen for help.

Elizabeth's face gave her amusement away. "I was just telling Catherine about your terrible ordeal," she said. "When I mentioned your name, she said she may have taken one of your classes . . . in . . ." She glanced toward the hills.

Gregory followed her glance. The clouds still hovered over the peak of Angel Mountain, but the white cross could be seen on the lower hillside.

"In chemistry. Or was it biology?" Elizabeth said finally.

"Biology," Catherine said. "I think it must have been 2005. You probably don't remember me."

He wanted to say he remembered her, but he didn't. "The undergraduate sections were large, I'm afraid, and I can't say I recall you, which is amazing given your . . . er . . . I want to say attractiveness, but we can't say that anymore can we?"

Catherine laughed, and Gregory thought there might be victory in the laugh. Such a beautiful smile, too! He hoped the awkwardness he felt was now gone for good. Humor sometimes put him at ease.

"Thank you, anyway," she said, looking at him with increased interest. "It was a fascinating class. I never forgot the research you described, the mapping of the genome and the future possibilities of editing DNA." She glanced at Elizabeth. "I'm sorry to bring that up," she said quickly.

"Did you go into science?" he asked, angling away from genetics.

"Library science. Not really science in that sense."

"Not chemistry or biology?"

"No. I knew I wanted to work with books, with words, with interesting others in books and words . . . and ideas. Then Elizabeth . . . Mrs. Jacobsen . . . hired me to organize her books."

He watched her speak as she shifted her weight from foot to foot. She tilted her head like a sparrow. She was possibly too slim, he judged with his physician's eye. Was she ill? But her skin looked good, no sallowness, and she was even slightly flushed as she spoke. But not too flushed. Just the right amount of flush, or blush. All of a sudden he realized she had stopped speaking and was waiting for him to say something.

"Wonderful," he floated out toward the vision of loveliness, trying to replay her words in his head. "Her books. Excellent."

Elizabeth watched them, clearly enjoying the connection they appeared to be making, at least, thought Gregory, a connection on his part, if not Catherine's. Was Elizabeth—and Catherine—amused at his discomfort and disarray?

Catherine looked at her watch and turned to Elizabeth. "I'd better try and catch the 4:30 train," she said. "Can Maria drive me to the station again? Otherwise I can call a taxi or Uber."

"Of course. I will tell her. It is late indeed."

"It was an honor to meet you, former student," Gregory said, as Elizabeth left the room. "How do you know Elizabeth?" Gregory hoped he didn't sound as lost and desperate as he felt.

"I didn't know her before this week. I answered an ad in the paper for this job."

"I see. How's the job going?"

"I've made a start. Dr. Worthington—"

"Please call me Gregory."

She smiled her beautiful smile. "Thank you, Gregory."

His name sounded different on her lips, as though it had found a new home, had entered a new country and wanted to live there.

"I . . . I . . ." Catherine glanced toward the kitchen, lowering her voice. "I was wondering if you could answer a question I have, a question about genetics." Something passed over her face fleetingly, an uncomfortable and awkward pain, as if she were pushing herself to ask the question.

"Of course. How can I help you?"

"Is it possible to trace relatives with genetics? Like ancestry searches? Real people, in the present day, not just racial percentages." She spoke quickly, as if to release the question before she locked it up again.

"Sure. To a degree, anyway. What did you have in mind?"

Elizabeth arrived from the kitchen. "Maria is bringing the car around."

"Perhaps we can talk another time," Catherine said, glancing at Elizabeth.

"At your convenience. I'm staying at present in Lafayette."

"I'm in Berkeley, but I'll be here tomorrow and Friday to work on the books."

"Here's my card. Call when you have a chance and we can get together." This was working out far better than he had hoped, even in his wildest dreams. Get together after one conversation? It usually took weeks and months of gentle approaches, always worried about harassment, using just the right words carrying just the right innuendos; not too much, not too little, just right. A balancing act.

They stepped into the entry, and Elizabeth opened the door for Catherine. "See you tomorrow, same time?"

Catherine nodded, smiling her thanks. "I'll be here." She turned to Gregory. "Nice meeting you, Dr. . . . er . . . Gregory." She sounded wistful, as though she were offered something that would disappear before she had a chance to take it. "Bye then."

He took her hand in his own, light as a feather, so smooth, so cool to the touch, so sweet. "A pleasure meeting you too." He watched her turn on her heel, descend the porch steps, and walk to the car where Maria waited.

As they drove away, he sensed his life was about to change, for better or for worse.

"Mrs. Jacobsen," Gregory said, abruptly turning to Elizabeth, "I nearly forgot why I came. I wanted to warn you. Abram is in danger. The crowd today was more threatening, antifa I think, or at least antifa inspired. We need to bring him home right away—as soon as possible."

Elizabeth frowned and shook her head. "He will not come home. And home is not safe."

"You need to talk to him. He needs to stop preaching."

"He will not listen."

"Why is this happening? Why do they hate him?"

"Catherine can explain. Catherine saw the graffiti." She looked out to the hills. "It is all happening again." She rubbed her hands together.

"What graffiti?"

"This morning, a swastika on the outer wall, to the side of the front door."

Gregory breathed deeply. "Did you call the police?"

"Not yet. What can they do? They cannot do anything. Maria removed it."

"The police can protect you."

Elizabeth raised her brow skeptically. "You believe that?"

"I do. You should call them. It's their job."

Elizabeth lowered herself onto a chair near the grandfather clock. You think the protesters are anti-Semitic? How would they know he is Jewish?"

"He's preaching Judeo-Christian morality, like an Old Testament prophet, and morality from any source is unpopular today. Reports are surfacing with his name, previous occupation, and heritage, although they also connect him to Saint Joseph's Chapel. But with that information they could easily research his background, and your association with him. There is often a ringleader that . . . well . . . leads, for whatever reason. We can't be sure if the swastika on your door and the mob on the mountainside are connected. Many protesters have no real idea what they are protesting against and simply join in. They protest against rules and authority in general. And there are many copycats that simply do as they please, rather like self-expression, or act simply because they enjoy power and chaos."

Elizabeth raised a wrinkled, spotted hand to her forehead. "I think I need to rest for a bit. I will think about what you said, Dr. Worthington."

"Gregory, please."

"Gregory."

"I'll let you rest." He could see she was exhausted, as though her life had been summed up in the last few days. He didn't want to make her worse. What if she had a heart condition? She must be in her eighties. "I'll watch over him. You both saved my life. It's the least I can do."

Elizabeth opened the door. "Thank you for your concern. I do appreciate it." Her voice was nearly a whisper.

"Are you okay?"

She nodded, touching her heart. "I need to rest. Maria will help me when she gets back."

As Gregory left, he glanced back to the front porch, waving with an open palm. Elizabeth stood in the doorway, leaning into the jamb, her face gray. He had seen that grayness before, and it didn't bode well for anyone.

THURSDAY

Chapter 33

It was troubling to Malcolm Underhill III that so much attention had been given to the little old man on the mountain rather than to the Sunday shooting at UC Berkeley, so carefully and brilliantly orchestrated. As he drove his new sport utility vehicle somewhat erratically, he considered the grave injustice of it all. The previous year he had crashed his 2016 SUV, changing lanes without care as he pondered injustice, especially injustice to him, but the memory lay buried and didn't trouble Malcolm at this moment of immense frustration and anger.

He had left his condo in the Berkeley Hills on Thursday in a fairly upbeat mood, until he saw another news flash on his phone about the crazy preacher on Angel Mountain. Social media was buzzing about the hermit, and the tweets Malcolm had sent flying into the cloud, loaded with delicious hashtags describing his Sunday massacre, had fizzled. What was wrong with these people? Were their attention spans really that short?

His girl of the night had made him breakfast so that he could take a few more antidepressants, and she hadn't batted a lash when he slammed the door behind him, carrying another stack of books from his storage unit to deposit in the van. It was the last stack, the last load, library books he had borrowed and not returned. They included classics and history—the Western canon, as they called it—which had no meaning in this day and age and were so harmful to so many, with their lack of inclusivity and intersectionality, not to mention the thousands of triggering microaggressions on every page. He, Malcolm, would do his part to bring the world into the twenty-first century. There was no need to look back—how dreary was that—for the past meant nothing and the future meant everything.

But even more important than the future was the present.

Malcolm needed to get control of the present, his present. The news media was on the wrong tack and should be encouraged to return to Malcolm and his righteous cause.

Malcolm emerged from the Caldecott Tunnel, cruising at a mere eighty, and took the off-ramp to the Orinda Village post office. He pulled out a small package addressed to the UC library—nothing like a little explosion to discourage the four-eyed book lovers. He would look forward to that news segment. And one day he would be congratulated for his list of accomplishments. He should definitely consider a run for president. He slipped the innocent-looking package into the postal box.

Next stop, Mount Diablo, a name he was determined to preserve, rather than the pretentious and soul-searching—ha ha—Angel Mountain that the hermit used, and now the media increasingly reported. Not a good development.

This Abram Levin, self-styled hermit, was really getting to him. Who did he think he was? Some kind of messiah? Some prophet or king? Reports of his previous life were surfacing, absurd reports of being homeless, of working at a chapel, of giving up a respected career as a UC professor. It was only right that he was booted out of UC, considering how he handed out grades, Malcolm thought, as he recalled the old man's lectures, and Malcolm's having to settle for an incomplete, not the grade to which he was rightfully entitled. Levin was clearly evil, not appreciating Malcolm's genius. And now the professor had become delusional, living in a cave on Mount Diablo. Malcolm had done his best to disrupt the gatherings in the meadow, but enough was enough.

The elderly really had to go, Malcolm reflected. They were a senile and unattractive bunch. The world didn't have room for their kind, not to mention the cost of their many infirmities, their encroaching weaknesses. The young should be living life to the fullest, hooking up randomly with whomever or whatever, gender or no gender, for one night, one hour. They did not need to be reminded of death—their own deaths—by senile seniors living too long.

Malcolm noted a recent report that claimed even middle-aged Americans were dying at a rising rate, so maybe there was hope after all for a future without the financial and social burden of the old weighing upon society. The report cited addiction and mental health issues as factors that had set back many gains made in longevity. Death rates were rising due to suicide, alcohol abuse, drug overdose including opioids, and chronic liver disease. Let them go, he thought. Let them die. Let others assist them in their frantic and sad efforts. Society could not afford their care.

Malcolm was grateful, as a proud Californian, that his state legalized assisted suicide, one of a handful of states so far. He had done his part in passing out flyers to the elderly, flyers that encouraged an easy death with dignity, overseen by a local clinic. He was doing his righteous part, a humble servant of the people and the times.

In recent years, Malcolm thought, smiling with satisfaction, suicides had killed more Americans than car accidents. Who knew? He swerved to miss colliding with a cement truck that insisted on crawling down the freeway in the wrong lane, his lane.

Malcolm was feeling better, more upbeat, as he recalled these bits and pieces from his files, neatly stored in his new and improved iPad. He inhaled his carefully rolled weed, now legal as well, and returned it to the cigarette holder. Life was looking up, as it should for a man of his abilities and finesse, not to mention his daddy's means. After all, he had a right to be happy, to feel good. He had the duty to nurture his self-esteem, to avoid triggers wherever possible—those words and phrases that judged him and hurt his delicate feelings—and to reward himself as he should be rewarded, to seek vengeance where vengeance was due.

Some of the books stacked in the back of the SUV had shifted weight, and he heard the gentle thud of books falling. Soon they would be *real* history. He chuckled at the image. So many more books to borrow and burn, so many more to turn to ash. Yes, his mission was a charitable one: to turn history into history, forgotten, burned, buried, scorching the Earth.

He grinned at his brilliance. And to combine this noble act with a lesser one of simple vengeance—now that was rewarding. He, Malcolm Underhill III, showed great promise. He still could sculpt power into a new art form, the modern art of the twenty-first century: terror. The presidency was child's play. He would become emperor or nothing at all.

Chapter 34

Abram awoke early Thursday morning to see the angel Michael peering over him. No longer did he shimmer and move as if dealing with Earth's gravity and rotation. He was at least seven feet, taller than any man Abram had encountered. This time the angel appeared solid, robed in pale gold. It was as if he had been given a real body, and Abram rubbed his eyes as he gazed upon the vision. Or was it more than a vision?

"Who are you?" Abram asked.

Michael smiled, and with the smile his eyes sparkled with love. And yet, Abram knew it was not the angel's love, but his Lord's love that wrapped him in warmth on this frosty November morning.

"I am Michael."

"Yes." Abram sat up, touching the stone floor with his feet, as if checking to see if he were still in the land of the living, still breathing the wondrous air and feeling the good Earth in this cold sandstone cave. He reached for the glittering sleeve draping the man's arm, or rather, the angel's arm. "Are you really an angel?"

"Do not touch me. I must soon return to the Father. Yes, I am Archangel Michael."

Abram withdrew his hand as if he might be burned. "Why are you here?"

"To tell you about the Judgment."

Abram rubbed his eyes again. "There really is a Judgment?"

The angel turned toward the icons that gleamed in the first light. He walked to the doorway opening onto the promontory. The world was quiet and dim and cold outside the cave, Abram thought, watching the bright figure look out to the valleys below. Early dawn crept slowly over Earth, one region at a time, as Earth rotated around her sun.

Michael turned to face Abram. "Of course there is a Judgment. How could there be justice without judgment? How could love be realized? How could goodness be protected from evil? How could wheat be parted from chaff, good seeds from tares? There is no room for weeds in the garden of Heaven."

Abram nodded. He had known this but had not known this. He had hoped for a Heaven of joy, but did not want to believe that it could only exist without the joyless. He had hoped for a Heaven of justice, but did not accept that it could never exist with the unjust hurting the just, those who hate hurting those who love. "How does it work? How does the Judgment work? Do they have second chances? Do I have a second chance?"

Michael nodded. "Of course. We can choose. We all can choose. Lucifer could choose, and can choose, even now. But it is unlikely, given the path of darkness he has chosen. There is little left within him that owns the power to choose love."

"Lucifer? Was the story true? About the great dragon and the war?"

"Lucifer's war in Heaven? Indeed. It was recorded. It was witnessed. He rebelled against the God of love, against love itself."

"And the Judgment?"

"You have been given the law and the commandments. You have been given all that the Spirit and the Son gave you, through Moses and the prophets, through the witnesses of Christ's life, death, and resurrection, all that has been given in word and song and sacrament through the centuries of your time. You have the light to see and to choose."

"Are we measured against the law, then?" Abram groaned within his heart.

"Indeed. Where you obeyed, where you disobeyed, where you gave true witness, where you gave false witness. There are sins of doing and of not doing, sins of speech and of silence, sins of assent and of denial, of life and of death." Michael raised his eyes to the cave's dusty ceiling, but Abram knew he saw far beyond, to Heaven itself. "When you die, when you leave your body and your soul takes wing, you will be given your own Book of Life. It is your history. You will see those you have hurt, the lies you have told, the laws you have broken, the places and times where you have not loved enough."

Abram held his head between his hands. "Oh, no."

"Oh, yes. You will see what you are: what you were, what you have become. You will see when you hid your light or let it shine in the darkness. You will see if you buried your coin or used it for good. You will see if you sheltered your sheep or scattered them, unprotected."

"I cannot bear it."

"That is as it should be. You must confess, repent, and our Lord will invite you into the cross."

"*Into* the cross?"

"When you are invited into the cross you will enter its wood—its woods—and you will follow a path through the shadows to the summit of the cross, where the woods part and the light and love of God await you."

Abram pulled away from the face of the angel, so stern and accusing. "So the Judgment is the time of cleansing, of preparation. Is this what they call purgatory?" Abram recalled Dante's *Purgatorio*. Many believed there would be a time of purging, of preparation, for how else could one bear the bright and burning light of Christ?

"Some call it that. We call it the time of Rebirth, when each Book of Life is rewritten with the tears of confession and repentance, a welcoming of the fire of God, fire to burn away sins, to clean and purify hearts and souls."

"Then all can be saved? If they repent?"

Tears formed in Michael's eyes. "They can but they will not. All are redeemed but must choose to be saved. Many—too many—choose not to be saved. They will not confess to failings. They are too proud. Most sins are born of pride. But all are given the choice."

"Free will again?"

"Love demands free will. Love demands sacrifice and suffering. Christ is the sacrifice and the one who suffers for us, even for those who choose darkness over light."

"But the cross—the wood of the cross—will those who repent be invited into those woods?" Abram focused on the saved, those who chose love over hate, life over death. He could not bear to think of those souls who rejected such love, such light.

"They will be invited. Every one of them. They will be saved, as some say, by faith alone."

"But their deeds count too, for there is the Judgment."

"Their deeds composed their Book of Life, a book they must read and rewrite to be reborn."

"And faith alone?"

"They know that only through faith in Christ can they rewrite and be born again. That is the repentance part—they choose to repent and beg for God's grace to rewrite their Book of Life. They will see all of the pages of their time on Earth, for they knew God's grace in their lives and will desire more. They will be in the habit of repentance, of calling upon God."

"So the good pagan? What happens to the good pagan?" Abram thought of the many good people, those who did good works, fed and clothed the poor, healed the sick, gave of their treasure, time, and talent, for noble causes throughout the world.

"Ah, the good pagan." Michael pondered the perplexing phrase. "I know whom you mean. His misdeeds will be shown him, but his pride in his good deeds may hinder, blind him, so that he cannot find his way into the woods of the cross. It is the justice of God to give each soul what he desires, what he chooses. Countless souls are leaving Earth as we speak, beyond numbering. I can hear the rustle of their rising at this moment and every moment. If I look I can see them—brilliant flashes like the wings of a dove in sudden sun. Each one must choose the light and repent. Each one must choose love."

"Are they lost forever if they choose the dark?"

"No one is lost forever. Heaven weeps for those souls who choose self over selflessness. Heaven intercedes again and again through the cross of Christ, re-entering Earth through the wood, a timeless and eternal sacrifice. Heaven awaits those souls to wake from their nightmare of self, to see the light of love, to be invited into the wood of the cross."

"Are there two Judgments, then? A particular and a general?" Abram recalled reading about that in seminary. One Judgment was this personal Judgment. Later there would be the Judgment of the world at the Second Coming of Christ, when Heaven and Earth became one.

"The dead shall awake, the paths will be made straight! Those who are already in Christ will sing his praises, as they have been doing at the river running by the throne of God, on the shores of the glassy sea, and in the Court of the Heavenly King. Those who are not in Christ will be judged on Earth in the Last Judgment."

"I see." But did he? Abram rubbed his face as though he could wake himself up. But he was awake.

"Good. Now proclaim what I have said. Proclaim the Judgment, that the days of Judgment are near. Proclaim the Year of the Lord that will make the crooked paths straight. Proclaim the End of Days and the sounds of the last trumpet. Proclaim the Second Coming of Christ, the Lord of All Creation, the King of Love, the Shepherd of Our Souls."

With those words, a sharp dart, like an arrow, burned into Abram's heart. He lay back on his hard bed and slept deeply, for how long he did not know, until shouts in the valley broke into his hearing. He opened his eyes, feeling strangely and wonderfully refreshed. Michael was gone. Had he been there at all? There was a second blanket that lay upon his old thin one, this one woven of a golden thread that shimmered in the early light. He pulled it to him and buried his face in it. It was fragrant with the aroma of roses . . . or jasmine . . . or both. He could not tell. He wanted to drink it in, to gulp it.

Abram recalled his dream. Was it a dream? Footprints had been left—burned into the stone floor, far larger prints than he could have made. The Earth had been branded. He looked around his cave. He rose from his bed and threw ice water on his face from the pitcher. He began his morning song, singing to his saints who glimmered and gleamed back at him, laughing with joy.

Chapter 35

Abram gazed over his meadow congregation. They numbered in the hundreds, he guessed, this Thursday morning. The rain and lightning of yesterday had not kept them away, and the hills remained dry in spite of the sudden downpour. His preaching, according to Caleb and Steven, had gone viral, whatever that meant. The world had passed Abram by, and yet the world now stood still for a time, to listen.

"Repent! For the Kingdom of Heaven is at hand!" Abram cried from his sandstone precipice. "Prepare ye the way of the Lord, make straight in the desert a highway for our God. Every valley shall be exalted, and every mountain and hill shall be made low: and the crooked shall be made straight, and the rough places plain: And the glory of the Lord shall be revealed, and all flesh shall see it together: for the mouth of the Lord hath spoken it."[15]

Abram observed the crowd and noticed his assistants waiting by the cross. Dr. Worthington was stepping up the deer path toward him, and the familiar sight filled Abram's heart with love for his brother in Christ.

The black-hooded ones on the periphery appeared like beetles crawling about the edges of his garden or wolves pacing the borders of his sheepfold. Abram could not see any news cameras. The skies were quiet and listening.

"Repent and believe. Repent and find joy. Repent and choose the path to Heaven."

A shout rose from those nearby. "How do you know these things? Who are you, Abram Levin? Who are you really? Who do you claim to be?"

"I am he who prepares the way for the King." Abram could no longer see Gregory, who had entered the cleft where the trail turned into the mountain before switchbacking to the cave.

"What king?"

"Jesus, the Christ, the King of Glory, the Lord of Hosts."

"Where is he? We don't see him."

"Repent, and you will see the face of God. Repent, and you will be invited to travel the only way to Heaven."

"How do we know the way?"

"Jesus the Christ is the Way, the Truth, and the Life."[16]

How could he explain about the wood of the cross? The woods that bridged Heaven and Earth? Whether literal or not, Abram knew truth lived in those words, in those woods, and in the images of Archangel Michael. In the end—and they were indeed speaking of the end—and the beginning—it was truth that mattered. There was no time left for lies and half lies. There was no time left for wrong choices.

A murmur rippled through the crowd. Some, Abram guessed, grumbled disbelief in the crazy hermit on the mountain. Others voiced assent, and Abram could see who they were. He could see the ones who believed, who turned a corner in their hearts to open a door to the Way, the Truth, and the Life. He could see it in their eyes, even from this high distance. He could see them repenting in the valley among the dry grasses. They believed, they repented, and they were saved, marked by Christ as his own.

Some folded their hands and knelt. Some wept. Others looked up to the skies as if angels would appear, as they had appeared to the shepherds so long ago.

"An angel spoke to me," Abram began, and he too looked up to the mountain that touched the sky. The tule fog, the thick ground fog from the San Joaquin Valley, was coming in, sliding toward Abram and his cave and the valleys below. He could see it roll in and away, and he knew time was slipping too.

"An angel told me to tell you—to warn you—about the Judgment."

The crowd grew silent. The hooded ones still moved along the edges, in the shallow shadows. Their ears were stopped. Their eyes were closed. They were deaf and blind, Abram thought, as he offered a prayer for their souls.

"When we die, when we leave our bodies, we will be given our own Book of Life, a book that we must rewrite. How do we do this? We repent and edit our sins, and make each sentence perfect. The red-lined deeds that cry out with blood must be erased clean with our love and our tears. Those we have hurt we must help. Those we have murdered—with our hands, with our words, or within our hearts—we must love."

As Abram tried to tell them of his conversation with Michael, the crowd began to sing. A few strong harmonious voices led them—or were there angels among them, Abram wondered—in a chorus of song.

All creatures of our God and King,
Lift up your voice and with us sing,

Alleluia! Alleluia!

Thou burning sun with golden beam,
Thou silver moon with softer gleam!
O praise Him, O praise Him!
Alleluia! Alleluia! Alleluia!

Thou rushing wind that art so strong,
Ye clouds that sail in heav'n along,
O praise Him! Alleluia!

Thou rising morn, in praise rejoice,
Ye lights of evening, find a voice!
O praise Him, O praise Him!
Alleluia! Alleluia! Alleluia![17]

As the seekers sang, the hooded ones shouted slogans and taunts, moving into the crowd. They carried signs and parted the people as though carrying weapons.

Caleb, Steven, and other friends made calls on their phones. Gregory arrived at the promontory and stood to the side of Abram.

And all ye men of tender heart,
Forgiving others, take your part,
O sing ye! Alleluia!

Ye who long pain and sorrow bear,
Praise God and on Him cast your care!
O praise Him, O praise Him!
Alleluia! Alleluia! Alleluia!

Praise God from Whom all blessings flow,
Praise Him all creatures here below,
Alleluia! Alleluia!

Praise Him above, ye heavenly host,
Praise Father, Son and Holy Ghost!
Alleluia! Alleluia! Alleluia!
Alleluia! Alleluia!

Abram looked up toward the mountain, where a helicopter droned through the thickening fog, whirling down and landing in the meadow. The people moved aside, as police arrived to keep the peace.

Abram turned to Gregory. "Thank you for coming, my friend. You can do me a service. Please, if you would, bring Elizabeth to me. I must see her—*today.*" He felt a bit out of breath and hoped he was not stammering. "Now I must be with my people." He breathed deeply, but his chest was tight.

"Of course, Father. But let me walk you down to the pond to Caleb and Steven. The fog is moving in."

Abram stepped slowly, leaning on Gregory and grateful for the doctor's arm supporting his back. Abram held his robes with one hand and laid the other hand on his heart. Slowly, the old preacher and the young scientist made their way down the deer path to the pond and the cross.

The police had surrounded the protesters and returned them to the periphery. Caleb and Steven joined Abram at the pond, and Gregory left to deliver Abram's message to Elizabeth. The penitents lined up to be baptized, to travel the way to Heaven, to take the first step toward the wood that would lead them out of the darkness and into the light.

Abram looked into the eyes of each of these his children and hoped they felt the love of God pour into their hearts, minds, and souls. He prayed over each one, baptizing them in the name of the Holy Trinity: the Father, the Son, and the Holy Spirit. He marked the forehead of each person with a cross, saying,

> We receive this person into the congregation of Christ's flock; and do sign him with the sign of the cross, in token that hereafter he shall not be ashamed to confess the faith of Christ crucified, and manfully to fight under his banner, against sin the world, and the devil; and to continue Christ's faithful soldier and servant unto his life's end.[18]

"Be happy," Abram concluded, "for Jesus has saved you from sin and death. God loves you so very much."

As noon approached, Abram saw the crowd had grown larger. Caleb led him back to his cave to rest. The tule fog had seeped around the meadow, not touching the people, but, Abram knew, they could not see him up here on the ledge in front of the cave. Perhaps they would come back tomorrow.

As he turned to the horizon, Abram saw that the air was clear, and he gazed over the sea of fog that blanketed the meadow and his people. In the distance Earth's rim touched Heaven. At that moment he sensed Earth's rotation as it rolled through the cosmos. At that moment he knew that one day, as Michael promised, there would be a new Earth and a new Heaven, and it would be glorious, ruled by the King of Glory, the King of Love, the Lord of Hosts.

Abram entered the cave and allowed Caleb to help him to his stone bed amidst the golden icons. Perhaps—after a sip of water—he would lie down and close his eyes to regain his strength.

As he dozed, he heard Caleb whisper to Steven and their friends. How blessed he was, Abram thought, to have such love in such a desolate place: the love of God, the love of the saints surrounding him, the love of the angels who visited, the love of these friends who looked after him, the love of these honest pilgrims who sought out Heaven itself, right here on Angel Mountain.

As he slept, Abram knew—somewhere in the heart of his soul—that this was the reason he was born into the world, to be one more voice crying in the wilderness to prepare the way of the Lord.

Chapter 36

Thursday morning Elizabeth awoke smiling. The nightmares were gone, at least for the time being.

A good dream beckoned her to return to the pleasurable depths of sleep, and she tried to slip back down and into the dream. Samuel had appeared, sitting on her bed by her side. He seemed at peace, content. His eyes were softer than she recalled, not holding conflicting hope and despair. He had let those things go.

"Be not afraid," he said, or she knew he said.

"Samuel? Samuel?"

"Heaven is real. Different than we thought. But good. You will see."

"Are you happy?"

"Yes, and there will be more happiness to come."

"More?"

"A new Heaven and Earth."

"But where are you now?"

"In God's palm. We are all in his palm, rejoicing in him until the last trumpet."

"You are waiting?"

"Waiting for the Kingdom of Heaven, which will be the Kingdom of Heaven and Earth. We rest, we see, we love, and we praise."

Elizabeth gazed at the vision. He appeared real. She tried to touch him.

"Do not touch me. You might be burned by the love of God. I do not have my new body yet."

"New body?"

"When the dead arise and are given their new bodies, when the Kingdom of Heaven and Earth is realized, the blind will see, the deaf will hear, the dumb will speak, and the lame will walk."

"I miss you."

"I love you."

"I love you too, Samuel. Do not leave me!"

"I must. But I am coming for you soon. Soon you will join me in Heaven. God is love. Remember this. Always choose love."

Elizabeth opened her gratitude journal and wrote down everything she could remember, words so precious, so glorious, that she did not think she would ever forget them, but just in case, they would be here to look upon. She knew how words could disappear, faces could disappear, people could disappear, even from the sacred places she guarded in her memory.

Laddie jumped onto the journal as she wrote. She pushed him aside. He pawed her arm that held the pen.

"Yes, yes. It is time for your shot."

Cradling her morning coffee, Elizabeth gazed through the kitchen window to the dry brown hills. This morning the tule fog was creeping around the mountain, like a ribbon of cotton batting, coming from the east to meet the wider coastal fog from the west. It was a view she never tired of, a weather drama playing out in her back yard. The white cross stood on the mountainside, a bright beacon of hope, though she had yet to believe in its promises as Abram did. Would it be engulfed by the fog?

She thought of Abram, his stubbornness, and his sense of destiny. Did he know what was coming next? Did he have so much faith? She did not. Her dream of Samuel was fading, but she treasured the slip of memory living in her mind and heart for a time. She would remember that feeling of protection and love, the security he had given her for all her married life. How fortunate was that? How grateful she was for their years together. And, she suddenly recalled, he was coming back for her, if she had enough faith to believe it was true.

She rinsed her cup and placed it in the dishwasher's top rack, then stepped into the entry and checked on her suitcase behind the ferns and the grandfather clock. She was ready to go at a moment's notice. But when Samuel came for her—if he did—she probably would not need her suitcase.

She heard a knock at the door and opened it.

Catherine stood on the stoop, her tote slung over her shoulder. Beyond, Elizabeth could see Maria backing the car into the garage.

"Good morning," Elizabeth said. "Ready for another day of books?"

The young woman smiled, nodding. "Looking forward to it."

Catherine stepped into the foyer and followed Elizabeth to her home office.

"I am worried about Abram." Elizabeth sat in an armchair and watched Catherine settle in to her work. "He is so foolish."

"Are the crowds causing trouble?"

"Dr. Worthington thinks so."

"Some are there simply for the entertainment."

"Are there protests like this at the university?"

Catherine paused. "Protests have been going on since the 1960s—even recently on Sunday at Sproul Plaza. They seem worse today. And," she added, "I've been part of them—when much younger."

"I find that hard to believe," Elizabeth said. Catherine seemed such a docile, civilized young lady.

"It was years ago, and I was swept into the idea of expressing your feelings rather than questioning them or holding them up to a standard."

Elizabeth nodded. "When I taught high school I saw that attitude. Protests can be a valid form of free speech, as long as they are peaceful. Think of Martin Luther King. But protests that break the law hurt democracy and free speech for everyone. As you say, opinions must be held up to some kind of objective standard. Without that standard, we have nothing."

"What is Abram saying exactly? Have you heard him preach?"

"I have not heard him. He has only begun recently, just this week. He is preaching Christianity, I believe: standards of right and wrong, the moral law which some call the natural law. Reporters say he is baptizing in the pool by the cross. One said he was another Billy Graham. That seems unlikely."

"Would you like to hear him preach?"

"Perhaps I should, and check on him again." Perhaps, Elizabeth thought, the last few days would prompt him to come home.

Catherine was fingering a slim volume by Richard Pipes. "*Communism*," she said, reading the spine and opening to the title page. "Would that be history? Clearly nonfiction."

"Yes. An excellent overview of what communism really is. Many in this country turned to communism as a reaction to Hitler's Nazism, which they equated with Mussolini's fascism. But communism and Nazism are two sides of the same coin: totalitarianism. They both purge and destroy, for they do not honor the dignity of the individual."

Recognition passed through Catherine's features and Elizabeth recalled the sudden awareness her students sometimes showed, as they linked facts, traditions, and histories to form a pattern of meaning. "Dignity," Catherine said, "was a key contribution of the Judaic tradition, wasn't it? Respect for the individual?"

"Because each person is made in God's image. Christianity continued and expanded the idea. All systems—*isms*, if you will—must be judged on how they perceive human rights. Do they respect and protect everyone, not just some, not just an elite? All genetic dispositions, all human lives, are worthy of God's love and thus our love. This became the Judeo-Christian heritage, the Western heritage that is so maligned and threatened today. And the threat is all too real."

Unfortunately, Elizabeth thought, without the foundation of belief in a God of love and his commandments to love, this heritage might not survive.

"Do you think Abram is preaching about that?"

"He knows as I know that we must be reminded of the law given to us by Moses and the prophets. I grew up with it, assumed everyone did, as they did in my generation, at least in the Western world. But others have not had this schooling, and this ethos must be witnessed to again and again. We start with the Ten Commandments, I suppose. 'Thou shalt not kill' is pretty important and covers a multitude of crimes against all peoples."

"Like the communists purges?" Catherine glanced through the slim volume.

"That is correct. We must confess and witness to our heritage of respect and dignity and the law that accompanies the Western ethos, the law of love. We must never forget what happens when we stop teaching the values of Western civilization. Hitler happens. Stalin happens. Mao happens."

Elizabeth watched Catherine absorb her words, and once again recalled the joy of forming minds to make better citizens, to be more human in our inhuman, subhuman, dangerous world.

Catherine looked at the books, then at Elizabeth.

Elizabeth realized she was distracting Catherine from her work. "I will let you do your job. I will come back later and see how you are coming along."

Catherine nodded and returned to her sorting.

Chapter 37

As Catherine worked in Elizabeth's office, sorting books, she thought about Gregory Worthington.

It was true their meeting was an opportunity, one she should possibly use to her advantage. Things didn't usually go well for her, and this chance encounter was too good to be true. It probably wouldn't lead to any new information about her father. But it might. Was it worth the time to contact her former professor? And what was he doing in Lafayette? She really didn't know much about him, and she needed to look after herself now. She needed to be on her guard. Aunt Pat couldn't protect her as her mother had done.

She wouldn't call Dr. Worthington yet. She needed to give it time—time to think and get perspective, not rush into anything. She knew little about him, except he had taught at UC, understood genetics, was a doctor, and had fallen on Angel Mountain.

She had to admit he was good-looking. He was about five-ten to her five-six with dark brows and eyes framed by brown-black hair neatly trimmed, thick and wavy. He had olive skin and high cheekbones. He seemed a bit awkward. She would keep their relationship, if there ever was one, purely professional.

If he could find her father, she might finally understand who she was, her roots, her true identity, not to mention her health history, so that she could take preventative steps in terms of serious illness.

But now Dr. Worthington was diverting her attention from an interesting job, one she wanted to see through. While at first overcome with envy when she entered Villa Tilifos, today, her third day there, counting the interview day, she was beginning to enjoy a sense of safety, as though the wealth surrounding her—wealth by her standards, by most standards, she guessed—could protect her. When she stepped across the threshold and into the entry, today wearing her mother's herringbone jacket, she felt as if she had entered another world, so different from her Berkeley world.

But to do the research she had in mind, Dr. Worthington—Gregory—would require some kind of payment on her part. She had better get that settled up front, so that she wouldn't feel obligated to him in any way. It was so important to not feel obligated, and this had been powerfully underscored by the #MeToo movement with its chorus of sexual harassment claims. She could see that, in the end, it was all about power in relationships, and she needed to be careful. He held too many cards, cards she wanted.

She had held the current volume, something by Jonathan Sacks, a British rabbi, for far too long as she sat on the carpet and leaned against the wall, watching the pattern of moving shadow thrown by the olive tree outside the louvered windows. She set the book alongside another Jewish author, Melanie Phillips, who wrote both fiction and nonfiction, it appeared. Her book *The World Turned Upside Down: The Global Battle over God, Truth, and Power* looked particularly interesting, and Catherine hoped she might borrow it one day. She turned to the table of contents and noted several intriguing chapters: "The Myth of Environmental Armageddon," "The Secular Inquisition," and "The Attack on Western Civilization."

Some of the volumes Catherine recognized. Many she didn't, and that was bothering her, especially since she had spent eight years as a librarian. Some were classics, and some seemed recent additions from the last decade. There were series like *The Story of Civilization* by Ariel and Will Durant (she had heard of them). Paul Johnson might take up a shelf of his own, his many titles seeming to cover Western civilization as well (she had not heard of him). There were biographies: *Saint Augustine of Hippo* by Peter Brown, who, Catherine noted, had taught at UC Berkeley (no recognition—yikes).

There were numerous titles by Roger Scruton, a British scholar also concerned with the decline of Western culture, who had experience with the Soviet Union. In fact, many of the authors had been survivors of fascism, Nazism, or communism who had escaped to America and, with a fierce sense of warning, wanted to witness to the murderous tyranny of these systems of government. Catherine picked up Alexander Solzhenitsyn's *The Gulag Archipelago* and turned to a marked page where she saw a passage underlined lightly in pencil: "But the line dividing good and evil cuts through the heart of every human being. And who is willing to destroy a piece of his own heart?"[19]

Catherine thought about the quote. It reminded her of the old idea of confession, of admitting one has sinned. Again, as Elizabeth had said earlier, it was like measuring one's heart against a rule of some sort, an objective standard, quite often a religious one, a Judeo-Christian one.

Catherine set the book down near Pipes's *Communism*. She turned to the next group of books. Several were by Gertrude Himmelfarb, who wrote about the Victorians, lauding their virtues, and warning that the world was losing its definition of virtue. Catherine recalled Aristotle saying that virtue led to happiness and thought Ms. Himmelfarb might be referencing the classical world. And here was Jonah Goldberg's *Suicide of the West: How the Rebirth of Tribalism, Populism, Nationalism, and Identity Politics Is Destroying American Democracy*. Other titles considered the state of American democracy and what was required for freedom to thrive, even survive—the need for liberty governed by law. In fact, the great American experiment that de Tocqueville wrote of, which Catherine did recall from Grace Academy, was forming a tall stack on its own: books about America.

The books on American history intrigued her, for they sought to understand what made America exceptional, sought to preserve those things that made her a beacon of hope and freedom in the world and discourage those things that thwarted that goal. Catherine considered this kind of thing useful history, practical history, history to help one understand today's challenges. Her teachers at Grace Academy had done this to a certain degree. But here, outside the classroom, in a personal library like this one, to see these questions asked and answered with such a moral and resolute purpose was something different. These books clarified her earlier education, amplifying and making sense of it all.

There was very little psychology or sociology, and few practical books on gardening, cooking, or decorating. No books dealing with travel, art, music, sports. She did find one title by Theodore Dalrymple: *Admirable Evasions: How Psychology Undermines Morality*. As she glanced through it, she noted more pencil marks, a few pages turned down at the corners, and a number of sticky tabs in varying colors. It was well thumbed.

Catherine spotted a book with the title *Imaginative Conservatism: The Letters of Russell Kirk*. She opened it and read a marked passage: "The rootless are always violent, and the lonely and bored find riot a welcome diversion." Was this true? It sounded like her own experience, finding excitement in protests and marches. They could become violent. Was rootlessness one of the causes of these protests? A lack of history that anchored one in society? Was this why there was an interest in one's own history, one's own genes—because generations hadn't studied history, had no cultural anchors or touchstones?

Catherine considered the crowds on Angel Mountain. The seekers wanted connection with something meaningful. Were they rootless? Was mob violence a possibility? Was Abram safe?

Catherine felt as if she had entered a wonderland of ideas—words and phrases and titles and covers that tempted her to open them and discover the thoughts living on the pages, voices of real people, forming a collegial choir. She sensed she had not been well served by her higher education. Grace Academy had begun something she had not continued, let alone finished. Was it too late to look for answers to her questions? Would these new friends, sorted and stacked, share their silent secrets?

She picked up Jordan Peterson's 12 *Rules for Life: An Antidote to Chaos.* It appeared to be a no-nonsense, old-fashioned approach to lauding the traditional virtues of work, self-discipline, and honor, laced with humility and respect for others.

Catherine noted a common thread among many of the jacket summaries. They advised not to trust feelings over reasoning, to discourage outbreaks of grievance and entitlement whining. She recalled her mother warning her about her ingratitude, considering all that she had been given, in spite of her absentee father—her life, a roof over her head, food on the table, clothing on her back, a mother who loved her. It made a lot of sense to count her blessings more often.

One of the books that mentioned the feelings issue was *The Coddling of the American Mind,* by Greg Lukianoff. She noted the authors wrote of cognitive behavioral therapy, once a popular route to lessen or even cure depression by rerouting negative feelings into positive ones. The idea was that you could actually retrain those instincts, or gut feelings, to make you happier. With the rise of self-expression at all costs, depression—and suicide—had soared. CBT made sense for anybody. Why not take control of your feelings if you could? Wouldn't that be a good path to walk on?

Elizabeth peeked in. "Lunch break?" She picked up a volume that hadn't been categorized yet, *Resurrecting the Idea of a Christian Society* by R. R. Reno. "This one intrigued me. And his argument was really Judaic as well as Christian. His point—or one of his points—is that religious traditionalists offer effective medicine to treat intolerance: dignity, respect. While I do not go to synagogue, I am inclined to agree with him."

"The Golden Rule," Catherine said.

"Precisely, or versions of it."

"Empathy, sympathy, compassion."

Elizabeth was crossing the room, working her way between the piles of books. "Roger Scruton, one of my favorites! *Conservatism: An Invitation to the Great Tradition.* As I recall, he defines freedom, as opposed to anarchy, as a trust formed by balancing freedom and order, a trust informed by history, religion, custom, and tradition. We speak of liberty being framed in law, for within the law lie the individual's sacred rights to liberty. It is almost a poem or a painting that is far more effective and compassionate than a tyrannical regime forcing behavior through political correctness, shunning, threats, and outright violence."

Catherine considered her words as she surveyed the many titles she had arranged, as well as the many ideas running through her head, ideas both competing with and complementing one another. "I guess it's all about how we are to live together, as human beings. And perhaps, what is goodness?"

Elizabeth smiled. "That is the great debate, the great question. And that is what a moral code is, simply a means to live with one another, a way to be human, in the good sense."

Catherine recalled Grace Academy and the scriptural commandment to love one another.

The phone rang. Elizabeth answered. "I will open the gate for you, Dr. Worthington."

Catherine was encouraged by the potential of Gregory's visit. This might be a chance to learn more about finding her father.

Things were looking up, unusual for her.

Chapter 38

It was late morning when Malcolm parked his SUV and headed to the meadow just to check on his little old man.

The crowd was larger than before, and the space oddly clear of haze, a phenomenon reported again and again in the news. The white-robed fanatic was already at the pond, pouring water onto heads. Some of the crowd were singing and swaying as though they had seen the second coming. *Really.*

He found his friends in black with their signs and masks. He nodded and handed their leader an envelope that would encourage their performance at least for the day.

He returned to his van and headed up the mountain. Examples needed to be set. Priorities needed to be established.

He wound up the hill to the summit, which he found oddly empty. The visitor center was locked, closed for the day due to other commitments, a note said, hastily scrawled and taped to the door. Malcolm guessed they had all joined the fun in the meadow.

Malcolm found an isolated area near the summit, well covered with brush. He unloaded his books and stacked them neatly. He considered one of his heroes, the man who set the Los Angeles library fire of 1986. They never convicted him. They spent a lot of time trying. That man was a genius, worthy of honor and emulation. Malcolm wished this would be as big an event. This would be his first book burning, but not the last. He would learn from this and see how he could improve next time.

This was the moment he loved, just before the last act, the last lines.

He looked over his handiwork. Probably two hundred books, at least. If they caught fire and the flames spread to the grass, it just might be something to be proud of. The ground and grasses were dry enough, in spite of yesterday's light rain, but to the east he could see the tule fog creeping in, which might dampen things a bit. Nothing was perfect.

He lay the fuse and set the timer for dusk when the gates closed. Fire in the dark was best.

He glanced around and saw no one.

Driving down the mountain, his euphoria soared. He was flying high—better than cocaine, better than heroin, far better than any of the new drug cocktails he'd tried. He had resisted the urge to stay and watch. That was far too dangerous for many reasons. He would have to enjoy the spectacle from a safe distance, but how far and how safe would be the question. This might be even better than shooting students in a quad—far more finesse required and, he anticipated, far more thrill.

He would find a safe vantage point. He didn't want to chance getting arrested when he was on such a roll, such a winning streak.

He needed to celebrate. The crazy hermit—his old professor—wouldn't be able to compete with this. Once again, Malcolm had made his mark on history, only a small sideline to the main revolution, but a brilliant one.

Chapter 39

It was midday when Gregory knocked on the door of Villa Tilifos. He breathed deeply. He wanted to sound calm and reassuring, but he didn't feel at all calm or reassured, given the seeming urgency of Abram's request to bring Elizabeth to him. The old hermit was exhausted, pale, and fragile. Gregory was grateful for Caleb and Steven and the others.

Mrs. Jacobsen—Elizabeth—was most vulnerable at her age as well, a widow clearly dealing with many sources of stress.

He wasn't too sure if Catherine would be there. On one hand, he hoped she wasn't, and on the other hand, he hoped she was. But he needed to focus on Elizabeth.

The door opened, and Elizabeth looked at him expectantly. "Gregory, good to see you, but has something happened to Abram?"

Gregory remained on the porch, watching her increased agitation. "That's why I came. He wants to see you."

"Oh, my. Something is happening." She rubbed her hands together. "Please, come in while I get my jacket. And we must not forget Catherine."

Gregory stood in the entry and glanced down the hall, following Elizabeth's gaze.

"She said she was interested in hearing him preach," Elizabeth said, hopefully. "Maybe she would like to meet him. He *is* quite remarkable." She raised her brows and nodded knowingly.

"Of course," Gregory said, not sure if it was a good idea or not. Catherine had not called him, yet it had been only one day since they met and had spoken about the genetic search. But was it safe on Angel Mountain?

Elizabeth was already heading down the hall. Gregory heard the two women speaking quickly. Soon Catherine appeared. She smiled and shook his hand.

"Dr. Worthington—Gregory—could I come with you to see Elizabeth's brother? I'm curious to hear him preach . . . and see his cave. Elizabeth has told me about him, and he's even been in the news."

"He's resting now," Gregory explained. "For some reason he wanted to see Elizabeth. I'm sure he would like to meet you. He loves meeting people." Gregory wouldn't mention the dangers, which he wasn't sure were dangers, after all. And this would be a short visit, and something he could do for Elizabeth and for Catherine too. This was an opportunity to act out his faith on so many levels, as Father Brubaker often said, echoing Aunt Jane as well. And Caleb and Steven would oversee things. Abram had many friends these days.

"I'm glad," Catherine said, smiling her beautiful smile.

Was the smile turned up a bit at one end? Did she have a lisp? He thought she might. How touching was that? And the mole was more like a beauty mark.

"Good," Elizabeth said. "We must go now. No, wait, let me get his supplies out of the pantry, in case he is stubborn and refuses to come home."

"I've got the supplies," Maria called from the kitchen. She handed two bags of snacks to Catherine.

"Good, then," Elizabeth said, nodding to Gregory. "We will bring Abram home."

Gregory didn't try to dissuade her, but he was pretty sure Abram wasn't coming home to Villa Tilifos.

Gregory watched the hermit's face as he slept, not wanting to wake him. He was deathly pale, as if laid out in his tomb, but he appeared to be dreaming, as his eyelids flickered slightly and he tried to speak. A pale gold blanket covered him, one Gregory didn't recall.

Elizabeth and Catherine stood nearby, watching and waiting.

Caleb had produced two canvas camp chairs and set them up near Abram's bed. "Please," he said to the women, "please, sit down."

They sat and waited silently in the dim cave. Gregory remained standing. He sensed another presence, several presences, and he glanced at the icons that glimmered in the half-light. Was this a holy sanctuary? He returned his watchful eye to Abram, whose lips continued to move as if forming words, with no sound.

Caleb approached and adjusted the blanket, laying his hand gently on the old man's shoulder. "They are here," he whispered, "as you requested."

Abram's eyes fluttered open and he glanced at his guests. With Caleb's help, he rose to a seated position, setting his feet firmly on the dusty floor and adjusting his robe. He placed his palms on his legs and leaned forward, eyeing each person in turn.

"Thank you, Caleb. Look at this! Elizabeth, and Gregory too, and another guest. How wonderful, another guest!" Abram tried to stand, but settled back onto his stone bed. "Not as spry as I once was."

"Please, don't get up," Catherine said quietly, seeming in awe.

"Abram," Elizabeth said. "I would like you to meet my new friend and assistant, Catherine Nelson. She is helping me with my library at home."

"My pleasure indeed," Abram said, nodding. "My sister has a lot of books," he added, winking.

Catherine laughed. "She does have a lot of books."

"How is it going?" Abram asked. "Are you sorting into stacks?" Caleb handed him a cup of water and he took a sip, nodding his thanks.

"I'm doing exactly that. Making stacks."

"She tried to make me sort them into stacks once, but I was not very faithful—or skillful—about it all. I found a title I liked, and I would begin reading, and well . . . you know how that might go."

Catherine grinned. "I do know. I'm finding myself in the same predicament, wanting to read everything." She glanced at Elizabeth. "But I'm trying to do better. I'm trying to maintain focus."

Gregory watched Catherine and Abram in their first explorations of one another's minds and manners, the nuances and tones and ways of speaking, ways of reacting to thoughts and feelings, as if in a dance. The unique complexity of each human being was truly astonishing, he reflected. Here in this moment in a cave on Angel Mountain, a moment in history that was fraught with danger, an old man and a young woman, upon first meeting, were chatting like they were longtime school chums.

Abram nodded. "Focus is important in many areas of life." He gazed at the icons on the wall. "I find my icons help me focus. Tell me, Catherine, are you a believer? A Christian?"

"I'm not sure. My mother was more of a believer than I have been. But she brought me to Saint Joseph's Chapel with her from time to time." Catherine glanced at Elizabeth. "I understand you might be familiar with the chapel?"

Abram nodded to Elizabeth. "The chapel saved my life. The chapel and Father Brubaker. You know him?"

"He's been good to us. He wrote one of my job references." She eyed Elizabeth again.

"That is correct," Elizabeth said. "A glowing reference from the priest, Abram."

"That is praise, indeed."

"I visited the chapel on Monday. The beauty, the music, gave me a sense of peace and meaning, difficult to describe."

"Our Lord has a way of doing that, giving us peace through beauty, through music."

She trusted Abram, Gregory could see. Abram had that way about him, that gift that unlocked hearts of others so that they could pour out their joys and sorrows. He had that gift.

"I found Christ in Saint Joseph's Chapel," Abram said. "Father Brubaker is a giving and sacrificial priest. He brought me in from the streets."

Gregory was surprised that Abram had been homeless, after his career as a classics scholar at a major university. Life could change instantly, it would seem.

The silence encouraged Abram to tell his story. "After my retirement, I had a bad patch and camped with the homeless at People's Park, down the street from the chapel. One day I stepped inside the chapel. It was so ethereal, so beautiful. My life changed. Eventually I was admitted to the seminary there, as a retired professor, and one would think too old, but they ordained me anyway. Father Brubaker said it was Christ whom I encountered and Christ who called me, but I knew Father made it all happen. He introduced us, if you will."

Abram turned to Gregory. "That reminds me! Did you know, my boy, that today, November 15, is the Feast of Saint Albert the Great? And here you are! My angels are laughing, having a little fun with us."

Gregory wasn't sure what Abram was referring to. "I'm sorry, I'm not familiar with Albert the Great."

"Why, Albertus Magnus is your patron saint, patron of natural sciences as well as philosophy. Thirteenth century. Brilliant Dominican but also humble. Taught Saint Thomas Aquinas. Studied and wrote about Aristotle, pulling Greek philosophy into Christian theology. A turning point in the history of Christendom, of the West. Faith and science united, and came to be known as Scholasticism."

Gregory nodded. "I had no idea. Saint Albert the Great may have been the one that inspired my lecture a year ago. I'm going to read up on him."

"I don't believe in coincidences, for the most part. Here we are on the Feast Day of Saint Albert, and here you are, my dear boy."

Gregory glanced at Catherine. She was processing all that she had heard.

"Aristotle," Catherine said, "thought the way to happiness was virtue. I remember that about him."

"Catherine, it all ties together—God's plan for each of us," Abram said, nodding. "He wants us to be happy. He loves us so! Father Brubaker rescued me on the Feast of Saint Albert. He was named after the saint—Albert Brubaker. And Saint Albert introduced Aristotle to the medieval scholarly world and, most importantly, taught Saint Thomas Aquinas. Just as I introduced Aristotle to UC Berkeley, for as long as they let me."

Abram's voice was growing hoarse, and he coughed slightly, clearing his throat. "Before I met Father Albert Brubaker, I had visited Greek Orthodox churches from time to time. I was a believer, but I had not fully encountered Christ."

Elizabeth nodded. "Eventually we found you, or Father Brubaker found us. We were so worried."

Abram grew quiet, thinking or praying, then said with a quiet urgency, "Gregory—please sit next to me here. I want to say something to you, to all of you." His tone had grown serious and he seemed to be measuring his words as well as his strength.

Gregory sat alongside Abram, feeling like an honored guest, facing the two women seated.

Caleb had retreated to the doorway that opened onto the sandstone tunnels. Steven guarded the entrance to the promontory and the deer path. Gregory could see that the brothers revered Abram and wanted to protect him from the crowds and the media. Several TV reporters, Gregory had been told, had tried to interview Abram by following him up the deer path to the cave, but Caleb and Steven had sent them away, as Abram had requested.

How long could this go on? Gregory asked himself. It was four days since Sunday when Abram first appeared on the ledge, since Gregory's fall, and his meeting Abram and Elizabeth.

They waited expectantly for Abram to speak, his eyes on the icons.

"Abram," Elizabeth said, breaking the silence, "come home. You need to come home with me."

Chapter 40

If anyone had the right to interrupt the hermit as he collected his thoughts—and his breath—Elizabeth had that right as his caring sister, but Gregory wished she had let him take his time to say what he wanted to say.

Abram leaned forward and took his sister's hand. Their hands were of similar size, ropy and mottled, like genetic twins, Gregory thought. He looked at their faces, so full of love for one another, so full of shared history. Elizabeth's hair was a coifed chestnut brown, short and curled, and Abram's hair was white, long and wavy down his back, but their features, Gregory noticed for the first time, resembled one another. They both had large blue eyes, full of reflection and purpose. Abram had not taken care of his teeth, and they were yellowing, while Elizabeth's were white, but their smiles lit up the room with their love.

"Elizabeth, dear Elizabeth, my own sister. I do not have much time. The angels have been visiting, and we know that happens toward the end. Now, be a good girl, and bring me my prayer book if you would."

Elizabeth's eyes were filling, and she wiped the moisture away with the back of a finger. Her lip trembled. She found the prayer book on a stand nearby and handed it to her brother. It was a small, thick book with delicate tissue pages, and it reminded Gregory of his Aunt Jane. She carried one like that and prayed its prayers daily.

Abram turned to Catherine. "I am glad you came, for I have something for you. Please take this old prayer book of mine. It will help you on your journey. You have many years ahead of you, but your friends will help." He glanced at Gregory and Elizabeth. "Go to Mass—regularly, to be fed with Christ and by Christ. You are an intelligent young woman. Ask Father Brubaker the whys of life and reasons for belief. Ask him all the questions, share all your doubts, pour out all your fears. He will help you, too. But most of all, my dear Catherine, in the Mass you will encounter Christ. When that happens, there is no turning back from such joy." He now eyed Elizabeth. "From such happiness."

Gregory watched Elizabeth as she listened to Abram, and for a moment pride in her brother ruled her features. But the pride turned to doubt, which then turned to love, and she cast her eyes down. Gregory saw this; he saw in Elizabeth a sister whose love would move mountains and open doors to faith if she desired it; he saw in Elizabeth that Abram would, one day, take her hand and lead her to Heaven.

"Thank you," Catherine said, "but I couldn't possibly take this. It's too precious, and you've only just met me." She looked to Gregory for help.

"I feel as though I have known you forever," Abram said, wheezing. "Please. Humor an old man."

Catherine nodded. "Thank you. I shall treasure it." She held the small thick volume in her palms, the delicate ribbon markers falling across her long fingers.

Gregory knew Catherine spoke these words from habit, from custom, but he also knew that what she said would come true. She would, one day, treasure the gift even more, and treasure the memory of this moment.

Abram turned to Gregory. "My dear boy, you too are to have something, to incline your heart to pray for me, now and when I am gone. Please bring me the Transfiguration icon."

Gregory breathed deeply. "But these icons are holy . . . how can you give me one?"

"Please," Abram gasped. "Do not question."

Gregory stood, removed the icon from the wall trellis, returned to his seat alongside Abram, and studied the painted wood cradled in his palms. The iconography formed a perfect triangle. Christ rose into the clouds, speaking to Moses and Elijah on either side of him. Peter, James, and John knelt before the vision. The colors were rich: reds and greens and golds. Gregory recalled that Scripture accounts describe Christ's face as altered, that it shone as the sun, and that his raiment was white and glistering.

Abram said to Gregory, "Your own face was transfigured, reflecting the glory of God, when you spoke to me of Christ. That is what Jesus the Christ does to us. He transfigures and transforms. May you always reflect the light of Christ. Pay attention to what our Lord tells you to do and the path you are to walk on."

"Thank you, Father," Gregory said, searching for words. Gregory looked at the glowing features of Abram, then at the icon and the transfigured face of the Son of God. This icon would open doors for him, of this he was certain. He would say his prayers before this icon and he would receive answers to the many questions he had. "I will pay attention as you say."

Abram patted Gregory's knee. "Good."

Abram turned to Elizabeth. "And now Elizabeth, my sister. Please, the icon of the Holy Trinity is for you. As you know, when we were children and we were separated, the Christian family who took me in—who protected and loved me in that terrible time—gave me this. They knew it was a Jewish story and a Christian story, and in this icon the full story of God's love is told."

He paused to catch his breath. "You know the characters, Abraham and Sarah and the three visiting angels of God, the three persons of the Holy Trinity—God the Father, God the Son, and God the Holy Spirit. And God the Son, Jesus the Christ, the Anointed One, in the middle, points to the lamb in the dish on the table. Who will be the lamb of God? Who will be the sinless sacrifice for the sins of the world? The Son of God will be the lamb of sacrifice."

Elizabeth made no attempt to refuse the gift. "Thank you, Abram. Perhaps one day I shall journey as you have, into your faith, but I am not there yet."

"I know, my dear."

Abram turned to Gregory and Catherine. "I must say goodbye—God be with you—until we meet again, and be assured, we will meet again. Please give me a little time alone with my sister. And tell Caleb and Steven I must speak with them afterwards."

Gregory turned to Abram and wrapped the frail form in his arms. He could feel his bones beneath the muslin robe, but the strength of Abram's embrace surprised him. The hermit held him by the shoulders and looked into his eyes. "Be strong. There is much to come, and much to accomplish. Do not forget the chapel and its pastor. The chapel is a holy place with sacred relics. I have often thought it might be one of the portals. Pray unceasingly. Keep watch for our Lord's return in glory."

Gregory wanted to ask what he meant about the chapel, but replied, "I will. Father, may I have your blessing?"

Gregory knelt. Abram stood and placed one hand on Gregory's head and with the other made the sign of the cross over him, saying, "May the Lord bless thee, and keep thee. May the Lord make his face shine upon thee, and be gracious unto thee. May the Lord lift up his countenance upon thee, and give thee peace. Amen."

"Amen," Gregory said.

Abram turned to Catherine, who was now standing, and kissed her gently on the forehead.

"Father, may I too have your blessing?" Catherine asked, and Abram blessed Catherine in the same manner. "Goodbye for now, Father. Thank you."

Gregory and Catherine stood in the doorway that led to the tunnels through the caves. They turned and looked back.

Elizabeth and Abram sat side by side on the stone bed. Abram's arm was around her as she gazed at the wall of icons, listening closely to his rapid, tender words. Her face was unguarded, and she appeared at peace. Now Elizabeth faced Abram and took his hands in hers, and she seemed to speak earnestly, with great joy.

As Gregory and Catherine stepped away from the door, Gregory heard the hermit laugh loudly, crying to his sister, "You saw Samuel! Samuel! How wonderful! Grace! Grace! All is grace!"

Chapter 41

With great care, Gregory placed the icon in his pack. Catherine wrapped the prayer book in a scarf and set it in her tote, in a safe corner.

The path through the caves led to the parking lot and campground. "Are you warm enough to walk for a ways on the trail? There's a nice vista point not too far up."

"Sure," Catherine said, buttoning her jacket. "The fresh air always clears my mind."

"Me too. And I promise not to fall off the mountain. It was quite a ways up, and I was diverted by a rattlesnake crossing the path."

"That would explain it," she said. "I'm glad you're all right."

"Thanks." He touched his forehead. "Still a bit tender. Have you ever hiked the mountain?"

Catherine shook her head. "I haven't, but I've been curious, since I can see Angel Mountain from Villa Tilifos."

They followed the trail through grass and chaparral, pines and manzanita, past the upper trailhead where Gregory had parked on Sunday, and were soon on the path that he recalled walking before he fell. Gregory returned in his mind to the image of the cave and the hermit, and, for the time being, allowed the silence to absorb their footsteps. But he was glad when Catherine spoke.

"What do you think Abram meant about the chapel? He said something about relics and a portal."

"I'm not sure. I heard a rumor once that holy relics are buried under the altar. I assumed they were relics brought back from Europe, which sometimes happens. Mary Magdalene's relics were on tour recently. It's possible."

"And the reference to a portal?" She slipped her hands into her jacket pockets.

"At first I thought Abram meant the tabernacle and our receiving eternal life through the Eucharist. But I'm not sure. The portal—doorway— might actually be through the dome above, literally. There may be passages on Earth that open onto Heaven." Gregory hoped he didn't sound too crazy. This was Catherine he was speaking to. This mattered. While he was nervous, it was a good nervous, a great nervous.

"Really?"

"We don't know, do we?" he replied, backtracking slightly to sound more normal.

"No one has returned to tell us," she said.

"Not to me, anyway."

"My mother passed away last year." Catherine said, glancing at him sideways. "I dreamed she appeared to me last night. Could it really have been her?"

They had entered a level portion of the path, shaded with oaks, leading to the lookout point.

"I'm so sorry about her passing," Gregory said, pausing for a minute. "She may have actually visited you. It happens. I've read numerous firsthand accounts."

"She said that Heaven is real and we would see one another again."

The lookout point faced northwest. Catherine sat on a weathered wooden bench, tilting on the uneven ground.

Gregory joined her. "Nice view up here, above it all."

"It's beautiful. So vast. So amazing."

The tule fog meandered like a thin white ribbon toward the coast, and here and there the low hilltops emerged from the mist, like islands in a sea of white. The sun arced over them, heading toward the western horizon. They had several hours before dusk, when the park would close.

"I believe Heaven is real," Gregory said, feeling brave.

Catherine eyed him seriously. "Why do you believe it?"

She is direct, he thought. "It's been a long journey."

"Tell me the short version," she said.

Were her eyes teasing or challenging or doubting? A little of all three, Gregory decided. "I'm a scientist. I saw faith as something out there for some people, but why bother? I was raised a Christian, but somehow I hadn't met Christ along the way." That was pretty honest, he thought. He even surprised himself. "As Abram said about his own conversion."

"Go on."

"In my studies of the genome and genetics, and my Stanford residency, I began asking meaningful questions, and finally connecting the dots, as it were. The intricacy and creativity and brilliance of our physical world reflected an Intelligence, a designer, and one thing led to another."

"But doesn't science explain our world? With evolution? We don't need God anymore. We don't need a religious explanation."

"That's the amazing part. Over the last few years, science has been effectively presenting a case for the existence of God."

Catherine looked thoughtful. "I thought it was a matter of faith, of belief, rather than scientific observation, data, and conclusions."

"Things have changed. In 1966, around the time of the 'God is Dead' movement, the astronomer Carl Sagan claimed two conditions were needed to support life on a planet. Without these two requirements, life could not exist. The first requirement was the correct star and the second was the perfect distance from that star. Calculations showed, based on this hypothesis, there were over a septillion planets that could support life, planets that had the perfect star at the perfect distance."

"I've never heard this, but then I took a minimum of science, and no astronomy."

"Science has made many more discoveries since 1966. But the announcement was exciting in the sixties, and it gave rise to all the space travel movies. There was a natural curiosity about aliens and life on other planets."

Catherine grinned. "Star Wars, Star Trek, ET, that kind of thing."

"Exactly. But science made new discoveries that never really made their way into the popular imagination, and people got stuck in that mindset that there is life out there. In that sense, they haven't kept up with science."

"What discoveries? Did they prove life couldn't exist on other planets?"

"Pretty much. Well-funded programs under the umbrella 'Search for Extraterrestrial Intelligence'—SETI—tried to identify life in the universe by tracking signals through radio telescopic networks. Nothing. Silence. Congress defunded the program in 1993 but private donors continued to search for life in the universe."

Catherine shook her head. "Let me guess. Nothing still?"

"Right. As of 2014, nothing."

"What happened then?"

"Sagan's requirements for life multiplied over the intervening years, way beyond two, which made the results more logical. Fewer and fewer planets met the increasing number of requisites discovered by science."

"How many planets today can support life? What did they come up with?"

"Actually, none."

"None except for Earth?"

"No, including Earth."

Chapter 42

Gregory watched Catherine's face. She wasn't laughing at him. She wasn't rolling her eyes. She seemed genuinely interested in his statement that it was impossible for planet Earth to support life, at least according to the math probabilities and life's necessary requirements.

"But—" Catherine shook her head in disbelief, at a loss for words to express her doubt. But she still seemed to take him seriously. She hadn't written him off completely. She was listening.

"Here we are," Gregory said. "We are life. Sitting under an oak on the side of Angel Mountain watching the incredible tule fog move through the valleys toward the coast. We are here—we are life—so how did this happen?"

"Go on."

Did Catherine sound intrigued or sarcastic? He wasn't sure if she believed him. "The latest data show that there are over two hundred requirements for a planet to support life. Each one must be met or else life cannot exist on planet Earth. For example, near to us, planet Jupiter has a gravity pull strong enough to divert asteroids away from Earth. It is clear—at least to this scientist—that the creation of life forms was not random but finely tuned. Extremely finely tuned."

"What about the creation of the universe? Wasn't that a result of the Big Bang? An explosion? Not God at all." She gestured to the broad landscape that reached to the horizon and the endless sky.

"Fine-tuning again. The universe was fine-tuned immediately after the Big Bang, which also had to have a cause in itself, as Aquinas argued. Today, astrophysicists claim there were four forces that needed to be fine-tuned and need to be continuously fine-tuned. If they had not been finely tuned, for example, no stars would exist. The odds are gigantic against the universe forming accidentally from an explosion, any explosion. The odds are something like ten quintillion to one."

"That's all encouraging, isn't it? Seems like meaning and purpose are now scientifically proven."

"Certainly in terms of probabilities, statistics. Many atheist scientists—the honest ones—have admitted that some kind of Intelligence had to be behind the creation of the universe."

"It doesn't seem to make the news."

"The general public is about twenty years behind. Also, belief in God isn't popular, considered too constraining in terms of ethics and behavior. The natural conclusion—not a great leap—is to identify this intelligent Creator as the God of Jews, Christians, and Muslims. All three religions make clear moral demands on our lives. All three proclaim a law. All three predict a day of Judgment."

"So what you're saying is that faith and science support one another."

Gregory nodded as they returned to the path. "They do. Absolutely." He grew thoughtful. "You're a better audience than my last one."

"How so?" She looked at him with expectant eyes, green eyes flecked with brown, almost hazel. She seemed genuinely interested.

"I gave a lecture at UC Berkeley, saying pretty much what I said to you, adding more information about Darwinian evolution and natural selection, but the end was similar, a supportive reconciliation between faith and science."

"What happened?" Catherine asked, and the urgency in her tone told Gregory he had touched a sympathetic chord.

"At first, shock. Then brutal questions, rhetorical questions. Then antifa protestors arrived from nowhere and the police did nothing except ensure I was safely removed from the lecture hall."

Catherine shook her head. "That's worse than why I resigned my job."

"You resigned from your last library job?"

"I defended the right to life of the unborn, in conversation with a group of colleagues at the library. They called me names, said I was a bigot."

A kindred soul, thought Gregory. "I'm sorry to hear that. Names can hurt, especially spoken in derision and anger. I was asked to take a sabbatical to write my book. Asked in forceful language by the dean. They didn't want any lightning rods, he said. UC Berkeley already had plenty of bad press."

"So that's why you're on sabbatical?"

"Wouldn't have been my choice at this time. But it's turned out for the better, all things considered." As he gazed at Catherine, with her delicate strength, her way of speaking, and her intricate interest in his own thought process, he meant every word. It turned out for the better, no doubt about it.

"We both spoke out for truth," Catherine said, "and paid the price."

"You for life and me for faith."

"Yes."

"So are you happy with the new job?" he asked, trying to lighten the mood.

Catherine's face lit up. "So far, it's been fascinating. All the authors I didn't read, never heard of. And Elizabeth is such a resource. I can ask her anything. And I love books."

Gregory grinned. "Good. I'm still feeling my way as to what I'm going to do. Write the book, of course. But what next? What underpins it? Academia or research or practicing medicine? Still some big questions ahead."

"Could you do all three? At a research hospital where you might teach as well?"

"The research does fascinate me. And the moral parameters are looming large. I'm not sure what I can do about influencing the use of genetics. That's the field where an ethical stand or viewpoint might make a difference."

"My mother and my Aunt Pat would say to go to the chapel and pray that God show you the path you are to walk on."

He laughed. "I think your mother and your Aunt Pat would have liked my Aunt Jane." He glanced at his watch. "We'd better return, find Elizabeth, and get back to Villa Tilifos."

As they stepped down the trail, Gregory recalled Catherine's interest in genetics. "You said you wanted to trace a relative through genetics?"

Catherine glanced at him quickly. "My father."

As Gregory heard the story about Catherine's abandonment, his heart cried. How similar these stories seemed to be—the loss of parents, the loss of a father or mother, or never having known them, as in his case. He sensed, however, she had not told him the full story—why her father left before she was born. He wanted to ask, but felt he was intruding.

"I understand," he said, careful not to pry. "I never knew my parents, at least not that I recall."

Catherine stopped alongside some low brush and pulled a strand of hair from her face, securing it behind her ear. Her braid had loosened and Gregory tried to imagine what she would look like with her hair worn down.

"I'm sorry you never knew them," she said, sounding genuinely concerned. "At least I had my mother. Who raised you?"

"My Aunt Jane, my mother's aunt, actually. So she was my great aunt. I loved her as my own mother. She passed away in 2003—I miss her. Parkinson's disease. I wanted to find a cure."

"So you went into medicine?"

"Yes, to discover a cure."

"I wanted to find my father," Catherine said. "Or find out who he was, is. To find myself."

"I had that urge once. Aunt Jane said not to worry about things like that. I let it go."

"Why? Isn't it a good thing to know your biological background? Isn't that who I am? A combination of my ancestry, genes from both sides, going back in time?"

Gregory smiled. "Sure, to a point. But it's not who you are if you are a believer. God shows us who we truly are, Aunt Jane said again and again. I wasn't sure what she meant by that, but I'm slowly seeing glimpses. I think it has to do with free will and choice, that we have many paths to walk on, no matter who we are, or where we were raised."

"Our choices are who we are?"

"We are our genes, and we are our environment. They call it nature and nurture. We are given certain things to start, but we have a lifetime to use those gifts, whatever they are. And how we choose to use them, that is the glory of creation, of using the intelligence we have been given to create our lives to be good lives, noble, worthy—of worth."

"I'll think about all that. I sent in my saliva sample to Ancestors.com, so at least I'll know what part of the world my ancestors called home."

"Seems a dividing enterprise, doesn't it?" Gregory wanted to say it encouraged racism, encouraged identities to be determined using the wrong factors. "Here we are trying to unify, find common ground, encourage world peace, and at the same time searching for that which makes us different from one another."

"I hadn't thought of that. You may have a point."

"Love your enemies, our Lord said. Be good to those who harm you. Look after the least of these. Unifying not dividing. Love. And as long as I'm preaching," he added, hoping to be forgiven, "I'll have to admit that the most I've learned about myself has been on the hard benches in Saint Joseph's Chapel, sometimes on Sundays, but sometimes during the week at a quiet midday Mass, singing with a few others, meditating on the tabernacle and the crucifix above. Sudden thoughts come to me in those times." Gregory stopped abruptly and gazed to the hills, feeling foolish, having opened his heart to Catherine when they hardly knew one another.

"I think I know what you mean," she said, looking at the ground and lacing her fingers together as though in prayer. She turned to him, her own face unguarded, and her eyes held affection, or so Gregory hoped. "I think I know what you mean," she repeated.

"Finding the path to walk on?" he asked quietly.

"Yes, finding the path," she replied.

They continued down the trail to the sandstone caves.

Chapter 43

They sat side by side, as they had done so many times in their childhood. But today Abram felt so much older than his sister, and his sister seemed a child.

"Elizabeth."

"Abram."

He turned to her and took her hand in his. "Elizabeth, I love you, my big and competent sister. I owe you so much. I owe you my life, my long life, but especially the first years."

Elizabeth nodded. "I love you too, Abram, my little brother over whom we worried and fussed."

"Soon I will know how much you and Mama and Papa did for me. I don't recall—I was too young. Only bits and pieces."

"You had a terrible fever when we hid on Mount Tilifos. You were vomiting and we had to keep you from crying in the dark and alerting the locals."

"I was only two."

"Yes," she said solemnly, "only two."

"And we escaped Crete and made it back home to Athens."

"And survived the war."

"Survived Hitler."

"Yes," she said, "barely."

"We joined our parents," he said.

"And the communists invaded Greece, a new terror. Papa lost everything, his homes, his business. We all had to be equal. The Greek partisans were our friends during the war, then they persecuted us under communism. No one wanted the Jews." Her voice rose higher with each phrase, and Abram squeezed her hand.

"No one wanted us. How did we live?"

"Papa sold honey door to door. I remember that time. I do not know how he managed to feed us in those post-war days. I have been told, but some things I have chosen to forget."

"It is better to forget some things."

"And be grateful for what we have, our lives."

"And America." Gratitude is good, Abram thought, a beginning, a kind of rebirth.

"We made it to America."

"Our parents encouraged us," he said, and he had a sudden memory of boarding a ship. "We went to America to college." He released her hand and folded his own, now deep in thought.

"We did pretty well here." She looked at him, her blue eyes large and confirming.

"Where did Papa find the money to send us here and pay for school?" Abram had not questioned this before.

"I do not know. We both worked part-time jobs. And we had American sponsors."

"I washed dishes. Ran errands for the local newspaper. Anything I could find."

"I was fortunate to find clerical work."

"I remember. I think God was looking after us."

"I am grateful."

"We returned to Greece later, with your Samuel, remember?"

She nodded, her features full of memory. "Many years later. Mama was dying. We said goodbye. I knew we would not see Papa again. He would not leave their room after she was gone."

"He died of a broken heart in six months. I feel bad that we were not there." Abram wrung his hands, shaking his head.

"Do you think they missed us—all the years we were in America?"

"They loved us," he said, "so they did what love does. They sacrificed, so that we could be free, so that we could live in peace and prosperity." Abram's heart wept. "I was not as grateful to them as I should have been. I should have done more, said more, loved more . . . and better."

"But your younger years were with the Greek Christians. To you they were your family."

"And I found them on that return trip. I found my brothers and sisters, or those who I thought were my brothers and sisters."

"And I found the families that helped us on the island of Crete—you did not remember them—and those later in Athens. I think of them as cousins. Most have passed on now. We kept in touch."

"It was good to go back," Abram said, "to thank them."

"They were good people. Heroic. They risked their lives, and their children's lives. They were righteous among the nations."

Elizabeth laid her hand on Abram's shoulder, turning to him. "All these years in America! Who would have thought? I am so grateful, Abram. So grateful for Samuel, for my teaching, even for the crossing guard job I had after I retired."

"My classics department was my life," Abram said, nodding, gazing again upon the icons on the wall. "Christ was born into the Roman world. I wanted to understand all of it, the Greek heritage that you and I owned, but also what came next, the world of Nazareth and Bethlehem and Jerusalem in the first century."

"Were you a believer even then?"

"Probably more of an intellectual seeker, a collector of ideas."

"When do you think you became a believer in Christ?"

"I know exactly when that happened or at least began. When Father Brubaker brought me in from the chapel porch. When he let me live in the old shingled house in back and gave me the title of Sexton, Keeper of the Keys. One of my jobs was to keep the red sanctuary lamp always lit, signifying that the mystical presence of Christ—the consecrated Host, the Blessed Sacrament—was reserved in the tabernacle on the altar. I loved keeping the lamp lit, and something happened over time. I met Christ—many times, as I was lighting that lamp."

"I can imagine you lighting that lamp. I can see it in my mind's eye."

"I was already old in those days. My Cal days seemed another world."

"You left Cal after decades of teaching," Elizabeth said.

"I had enough of the speech and thought police that controlled the faculty and public debate. I needed air to breathe."

"Too much like Nazism, you said when you retired."

"But I needed to work. Work occupied my mind and my memory. I was drifting when Father Brubaker found me sleeping on the porch."

"We would have brought you home to live with us sooner, but we could not find you."

"I would never have listened to you. I had much to learn about humility. I was full of myself. Full of pride. Pride rots the soul. I was rotting inside."

"And People's Park?"

"Ah, Elizabeth, I have forgotten much of those years, so drug-addled I was. But the pastor found me. You found me. God found me and pulled me in with a twitch upon a string."

Abram was tired, so very tired. "I need to rest, my dear sister. I need to close my eyes for a time." He kissed her on each cheek and on the forehead.

"We will meet again soon. Of that I am sure. Wait here for Gregory and Catherine to return. Watch over me with the icons until then."

Elizabeth fell into her brother's embrace. "Yes, of course. Until we meet again, my dear Abram." She took a seat in one of the canvas chairs, near the wall of icons.

Abram stretched out on the stone bed, pulling up his golden blanket.

Soon he was deeply asleep, covered with the blanket and guarded by the love of the saints and his big sister.

Chapter 44

That same Thursday afternoon, Malcolm Underhill III had a few drinks in a local pub, congratulating himself again and again.

But slowly, as he downed one more shot—in celebration, of course, and most deserved—he grew more and more concerned that he might not have set the fuse right or the timer right. He fought the urge to return to the summit and check.

Finally, he decided to be safe not sorry and headed back to the park. The gates wouldn't close until dusk, hours away, so he had plenty of time. Anyway, he might want to spend the night watching his handiwork. Fires were best in the dark. He could take photos and post them on social media, the great equalizer. Once he was in power, he would need to shut down social media and the internet as well, but they could be effective weapons for now. He headed to the summit, full of the righteousness of his cause, just as the sun began its descent into Earth's horizon.

As he approached the stacks of books—so beautifully arranged—he saw a flame. His memory had served him well. He realized he set the timer too early and arrived too late to change it—what a fool. A flame was shooting up near him, way before sunset. But no matter. Now he could watch the show.

He sat on a bench nearby and grinned as the flames crackled, leaping into the sky, the pages devoured, the words eaten, destroyed. Was he brilliant or what?

He pulled out a pint of single malt and took a swig. He rolled some weed. His van was nearby for a quick exit if things got too—ha, ha—hot.

He was on top of the world, between Heaven and Earth, and he was in control.

He stood and raised his hands to the skies, challenging anyone who might question his authority. No voice came from above. No challenger appeared. Those fools in the meadow listening to the crazed Jewish prophet. Ha! They were all delusional and needed to be locked up for a very long time.

It was when he reached for the whisky for another celebratory swig that he felt the quake. The land shifted and rumbled and he sat down and held onto the bench, but it toppled over. Now, finding himself sitting in the grass, waiting for the shaking to stop, he noticed his pant leg was on fire. He dropped the joint and poured the rest of the alcohol over his leg, hoping to quench the flame. Fool! Alcohol!

The Earth shook again.

Malcolm ran. And as he ran the fire spread up his leg. He tripped and fell into a ditch that appeared without warning. The ditch became a gully that became a chasm. Malcolm tumbled into the dark void, into the mouth of the mountain, screaming in anger and pain, cursing Heaven. Soon he was silent, and Malcolm Underhill III was no more, his ashes buried deep inside Angel Mountain, ashes that would feed the spring grass.

Chapter 45

Abram did not know how long he had slept, nor the hour of the day, but sensed it was late afternoon by the feel of the light. He awoke, recalling Elizabeth. She was gone.

He had heard the careful footsteps of Gregory and Catherine as they led Elizabeth out through the doorway to the sandstone tunnels. They were quiet, Abram thought, not wanting to disturb him. He had tried to pull himself out of the depths of his sleep but could not manage it.

He sensed it was the last time he would see her in this world. Soon he would go to his true home. Soon he would be released from this bondage, this sweet bondage in this wonder-filled and terror-filled world, this awesome and awe-full world. His work was nearing its end and just in time, for his body longed for release too, or at least transformation.

As Abram prayed the Lord's Prayer, he commended his sister to his Lord and prayed for Gregory and Catherine. Somehow they fit into God's grand design, and while Abram did not believe in predestination—free will was cherished by his God of love—God did have a plan for humanity.

The question that remained was how each person chose to contribute to that plan, the redemption of mankind. Did the sinner repent and start anew? Did the sinner seek to be fed with sacraments and Scripture? Did the sinner open his or her heart to the love of God, allowing transfiguration and transformation? Did the sinner trust and obey God and his commandments? How confounding it was for many that to find oneself, one must lose oneself. How confounding it was that to have faith, one must be faithful. To know truth, one must speak truth. To be loved, one must love. To find, one must seek. To see, one must open one's eyes. To hear, one must listen.

Mankind was confounded, lost, scared, and too proud to admit it, walled within a fortress of self.

But the Holy Spirit roamed the world, blowing through the low valleys and the high mountains, breathing into every heart the hope of eternity, the promise of Heaven.

Abram stepped outside, onto his promontory.

The fog swirled below, but the sun had come out and was bathing the mountainside.

"My children," he cried into the fog bank below. "My children!"

Abram could see movement, and slowly the sun parted the fog. The crowd had lessened, but many remained, waiting by the white cross and the waterfall as though knowing these places would be safe, watching for the holy hermit's return. He began to sing his Psalm to the Earth, to the heavens, and to his God:

> The heavens declare the glory of God; and the firmament showeth his handy-work.
> One day telleth another; and one night certifieth another.
> There is neither speech nor language; but their voices are heard among them.
> Their sound is gone out into all lands; and their words into the ends of the world.
> In them hath he set a tabernacle for the sun; which cometh forth as a bridegroom out of his chamber, and rejoiceth as a giant to run his course.[20]

The sun was burning the fog into an aqueous swirl of moisture and light. Yet Abram knew they could see him as he sang, that they could see with their own eyes Angel Mountain's glory, the gentle slopes rising to / Heaven. With a full heart, he picked up his robes and descended to the pool, Caleb leading him and Steven following.

"Be baptized today!" Abram cried. "Come to the waters of life, to the spirit of truth! Be reborn by power of the Holy Spirit. Come to Jesus, our dear Lord, who welcomes you with open arms. Come to the waters of Heaven poured on your parched souls. For great is your faithfulness and the fruits of the Spirit will be yours as you travel the road to Heaven. For Heaven is now! Eternity is now! Free for the asking."

"Brother Abram, what are they? These fruits?" It was a tiny reedy voice.

Abram nodded to a woman who carried a child on her hip. The boy snuggled into the hollow of her shoulder, asleep.

"Be not afraid," Abram said, approaching the woman, whose eyes darted about as if fearing discovery. "There are twelve fruits of the Holy Spirit and you will see the thread of love that weaves them into a cloth of beauty, of baptism. They are love, joy, and peace." He paused, nodding and smiling, opening his palms in offering, meditating on each gift. "They are patience, kindness, and goodness." He folded his hands, his gaze roaming the faces present, uniting each gift with each face. "They are generosity, gentleness, and faith. They are modesty, self-control, and chastity." Abram walked to the waterfall, raising his voice to be heard against the pouring of the waters into the pond. "These are the gifts God gives you when you are baptized with the power of his Holy Spirit. These are the gifts that lead you on the path to joy and happiness."

Abram baptized as he had been commanded.

Caleb and Steven handed out cards with the words of baptism and the fruits of the Holy Spirit listed to remind the newly baptized of their gifts of life. Also on the cards were the names of local churches, where they could continue their journey to Heaven.

As dusk approached, Abram glanced behind him, up to the mountain outlined against the sky. He turned his eyes to the north, where he knew fires still burned, and, as the sun began its descent in the west, he felt a bit of ash on his robe. It floated white and landed black, smudging the muslin.

Caleb warned Abram. "We need to go back to the cave. The ash is blowing in. It is time for the people to go home. Twilight is nearing."

Abram blessed the crowd, and they peacefully dispersed. As he stepped up the deer path, he sensed his heart was like his cave, a tabernacle holding God within. His heart was a tabernacle within his body, as the cave was a tabernacle within the mountain, all pointing to Heaven, for the Kingdom of Heaven was within each person, anchored by a white cross on a hillside, and refreshed by holy waters.

After the young men left, and after he said his evening prayers, an old tune came into his head, and he sang to his saints on the wall. Holding his sister close to his heart, he commended all those baptized to God's mercy and love. He prayed for Caleb, Steven, Gregory, and Catherine. As bits of the hymn came to him, he pulled the tune and the words from his memory,

Crown him with many crowns,
The Lamb upon his throne;
Hark! how the heav'n-ly anthem drowns
All music but its own:
Awake my soul, and sing
Of him who died for thee,
And hail him as thy matchless King
Through all eternity.[21]

Where did that hymn come from? He could see Saint Joseph's Chapel where he had been a postulant, where he had been ordained deacon and priest, where his robust and towering bishop had sung to the tabernacle with his boisterous baritone and the tune had echoed through the barrel vault high above as if singing to the streets of Berkeley. The bishop was gone now, or was gathering by the river that runs by the throne of God, as he often said. Was he watching from Heaven and helping the angels guide Abram in his final hours and days?

How did the rest of the hymn go?

Crown him the Son of God
Before the worlds began,
And ye, who tread where he hath trod,
Crown him the Son of Man;
Who every grief hath known
That wrings the human breast,
And takes and bears them for his own,
That all in him may rest.

Crown him the Lord of Life,
Who triumphed over the grave,
And rose victorious in the strife
For those he came to save;
His glories now we sing
Who died, and rose on high,
Who died, eternal life to bring,
And lives that death may die.

Crown him the Lord of Lords
Who over all doth reign,
Who once on earth, the incarnate Word,
For ransomed sinners slain,
Now lives in realms of light,
Where saints with angels sing
Their songs before him day and night,
Their God, Redeemer, King.

Crown him the Lord of Heav'n,
Enthroned in worlds above;
Crown him the King to whom is giv'n
The wondrous name of Love.
Crown him with many crowns,
As thrones before him fall,
Crown him, ye kings, with many crowns,
For he is King of all.

And what was the phrase the bishop used as the reason he sang? Because his heart was speaking through song. With that thought, Abram the hermit, priest, and prophet, drifted into a deep sleep on his hard bed of stone, the music dancing in his soul.

FRIDAY

Chapter 46

Abram had been sleeping deeply—unaware of the earthquake—when Michael called him out of his body, sometime in the night between the fifth and sixth day (known as Thursday and Friday) of the third week of the eleventh month (known as November), 2018 Earth years AD, *Anno Domini*, after the Year of Our Lord, Earth time.

"Abram Levin! It is time," the angel said. "Do you want to see Elizabeth before we begin?"

"See her once more?"

"On Earth, yes. You may choose whom to see, or not to see. Then we must leave Earth, that is, if you still choose Heaven."

Abram found himself standing at the foot of his sister's bed.

"Elizabeth."

She stirred awake, and Abram smiled when he saw the tabby sleeping in the hollow of her arm. She stroked the cat, who, Abram recalled, bore the name of Laddie.

"Elizabeth."

She opened her eyes. "Abram!"

"Elizabeth, I am all right. It will be all right. Just like Samuel said."

"Oh, no, Abram, what do you mean? Do not leave me."

"All will be well. Your guardian angel will come—mine is named Michael."

Laddie did not seem to see him.

"Are you in Heaven?"

"Not yet, but soon." Abram thought that might be the case.

"I love you," she said.

"I love you, too. We will gather by the river that runs by the throne of God."

"Yes."

"How is Laddie?"

"He is doing well, Abram, all things considered."

"Good."

"Are you ready, Abram Levin?"

Abram was back on his rock bed in the sandstone cave.

"Yes, oh yes." Laddie would comfort Elizabeth. And there were Gregory and Catherine to help her. God was so very good, so full of grace.

"Do you see the fire?"

"I see it," Abram said to the shimmering image of the angel that was beginning to take shape. Beyond, he saw through the cavern ceiling, to the top of the mountain, and to the flames leaping in the dark. "What is happening, good Michael?"

"Books are burning, and the ash you felt today was words on paper, man's story, his history of life on Earth, at least as he has recorded it."

"History books? But why?" The flames leapt high, as though escaping the mountain, trying to run away from Earth.

"Also poetry and art and philosophy. Theology. Sacred texts of Jews, Christians, and Muslims, Abraham's children."

"Who is doing this?"

"His name is Malcolm. We have tried to love him enough. But he turns away with scorn."

"Is it always a matter of love?"

"You know it is."

"Love that moves the stars and moon and sun?"

"Love that gives life. Love that lives."

"And takes life too?"

Michael now appeared angry. "Never!"

"But we die. Our bodies—"

"Adam chose. Adam fell from grace."

"Adam and Eve?"

"Yes."

"But why did Malcolm do this thing? Why burn books of truth and joy and meaning and freedom?"

"He said yes to Lucifer again and again. He understood no other way. He could not remember any other choice. He could not hear and he could not see. He became deaf and blind."

"Did he know this?"

"In some way he knew. He separated himself from truth. He sought power and revenge. He did not think in straight lines, but in crooked ones.

He complicated the simple and true. He wove self-pity and self-hate into his life. But the mountain—my mountain—opened and claimed him. Did you feel the earthquake?"

"No. There was an earthquake?"

"It opened up the Earth. The Earth was angry. The man named Malcolm is no more, but Lucifer may claim his soul."

Abram tried to follow what Michael was saying, but wanted to go home, to Heaven. He sensed his body was still on his stone bed, and his soul was still within that flesh. Was he dreaming again? Would he wake up and see that this was all a vision like the other dreams?

"Come, it is time."

"Time?"

"Time to leave time. Time for eternity. Do you wish to come with me? It is your choice, your choice you are free to make. You are free to love and to know the King of Love."

Abram saw that he *was* dead, after all. Or his body was. All flesh is grass . . . the grass withereth, the flower fadeth: but the word of our God shall stand forever . . .

"I want to come with you. Take me. Take me home."

Chapter 47

In the twinkling of an eye the cave disappeared, and Abram looked behind to see his wall of icons grow smaller and smaller. He saw Elizabeth kneeling beside his bed, touching his cheeks, and Catherine and Gregory nearby. A translucent iridescence emanated from his body, which seemed to be much younger. The golden shimmering danced with the icons, throwing their own light into the illuminations. He saw the sandstone caves now from outside, from above the mountain, as he rose high like a bird, and he saw the bright wings of Michael ahead of him. Soon other angels flew alongside Abram, escorting him on his journey, pallbearers of his soul.

He tried to look back, to Elizabeth and Angel Mountain, but all he saw was fire on its peak leaping to singe the skies, the grassy flanks of the mountaintop now blackened and blanketed with the ash of pages and words, the writing on paper and parchment bits holding humanity's hopes and dreams, the answers to the sorrows and joys of life—the whats, the whens, the wheres, the whys.

Abram felt the wind winged by Michael and the angels as though cradled in the crèche of God's hand. A happy certainty filled him, and he thought his soul might burst with joy. Trust and obey, for there is no other way . . . the words calmed him as though he had sipped a fine wine and the warmth of the wine filled him with acceptance of the moment, acceptance of this, his heavenly journey home.

He chose not to think too much, but to simply en-joy.

Abram found himself at the entrance to a forest. Michael was now half-formed, and he could see the golden curls that crowned his head, the sword that fought the dragon of old, the brilliant cape and clothing of battle. He held a book, which he handed to Abram.

Abram noticed also that he, Abram, had grown into some kind of form, a filmy version of his younger self, an image of substance—some kind of substance—that comforted him. He reached for the book and read the spine. His name was engraved in golden script.

"This is your Book of Life," Michael said, nodding. "Open. Read. Do what must be done. Confess. Repent. Enter the woods of the cross. You are near the first Heaven."

With a sudden gust of wind, Michael was gone.

Abram opened the book, and as he read of his birth and early child-hood, his mother filled his vision. He closed the book and entered the woods, tears streaming down his face.

"I am so sorry."

"Oh, Abram, how wonderful to see you again!" His mother wrapped him in her arms, and as she did, he knew he was forgiven.

"I love you," Abram said, seeing her face for the woman she truly was, the mother who gave him up so that he could live. "Thank you for saving me. You sacrificed your need to have me with you."

"I love you too, my son. I did what love commands." She glanced side-ways, and Abram saw his father, whose hand held hers. "He is here, Leon. He is here!"

"Welcome, my son," his father said, holding him tightly with a strength Abram did not recall.

"Is this Heaven?" Abram asked.

"It is the beginning of your journey into the woods, the first Heaven," Jacob said.

"Will you come with me? How many Heavens are there?"

His mother nodded. "We have been assigned to meet you, but you will travel with others as well." She had Elizabeth's chestnut curls, and Abram felt a sudden joy.

"Others?" Abram asked.

"You will see, son," his father said. He was short but strongly built, with a face of wisdom and beauty.

"Not to worry, my child," his mother added. "We made the same jour-ney. There are many by the river waiting for you."

"The river?"

"The river that runs by the throne of God," his father said.

"There really is a river that runs by the throne of God?"

"Now," his mother said, "no more questions. Remember, always re-member, choose love; always choose love. We will meet again."

There were others Abram met as he followed the path through the shadowy woods, others he had not loved enough. His tears were many and his confessions many and his repentance great and heartfelt. These souls of his past, written into his Book of Life, joined him as he stepped on the path that parted majestic firs, thick as the California redwoods. As he moved, more souls of his past emerged from behind the trees, or from the wood of the trees—Abram was not sure—to encounter him, waiting for Abram to respond with recognition.

Abram journeyed on, choosing the way of love at crossroads of hate and selfishness and pride. The souls that formed his past helped him to remember, to repent, to rebirth his life. Soon all wrongs had been righted, all sins reconciled. Soon, soon, all had been forgiven in the woods of the cross. Those he encountered on the path through the woods seemed to follow him, or did they lead him, encouraging him on?

As he moved up the trail through the forest, green shoots grew from the brown trunks. The leaves brightened, lightening the shadows with their shimmering, until, after many encounters, many scrubbings and healings of his soul, Abram emerged from the woods and looked back.

He realized the woods were indeed the wood of the cross. How could that be? He had emerged from the top of the vertical beam of the cross that became the crucifix scarring and shaming Golgotha, planted outside the walls of Jerusalem in the Year of Our Lord, Earth time. He looked down, past the horizontal crossbeam. The vertical beam was rooted in the Earth's horizon that rimmed Heaven. The dark wood of the cross was sending out green shoots, and soon the cross became grassland with a river running through it. The transformation was swift and welcome, and Abram had the overpowering sensation he had come home.

Abram waited on the banks of the swiftly rolling river. He was alone now, the followers scattered, or so he thought.

Soon he saw those he had been searching for. His parents waved from a meadow bordered by a stand of pines where the river pooled under a waterfall in the distance. Other familiar faces waited there too.

Abram walked quickly, his form growing more solid with each step, his white robe billowing in the high green grass. The air was piercingly clear and clean, like the high country in Greece, or like the salt breeze from the San Francisco Bay, when the fog was blown by wind coming from the sea, through the Golden Gate.

Abram ran—for he remembered he was young again—to the gathering of his friends and family by the river, the river that runs by the throne of God.

Chapter 48

Elizabeth awoke at dawn on Friday, the clock reading 6:23. She smelled smoke. Sitting up too abruptly, pain shrieked through her lower back. More slowly now, she reached for Laddie, a shadowy form curled at the foot of her bed.

She recalled an earthquake in the early evening as she slipped into sleep.

But now something was burning. Had the northern fires turned south? But it was not the smoky smell that awakened her, nor the first light. Of that she was certain.

It was Abram, Abram she saw, Abram who spoke to her in the night. Was it a dream? Was it real? What had he said? Elizabeth could not recall, could not breathe the memory to life and, with a quiet urgency, pulled Laddie close, cuddling him. Soon the old tabby was deeply purring, and Elizabeth could feel the low-pitched rumble thunder through his chest and into his throat, a sort of speech that massaged her palm as she stroked him. His golden eyes blinked with what she assumed to be pleasure and, she liked to think, a happy gratitude, possibly love.

Love. Gratitude. The image of her brother remained with her. How grateful she was for this memory, although it was dimming fast. She was not sure if he had spoken, but she recalled his arms reaching out to her. What did that mean? Had he passed on? Was he with Samuel?

A slow panic took hold of Elizabeth. Her heart quickened its beat, and she set Laddie down on the bed. She stood carefully, reached for her robe on the chair, stepped to the window, and parted the panels.

She gasped.

Smoke billowed from the top of Angel Mountain, and she could see flames moving down its upper flanks. Did the quake fell a utility pole, showering sparks on the dry grass? Had there been a lightning strike during the night? Had a hiker thrown a cigarette into the brush, or was a campfire left untended? Campfires had been prohibited since the firestorms in the north. It appeared that the fire had not reached the white cross, barely visible in the thick haze. She should be grateful for that, she told herself.

Where was Abram?

A knock on her bedroom door reminded her that Catherine had spent the night, agreeing to Gregory's suggestion. Elizabeth had been upset by her conversation with Abram, his clear sense of death coming, even his gift of the icon as though it were the last time she would see him. Dr. Worthington had taken her pulse and was worried.

Elizabeth breathed deeply, hoping to calm her fluttering heart.

Catherine peeked in. "The mountain's on fire," she said, holding up her phone. "And there was an earthquake last night. Did you feel it? We'd better evacuate your brother. The firefighters are working to contain it—it appears to have started on the peak. The story is all over the local news and going viral."

Elizabeth laid her hand on her heart. "We need to reach Abram. I will get dressed, but first I have to give Laddie his shot."

"I'll call Gregory. He might know more." She tapped a number, and Elizabeth could see there was no answer. Catherine spoke quickly into the phone. "Left a message," she said. "You want to wait here? I can take your car, and bring Abram back, or Maria can take me."

"I am coming with you."

"I'm sure he's all right."

"I will meet you downstairs," Elizabeth said, "and I will drive."

Elizabeth drove with a calm that surprised her. She expected the worst, but was not sure what that would be. They arrived at the park entrance, closed until further notice due to fire danger. Elizabeth pulled out a small remote and pointed it toward the gates. Tony was on duty and came to her window.

"Better not go in, Mrs. Jacobsen. The fire is out, but we haven't been given the green light to let you through."

Elizabeth shook her head. "The fire is out but we need to see Abram. I am sorry, but we are going to the cave." She drove through the open gates.

Catherine looked back. "He's frowning and shaking his head, but I don't think he's going to stop us."

"He will have to understand. The rangers have been kind," Elizabeth said, glancing at Catherine, "so I hate to go against them, but this is an emergency."

Catherine nodded, and they followed the road to the parking lot, the campgrounds, and the sandstone caves.

Elizabeth got out and ran ahead, surprising herself at her sudden agility or foolishness or both. It was a moment of carelessness, of not caring about herself, to rescue her baby brother who needed rescuing. She would act and face the consequences later. She had no choice.

When she reached the entrance to the cave, she stopped and raised her hands to her eyes to shade the bright light that emanated from the interior. Had the fire reached Abram after all?

"Abram!" Elizabeth screamed. "Abram!"

Catherine arrived and reached for Elizabeth, steadying her. "Don't go in there. No, Elizabeth, don't go in there."

The two women stood and watched, but as their eyes adjusted to the brilliant light in the hazy morning—the sun darkened by smoke—Elizabeth knew it was not fire. It was something else.

They approached the entrance. Elizabeth stepped inside first. Catherine peered around her shoulder, her hand still on Elizabeth's arm. The sweet aromas of roses . . . and jasmine . . . filled the cave.

The inside was lit with a light both opaque and sheer. The light seemed to move, shimmer, and Elizabeth watched, mesmerized, shading her eyes with her hand. The beauty of the light entranced her, and for the moment she forgot Abram. The light held colors she could see, every color of the rainbow, and yet it was still a white, bright light. She wanted to step into the light and live there. Her yearning grew, until the longing nearly propelled her farther inside, but Catherine took her hand. Elizabeth glanced at Catherine.

Catherine's gaze was not on the light, but on Abram.

Elizabeth turned to her brother on the sandstone bed. It was Abram, for sure, but the form that lay under the golden blanket glowed. The light in the cave clearly came from this source, and Elizabeth drew closer to Abram's face and closer to the fragrant aroma.

Her eyes filled with tears, for Abram appeared as a young man, all lines and age spots gone from his face, his hair and beard a chestnut brown. His eyes were closed, but his lids fluttered. Was he alive?

"Abram," Elizabeth whispered, kneeling by the form on the stone bed. "Abram, are you sleeping?"

She laid her hand on his chest, but found no heartbeat. She touched his face and it was cold. His body was no longer living, but his soul—where was his soul? She knelt there, with Catherine standing beside her, for what seemed a long time, watching his face, so full of happiness and joy, and then lastly, of peace. Yes, all these emotions danced through his features, until finally his features were still.

Elizabeth looked at Catherine, who remained calmly waiting. "Did you see that?" Elizabeth asked.

"Is he sleeping? Is he all right? Should I try to reach Tony at the gate?"

Elizabeth asked again, "Did you see Abram's face? How it changed in the light? The moving light?"

Catherine shook her head. "No, are you sure? Is he breathing, Elizabeth? He is very still, isn't he? I'll try Gregory."

Elizabeth knew her brother was gone. Somehow she knew she must face his death, face his death with words. "He is not breathing. Catherine, I believe he has passed away. Abram has left us. There is no need for Tony now. He has enough to do."

Suddenly she felt overwhelmed. It was as if a mighty river rose within her, flooding her heart and soul with a torrent of loss. Elizabeth held her brother's face in her hands. "Take me with you, Abram. Please, oh please, talk to this God of yours—of ours—and take me with you." She laid her cheek alongside his and wept, longing to travel with him. "Do not leave me, Abram. Do not leave me here." But her only answer was increasing cold— the cold of his face and her own cold. She shivered and drew away.

The light continued to dance in the cave. It seemed Catherine didn't see it. Why did she, Elizabeth, see it? Bewildered, she looked again upon her brother. The form and the air around the body and the bed and the blanket continued to glow, and Elizabeth was overwhelmed with something she could not define. It was all around her, settling upon her, entering her very being. It felt like being in love, like finding safe shelter after running and hiding, like drying a child's tears and seeing him smile again. It was like holding Laddie and feeling his joyous purr. It was all of these things, these full-of-life things. It was simply and purely love, a greater love than she ever imagined there could be.

Elizabeth felt a fluttering wind, as though giant wings were batting the air in the small space of the cave. She turned and looked up, toward the sound of flapping. The ceiling of the cave, a dome of craggy sandstone, appeared to open, and she saw in the gap a sky of blue. Through the opening a white dove flew out, growing smaller in the patch of blue. Elizabeth could see no haze nor ash, only brilliant blue, the azure sky of a summer's day.

Chapter 49

Catherine couldn't get a phone signal, even on the ledge. Ash still drifted down, obscuring the valley. What was happening? The air here on the promontory was clear, and there was even a ray of sun landing upon the beginning of the deer path to the cross and pond and waterfall.

She recalled she had never heard Abram preach, nor seen the crowd that gathered. But there had been videos online from many angles, some with hymns in the background, some with the angry shouts of protesters. Groups swayed to the music, their souls singing while their bodies danced.

Now she tried to peer through the haze to the meadow below but could see nothing.

The gates were closed. There would be no one in the meadow this morning.

Catherine peeked into the cave. Elizabeth was weeping, her cheek next to Abram's. Catherine entered and placed a hand on her shoulder. "I haven't been able to reach Gregory," she said. "I can't get a signal."

"What will I do without Abram?" Elizabeth cried, her eyes on the top of the sandstone cave as though she expected him to appear.

"I'm so sorry, Elizabeth. I'll stay with you as long as you need me."

Elizabeth stood and took Catherine's hand. "Thank you. Abram is my baby brother. Samuel is gone. Now Abram is gone too."

Catherine heard her sense of abandonment. Elizabeth's cheeks were streaked with tears as she lowered herself onto a canvas chair.

At that moment, Gregory arrived through the sandstone tunnels. "They let me through the gates with my medical credentials. The fire is out." He stared at Abram. He glanced at the women, then drew near Abram's body. He touched his pulse and felt his forehead. He stood back, looking both puzzled and in awe. "I'm sorry, but I believe Abram has passed away.

There's no pulse. But look! His face, his form, are full of light," he said. "He's young. How can this be?"

Catherine could see the change as well. His features were smooth, the deep lines gone, and a light emanated from his form. "Gregory, a brighter light shone from the doorway—the doorway you came through. Did you see it? I thought it was the fire, but soon realized it was a light of a different kind."

"I saw it," Gregory said. "And the aroma! The fragrance is of roses . . . and jasmine."

"The light is less now," Elizabeth said, her voice faint.

Even in the whisper, Catherine thought that Elizabeth sounded more in control, as though she had absorbed the reality of Abram's death.

The aroma was increasing, as though they were deep within a garden of blooming flowers.

"Where's the fragrance coming from?" Catherine asked.

"From Abram's body," Gregory said. "It's a sign of sanctity. And the light as well. Remember how Moses was veiled when he returned from Mount Sinai? He had seen God and his face was so transfigured that it was blinding to those who looked upon it. Saint Paul wrote about unveiled faces . . . what was it?"

"I don't know," Catherine said. "Like the Transfiguration icon?" She turned to Abram's icons, but recalled that Gregory had been given the Transfiguration icon.

"Something like that," Gregory said, nodding. "It all fits together to form a whole."

Elizabeth turned to Gregory. "I saw Samuel the other night in a dream, but I am not sure it *was* a dream. Is it possible he visited me? That it really was him?" She looked at Abram. "Maybe Abram will visit me now? But—he *did* visit early this morning. I had forgotten."

"Abram visited you?" Catherine asked.

Elizabeth nodded, seeming more certain.

"I saw my mother the other night," Catherine said. "I don't know what it means."

"These visions or appearances do happen," Gregory said.

"Abram believed my vision was truly Samuel," Elizabeth added. "He laughed with happiness when I told him yesterday."

Gregory moved closer to Abram to observe the shimmering glow. "It's not a blinding light now, but it might have been earlier." He looked around the cave, then to Elizabeth, his face full of compassion. He had been through death and dying before, Catherine guessed, and had cared for those left behind, the mourners.

"There have been many accounts," Gregory said, "of loved ones returning to comfort spouses or children. Father Brubaker insists that his old bishop appeared to him shortly after he died. He stood at the foot of the bed, smiling."

"Has it happened to you, Gregory?" Catherine asked, guessing Elizabeth wanted to ask the same question.

"Has it?" Elizabeth whispered.

Gregory shook his head. "I'm afraid not, at least not that I remember. And that's the problem. Many heavenly visits could be forgotten upon waking."

"Your Aunt Jane?" Catherine said, watching his reaction.

Gregory nodded. "I've always been sure that she's okay, that she's in Heaven, or wherever we go, sleeping, waiting for the new Heaven and new Earth. Maybe she did visit me. Maybe I've forgotten . . . it's coming back to me, the quote from Saint Paul: 'But we all, with open face beholding as in a glass the glory of the Lord, are changed into the same image from glory to glory, even as by the Spirit of the Lord.'"[22]

Catherine thought about the words. "We are changed into an image of Christ?"

"In some mysterious glorious way, yes, while still being ourselves, so that we remain who we are, but are full of the light of Christ. I was entranced with that idea when I took confirmation classes and tried to memorize the verse. The glass Paul refers to would have been a mirror, and some translations use 'unveiled face,' recalling the veiling of Moses."

Elizabeth drew closer to Abram, and as she did, she shielded her eyes. "It is bright; it really is bright. Almost like looking into the sun. Oh, Abram, what has happened? Will I see you again?" Her voice caught on the words and she trembled.

Catherine put her arm around her shaking shoulders. "Come sit with me."

Gregory moved to the outer doorway. He pulled out his phone and tapped. "Father Brubaker, glad you picked up. We need you on Angel Mountain . . . sad news . . . Abram has passed on. I'm sorry too, but I don't think he's sorry . . . Yes, please come and help us with what needs to be done. I'll meet you at the park gates to let you in—they're closed because of the fire on the summit."

Gregory laughed at something the priest said.

"What did he say?" Catherine asked.

"'All is grace. All is grace.' It was a phrase used by the bishop again and again. And by Father Brubaker. And by Abram. And it's true. All *is* grace."

"Should we wait here?" Elizabeth asked.

"If you wish, or come with me."

"You go, Catherine," Elizabeth said. "I need a few more minutes with my Abram before I say goodbye, at least goodbye to his earthly form."

"I understand," Catherine said, although not wanting to leave her. She followed Gregory through the sandstone tunnels to his car.

Chapter 50

"I saw the smoke on the mountaintop," Gregory said, as they drove down to the park entrance, "and came as soon as I could. I was glad to see that you and Elizabeth were already there."

"You got through the gates with your medical credentials?"

"It took some fast talking. I said I knew the hermit in the cave and needed to find him to check on his safety. The ranger seemed relieved, since he had been told to guard the gates and hadn't been able to check on Abram. And I sounded desperate."

Catherine listened quietly, watching him from the passenger seat. "It's all so sudden, and so amazing. The light coming from the cave, coming from Abram! It was even brighter earlier. And his being young again. Was that really Abram?"

"It was. Elizabeth recognized him. I recognized his features. How long were you there before I arrived?"

"I'm not sure, maybe thirty minutes."

"And the light you saw earlier? Can you describe it?" Gregory asked, as he parked near the gates to wait for Father Brubaker.

"The light glowed. It was both fierce and gentle," Catherine said reverently. "And it came from Abram. What does that mean?"

"He was reflecting the light of Christ, the light of love. His image was becoming like Christ's, like the Creator, as Saint Paul wrote. He had the beatific vision—the vision of God, seeing the face of God. And we saw God's reflected light in Abram's face, his young face." Gregory fumbled for the right words as he watched her reaction, but with Catherine he was encouraged to risk anything, to bare his soul, to even look ridiculous.

"The light was love?" She sounded genuinely interested, curious.

Gregory looked up to the mountainside where burn paths had scorched the grass. He nodded. "Uncreated love, the energy of creation. Light in the darkness. Even the Big Bang, the forming of the stars and constellations, the sun and the moon. Uncreated energy. Uncreated love. We don't have the words—theological or scientific—to describe the indescribable."

"Maybe, in the beginning was the Word . . . God created light . . ." Catherine said, as if she were reaching for the right words as well.

"It's where poetry and faith and science merge as they did centuries ago and later separated. Some religious scientists believe that the universe was created and is kept in existence—actually held together—by the love of God."

"Didn't Dante say something about that?"

"How did that stanza go?" Gregory said, searching his memory. "I'm no poet, but I think Father Brubaker quotes it often: 'Yet as a wheel moves smoothly, free from jars, my will and my desire were turned by love, the love that moves the sun and the other stars.'"[23]

"Does that have anything to do with the music of the spheres?"

"Exactly, from Pythagoras. Did you study the early philosophers? You mentioned Aristotle."

"I recall Aristotle from high school, but Pythagoras caught my attention when I was sorting Elizabeth's books. Something about ratios and perfect harmonies."

Gregory nodded. "All part of the miracle and beauty of creation, an intelligent design."

A line of cars was forming at the gate and being diverted into a parking area.

"Look at the crowds arriving." Catherine checked social media on her phone. "The fire on Angel Mountain is being shared and reports reposted, mainly because of Abram living here and preaching. I should have stayed with Elizabeth."

"She should be okay for now. And she needs time with Abram." She may not have another chance, he thought, watching the pilgrims being turned away.

"How long will it take for Father Brubaker to get here?"

"He was on his way . . . he heard the reports of fire. He must have figured Abram was on the mountain, from the news postings and my messages."

"I think this might be him now."

"Good."

Gregory and Catherine stood by the car, waving at the portly priest who raised a thick hand in return, his ruddy face looking determined. Gregory recalled how he moved about the chapel—and the altar when saying Mass—with a combination of reverence, patience, and delight. He was a solid, assured man, dedicated to God and to those who came through his chapel doors. "I want to introduce them to our dear Lord," he would often say, pointing to the tabernacle on the altar. "Once introduced, all is grace— I've done my job." Some stayed and some left, but all were introduced. Gregory had been introduced to Christ by Father Brubaker and would be forever thankful.

Gregory called to Tony at the gate. "Let him through. He's with me."

Tony Mitchell and the priest approached their car.

"I believe," Father Brubaker said to Tony, raising his brows and glancing at Gregory and Catherine, "Abram the hermit has passed into Heaven. May his soul rest in peace." The priest made the sign of the cross prayerfully. "Dr. Worthington can document the death properly for you."

"Father Abram?" Tony also made the sign of the cross. "How did he die? Not the fire?"

"No, I think his heart gave out. It was time," Father Brubaker replied.

"I'm truly sorry!" Tony said mournfully. "He was a holy man. He baptized my son who refused to attend church with us, but Matt responded to Abram. We here on the mountain watched over him as best we could. We will miss him." His gaze turned toward the sandstone caves.

"We will indeed miss him." Gregory helped Father Brubaker into the back seat and Catherine took the passenger seat in front.

"How is his sister taking it?" Tony asked Gregory. "Mrs. Jacobsen?"

"As might be expected. Not well. But I think she believes in Heaven. That will help."

Tony motioned to the line of cars at the gate. "They want to see him. They want to see the body of the saint, they say. They want to touch him. They want relics. I asked for some assistance from the Danville police, and Officer Riley can advise us how to handle the crowds."

"I'll check with Mrs. Jacobsen." Gregory shook his head. "I'm not so sure—"

A female police officer had joined them. She was heavyset, middle-aged, with an air of authority. She rested her right hand on her holster, standing straight and tall. She spoke with a New Jersey accent. "I'm Officer Riley. I'll arrange the permits—there are always permits—and I'll fast-track the request to the right people. We have two jurisdictions here—city police and state park rangers—so we need to do this right."

"What do you suggest?" Gregory asked, seeing she appeared to know what she was talking about.

She nodded, gesturing with her left hand. "Have them form a line, an orderly line, controlled by the police and rangers." Her face was encouraging, matter of fact, as though she encountered hermits dying all the time in caves on mountainsides, and this what was done. Her subtext was, "Hey folks, this isn't rocket science. Just do it."

"If Mrs. Jacobsen agrees," Tony added. "And thanks for answering our call for reinforcements."

"Of course," Officer Riley said, "but it might be wise to let his fans—or worshipers or whatever—have a look." She pointed to the caves, which could be seen in the distance. "I could rally more of our local police to control the lines and any unwanted visitors. I never had a chance to hear him preach. He must have been really something, a kind of Billy Graham. The phones keep ringing at the station. We're getting lots of publicity for the area—for local businesses and such—and for the state park."

Gregory could see her point and could also see her own curiosity. An orderly viewing might be acceptable. What would Abram want? Who was he, after all? Gregory hadn't known him long, only a few days, and yet he felt he had known him much longer. This man of science would treasure his conversations with this man of God. He would write them down, so as not to forget. And the icon of the Transfiguration! It would remind him of Abram's own transfiguration and transformation into a young man, that amazing unveiled reflection of Christ.

"Tell them to return on Saturday," Gregory said to the officer, "and send them away for now. Viewing will be Saturday." He would speak to Elizabeth and cancel the viewing if she wanted to.

"Where?" Tony asked.

"In the sandstone caves," Officer Riley replied. "That should satisfy them. I'll provide police protection and permits. We might need the coroner's office to sign off. We won't 'stand down' if there's trouble. You can count on that." Her voice was gruff but commanding, and Gregory could see she had experience she was putting to use. She also appeared to have seniority, some kind of authority at least, being probably in her early fifties. "I spent many years on the Berkeley force until I had had enough of city and university politics. I can help you here. I can do crowd control and do it right." She handed him her card. "Let me know."

"Thank you. I'll get back to you soon." Gregory lowered himself into the driver's seat as the ranger and officer headed back to the gate. "Let's return to Elizabeth," he said to Father Brubaker and Catherine. "We've left her alone too long."

"Here we are," Gregory said, parking in the lot near the sandstone caves. "Follow us, Father, through the passages."

They entered the tunnels. The interior light was dimming but still shimmered with an incandescence that Gregory could not explain. They stepped carefully, turning left and right, and Gregory was glad when they finally reached Elizabeth, sitting alongside her brother as though she were waiting for a ride home.

SATURDAY

Chapter 51

Saturday morning Elizabeth awoke, full of a deep longing, her hand on her heart. She parted the damask panels that covered the window. The white cross could be seen through the hazy light, Angel Mountain rising beyond in the dawn.

Laddie nuzzled her ankles, his golden eyes peering up at her. Elizabeth smiled at him, then turned to the white cross, searching for Abram's cave. How grateful she was that Gregory had offered to organize today's pilgrimage.

She could not see the sandstone formations from Tilifos, but she knew they were near the cross. Soon the pilgrims would come. Soon they would look upon her brother Abram, say a prayer, try to touch the holy.

Elizabeth did not recall exactly what the Jews believed about Heaven. What difference did it make now, anyway? She had no power to change truth, nor did she desire to.

Her teaching career had been about truth, about the belief systems of the West that inspired, and were foundational to democracy: freedom of speech, of thought, and of belief; equality under the law; human dignity and the value of each person regardless of age, gender, race, or creed. She hoped she had imparted some of this magnificent legacy, this legacy of life. She did it for Samuel and for Abram and all those lost in the Holocaust, all those persecuted. She did it for her own sanity, and for the truth, as both Samuel and Abram often reminded her.

Samuel. Abram. No one visited her last night in her dreams or her wakings. There were no visions of husband or brother. They had moved on, she guessed, to gather by the river, as Abram often said. She summoned the face of Samuel, recalling his recent visit in the night. She summoned the face of Abram who reached to her with arms of love. Those memories would have to do, and those summonings would feed her heart until it was her turn to make the crossing, the passing into Heaven.

In spite of the remaining haze from the fire on the mountain, the area around the cross remained clear. Many had commented on the strange phenomenon. Many had read meaning into the event, the old hermit's death, the light in the cave, even the earthquake and fire. Let them, Elizabeth thought, for it helped them make sense of their own lives, their own sufferings. It gave them hope.

And maybe they were right. Maybe, just maybe, her brother was a saint, as the Christians called the holy ones. Maybe he was so full of the love of God that he glowed, reflecting the glory of God, as Father Brubaker said as he gazed upon Abram's body in the sandstone cave.

Maybe there really was a God who loved mankind, his own creation, loved them enough to die a painful, public, and shameful death on a cross to atone for their sins. Maybe the long-awaited Messiah of the people of Israel was Jesus of Nazareth. Maybe it was all true and there was a happy-ever-after ending, a new beginning, another chance—in eternity.

Elizabeth lifted Laddie and held him close. "What do you think, Laddie? Are you a believer?"

The purr thundered through Laddie, the vibrations moving along her arms and into her heart, merging with the beat of life.

Elizabeth prepared the syringe of insulin and made a pocket of furry flesh. She inserted the needle and pushed in the plunger. Laddie did not seem to mind, and for that she was grateful. She kissed him on the forehead, scratched him behind his ears, and set him down gently.

It was Saturday morning, and they would join the pilgrims at the cave. They would see what arrangements Father Brubaker and Dr. Worthington had made to allow this all to happen.

She pulled out her gratitude journal and wrote:

> Saturday, November 17, 2018
> I am grateful to be on this good Earth one more day.
> I am grateful for Laddie.
> I am grateful for Gregory and Catherine.
> I am grateful for my home and Maria and my books.
> I am grateful for Abram, my little brother, who has gone home to God.
> I am grateful for my life with Samuel and for the hope to see him again.

She heard stirrings in the kitchen below. Catherine was making eggs, as she promised—her specialty, she said—scrambled with tomatoes.

Chapter 52

Arriving at the park gates, Catherine could see that a line of vehicles was already forming. Elizabeth motioned to Tony, who was walking along the line, checking identification.

The ranger spoke through the open window, his squinty eyes friendly, his manner serious. "Dr. Worthington and Father Brubaker are making arrangements at the cave. You are to join them. There are others helping too. They will guard the pilgrimage route and watch over the crowd." He saluted and waved them ahead.

The women parked near the sandstone tunnels and made their way to Abram's cave. They waited in the doorway, watching Gregory instruct a young man.

Father Brubaker approached them. The priest wore his black clericals and white collar, and the uniform comforted Catherine, as though she were protected from chaos by order. "We have a place for you to watch the pilgrims, if you like." He motioned to chairs in the corner, roped off.

"Thank you, Father," Elizabeth said.

Catherine nodded. "I'll stay with her." As they took seats, Catherine noticed that the aroma of roses and jasmine remained. Abram looked the same—young, at peace. The light around the body had lessened, but was still extraordinary.

"What is the plan?" Elizabeth asked, as Gregory joined them.

"The pilgrims will gather in the meadow," Gregory explained. "Caleb and Steven and other helpers will ask each person to sign in. We won't be carrying candles or lanterns due to the fire hazard."

"At least the summit fire is out," Catherine said.

"How did it happen? Do they know?" Elizabeth asked. "I have worried about fire on this mountain."

"Arson," Gregory said. "The fire was intentionally set: a bonfire of books, mostly library books, lit by a timed fuse."

Elizabeth shuddered, and Catherine put her arm around her. "Like Savonarola," Elizabeth said, but Catherine didn't recognize the reference. "And Hitler," she whispered under her breath.

"And like the Los Angeles library fire," added Catherine. Was there a connection between the two fires and the shooter from the Berkeley library? The books that went missing? It all seemed so outrageous and unlikely, and yet it formed a pattern, a crazy one, but a pattern nevertheless.

"So what happens next?" Elizabeth asked.

Gregory explained. "The pilgrims will receive a memento prayer card and bit of stone from the cave, sealed in plastic, at least as long as supplies last. Abram's many helpers have been working on this over the last day. The pilgrims will file past the pond and waterfall, up the deer path to the ledge, and enter the cave. They may light a candle, place it in a sand tray, and offer a prayer. They will exit into the tunnels and the parking area. A shuttle will take them back to the gate lot."

"And the body? Abram's body?" Catherine asked, seeing that the glow still emanated from his features, around the bed, and through the golden blanket. He looked happy, at peace.

"I'll guard the body," Gregory said, "once we arrive in procession. Caleb will help. His brother Steven will guide the pilgrims from the deer path to the ledge and to the entry."

"In procession?" Elizabeth asked.

"We will begin with a procession," Father Brubaker said. "I will lead—with Mrs. Jacobsen and Catherine if they so desire—carrying a single lantern and singing."

"I'll carry the cross," Gregory said.

"We can follow you," Elizabeth said, and Catherine nodded.

"His assistants will come next," the priest added, "guiding the pilgrims, single file."

"Will there be guards, a police presence?" Catherine considered the arrangements and feared a public viewing like this could invite trouble.

Gregory nodded. "All along the route. Park rangers too. And remember that each person has produced ID at the gate, and signed in at the gathering place in the meadow."

"It's the best we could do with such short notice," Father Brubaker said. "Not perfect, but nothing ever is."

"And after the viewing?" Elizabeth asked, her voice halting, unsure. "When will the body be taken for burial?"

"We will decide that at the end of the day," Gregory said, glancing at Abram's face, then at the priest.

Chapter 53

Gregory carried the cross high, a bronze processional cross Father Brubaker brought from the chapel.

As a boy, Gregory Worthington had been a crucifer from time to time at Saint Mary's Denver. In the last few years, he had carried the cross in procession in Saint Joseph's Chapel. But he had never carried one outside, in a state park, through a meadow, past a pond and waterfall, up a deer path, and into a sandstone cave. He had never carried the cross to the bed of a hermit—to the body of a hermit—one who might be a saint.

Saints, Gregory had read, were men and women who were so full of God's love that it burned through them, lighting the world, transforming everyone they met. It was a mystery and a miracle, the intersection of the immortal and mortal, the eternal and time, as Father Brubaker often said, quoting his bishop of blessed memory.

They were singing "Great Is Thy Faithfulness"—printed on the back of the prayer cards—as they moved from meadow to pond, following Father Brubaker, robed in black. Catherine and Elizabeth walked behind Gregory, and he was glad that the younger woman was caring for the older, a fact that endeared her to him even more.

The procession of pilgrims sang, and their chorus swelled and echoed in the cold morning air. A low breeze, rippling the surface of the Earth, had cleared the air in the meadow, and the sun, given a window of time to light the land, turned the grays of smoke into the greens of foliage and blues of sky. The pilgrims approached the pond and the falls, now sparkling in the sun, the waters pouring down from the outcrop above. Soon they stood before the white wooden cross on the hillside.

Father Brubaker led the people in prayer: "Our Father, who art in Heaven . . ."

As they prayed, Gregory exchanged glances with Catherine. Her arm linked with Elizabeth's as though supporting her. She smiled her tilted smile and returned her gaze to the cross, reciting the prayer she seemed to know.

As the priest welcomed the pilgrims, blessing them, Gregory wondered how Elizabeth felt about her brother's conversion and these Christian rituals. But then she didn't go to synagogue, he recalled. Perhaps she was an agnostic, with residues of faith lining her heart and mind. Residues, linings, could be powerful: those early words heard and deeds done, candles lit and hymns sung, histories retold to be remembered in story and song, a culture passed from generation to generation, sometimes surfacing into the present, surprisingly, and penetrating it with meaning and beauty.

It had happened to him, after his agnostic-atheistic college years, this rising up of his Denver childhood, experiences pulled to the surface by the familiar rituals and melodies he found in Saint Joseph's Chapel. It was a moment of clarity, seeing that faith and science blended into one intelligent design for mankind. Just so, his belief was reborn. Christianity gave him systematic reasoning that led to a creed that was supported by logic and historical witness. This reflected naturally the elegance of design he observed in both the great and small, the cosmos and genome, through telescope and microscope. Such a convergence of past and present probably happened to many who were open to change and open to their own power to choose.

The priest turned up the deer path, and Gregory followed with his cross held high. The curious and the faithful processed behind Catherine and Elizabeth, glancing up to the sandstone formations.

Upon arriving at the promontory where Abram had preached during the week, Gregory followed Father Brubaker into the cave and set the cross against the wall, near Abram. The light still emanated, a soft glow filling the space. Gregory and the two women took their places on the far side of the room. The pilgrims entered and were given a votive to light, which they set in a large iron stand that Caleb tended. They prayed before the body of Abram the hermit and exited through the sandstone tunnels to vans that shuttled back to the parking lot.

All the while the song was sung outside, and the chorus rose from the meadow and into the room of wax and flame and glow. Some took photos, but most paid their respects without recording the moment, as if this were more respectful. They stared, stunned, at the body of Abram. Some made the sign of the cross and some knelt, their lips moving silently.

Those friends who had helped Abram in life now helped him in death. They guided and watched and assisted with the lighting of each candle, with the saying of each prayer, and led the pilgrims silently into the sandstone maze.

Gregory wondered at what he witnessed here in the half-light, the glow of the holy that could not be scientifically explained. But more than the light and the form of Abram were the faces of the pilgrims. They had heard him preach or seen online videos of his preaching. Some had been baptized. Some had changed their lives and their ways. They had chosen a different direction, one of goodness and truth, righteousness and compassion. They had chosen the way of love and of life. Their features were unguarded, as though a veil had been lifted, or pierced, and in this sense they had become young again, open to mystery and miracle, open to transfiguration by the love of Christ.

As they left, did they think they would tell their grandchildren what they saw and did on this wintry November day? Did they sense they were part of a moment in history? Young and old, men and women, parents and children, filed through the meadow up the path to this promise of eternity, where love shone through time in a sandstone cave.

Gregory glanced at Catherine. She too had an unguarded look on her face. Her features were open, full of awe. Elizabeth sat, fingers laced on her lap, her focus on her brother's body as if she would not miss one moment of this last day together, even if his soul had moved on. A tear slid down her cheek, but she seemed unaware, and Gregory handed her a tissue. He thought the tear might be one of joy not sorrow, thanksgiving not loss, at least for the moment.

ETERNITY

Chapter 54

Abram found his parents gathering with others on the banks of the river. Soon he met his ancestors, cousins, aunts, and uncles who had arrived earlier. The Greek families that harbored him in the time of terror greeted him with tears and laughter. It appeared many families through many ages were gathered by the river, upstream and downstream, along the banks and up toward the foothills and the mountain beyond. Many faces he knew, but many he did not know. Would he one day know them all?

Far in the distance Abram could see a high mountain, and on the mountain peak he could see the throne of God. Around the throne was a rainbow, and Abram knew that on the right hand of God the Father was seated God the Son, Christ the King, Creator of All, Judge of the World, King of Glory, Lord of Hosts, Alpha and Omega. Waters poured down the mountain, into the streams, and into the river that ran before him.

As Abram contemplated the scene, the joy of the Holy Spirit pierced his heart. He knew the Father and the Son and the Spirit were one, embodying the Holy Trinity, the perfection and realization of love. Abram could see this mystery. He could now know this marvel. These truths were written—or being written—on his heart in language he could understand.

Abram also knew there was a book in which his name had been scripted, a book with the names of those redeemed by Christ (which he knew encompassed all humanity, born and unborn), and those who accepted the redemption and experienced salvation, those who chose to say yes. He knew that the unborn, and those who died as children, were here by the river too, but fully realized as adults. He could see that those gathered together appeared to be the same age, and Abram knew the age chosen, with a clarity that astonished him—thirty-three, the age of his Lord when he sacrificed his mortal life to save mankind.

The river was wide and deep and rushing. Those gathered appeared joyous to see one another, to understand the mysteries of creation and the love of God, the love that moved the stars that sang to the music of the spheres.

Abram looked up to the vast sky where new stars shone. He could see galaxies and solar systems, universes, planets, suns, and moons. He recalled Saint Augustine's words: "There we shall rest and we shall see; we shall see and we shall love; we shall love and we shall praise. Behold what shall be in the end and shall not end."[24]

As he marveled at these things, he knew that more truth was being written on his heart. More wonders. More love creating more wonders. His heart was being written upon like his Book of Life and the Book of the Redeemed, only this time it was being written with the love of God. Words burned into his soul, forged by God's love. And with the words etched and carved, he could see visions of Heaven, as he waited for the new Heaven and Earth to become one, after the final Judgment of the world.

Abram then saw twenty-four elders in white robes and gold crowns, all around the throne. Lightning flashed, thunder rolled, and seven lamps burned, the seven Spirits of God. He saw a glassy sea and four beasts—a lion, a calf, a man, and an eagle—with wings and eyes, and they never rested from praising God.

Abram longed to join them, to sing with them the song of praise, "Holy, holy, holy, Lord God Almighty, who was, and is, and is to come." Abram longed to sing too, to give glory and honor and thanks, forever and ever.

Abram saw the elders kneel before the King, casting down their golden crowns around a glassy sea.

The music was carried by the emerald waters, sparkling and tumbling toward those gathered in the meadow. As the river rolled by, Abram had the sense that the waters were singing too. Each person soon joined in the song, and Abram lifted his heart and voice with the others:

Holy, Holy, Holy! Lord God Almighty!
Early in the morning our song shall rise to Thee;
Holy, Holy, Holy! merciful and mighty!
God in three Persons, blessed Trinity!

Holy, Holy, Holy! All the saints adore Thee,
Casting down their golden crowns around the glassy sea;
Cherubim and seraphim falling down before Thee,
Which wert, and art, and evermore shalt be!

Holy, Holy, Holy! Lord God Almighty!
All thy works shall praise thy Name, in earth, and sky, and sea;
Holy, Holy, Holy! merciful and mighty,
God in three Persons, blessed Trinity.[25]

Abram was outside time and in eternity. He was with God, in God, held in God's palm. He saw past, present, and future, all as one, yet he knew much more was to come, for he waited for the Second Coming of Christ upon Earth to rule the new Heaven and Earth. In the meantime Abram sang with his family and friends, as they gathered in the meadow and the pines, on the banks of the river that runs by the throne of God.

SUNDAY

November 18

Chapter 55

On Sunday morning Elizabeth gazed upon Angel Mountain in the early dawn, focusing on the white cross anchored in the brown grass on the hillside. The haze swirled in the valley below, but the area around the cross remained partially clear, as if favored and protected. The sky above the summit waited for the light of the rising sun, and with a pang Elizabeth realized again she was alone, separated from not only Samuel but Abram too.

She gave Laddie his insulin shot and turned to her gratitude journal. She was thankful for Maria, Catherine, and Gregory. She was thankful for another day, sort of. She was thankful they were returning to Abram's cave this morning, and thankful that the viewing was over. She would have a few more moments with Abram before they moved the body for burial.

Catherine had suggested that she consider burying Abram at Queen of Heaven Cemetery, where her mother was buried. They prayed for the dead there, she said, for it was a Christian cemetery with a chapel. There was an attractive expanse of lawn with flowers and graves. There were marble headstones. There was a mausoleum where cremains were honored in wall tombs. It was a place of quiet and grace, surrounded by hills like those surrounding Angel Mountain, and Catherine said she went there occasionally with her Aunt Pat to visit the grave of her mother.

Father Brubaker said that location would be fine and he could arrange it. He could also arrange a Requiem Mass if Elizabeth desired one.

Elizabeth stepped down the stairs slowly, her hand on the bannister. How strange she felt this morning, as though she were embarking on a new adventure. But she was far too old to have those feelings. She decided it was her sudden isolation from the two men she loved, that they were no longer the center of her focus and her life, the subjects of her desires, her worries, and her fears. How would she organize her time? She only had herself. It was a strange experience to be so alone for the first time. What would she do with such freedom?

She stepped into the kitchen and gratefully received a mug of strong tea from Catherine. "Good morning. Thank you," she said.

"Good morning," Catherine said. "Come sit down and have your breakfast." She moved to the table and pulled out a chair for Elizabeth.

Gregory was at the sink, and he turned around to greet her. "Did you sleep well?"

"You are washing dishes?" Elizabeth asked. His long sleeves were rolled up and he wore an apron.

"They needed washing. I used to help my Aunt Jane all the time. I like doing dishes. Anyway, I got here early, couldn't sleep last night thinking about things, and well, thought I might as well lend a hand."

Catherine gazed through the glass doors in the nook. "Soon we will head to Angel Mountain. The sun is rising. The fires in the Paradise area are still burning—they've done great damage to several communities. Heart-breaking to see it on the news. We need a good rainstorm. We need to pray for rain."

Sitting at the pinewood table, nibbling toast, Elizabeth smiled. God was good, she thought, just like Abram always said. Her new friends covered her with a protective blanket of love. Yes, God was very good, and maybe all was grace, after all.

Elizabeth followed Gregory, and Catherine followed Elizabeth, through the sandstone tunnels to Abram's cave.

They stepped inside. The hard stone bed was empty. Abram's muslin robe lay neatly folded. An indentation in the shape of his body could be seen.

Elizabeth gasped, feeling faint. "What has happened? Abram is gone!" Her legs were buckling and she feared she was falling. Catherine supported her and guided her to a chair.

Caleb was sleeping on a cot under the wall of icons. He had been on guard during the night.

Gregory stepped closer to the stone bed, his gaze scanning the cave's interior as though he might find a clue. "What could have happened?" He walked about the cave as though Abram would materialize from the walls.

"Where could he be?" Catherine asked, her voice low but intense, her arm around Elizabeth who had begun to shake.

"Caleb was on guard," Gregory said, turning to the boy on the cot.

Caleb awoke from the commotion and sat up.

"Caleb," Gregory said, quietly and firmly, "where is Abram? Abram's gone. Who's been here?"

Caleb rubbed his eyes as he saw what happened. "He couldn't have disappeared—"

"Did Father Brubaker come?" Gregory asked. "Perhaps with the coroner?

"No one's been here." Caleb stumbled out of the cave, to the ledge to search the hillside.

"Look at the icons," Elizabeth said. The shimmering light was growing stronger.

"They're brighter than usual," Gregory noticed.

At that moment the shimmering took a shape, and Elizabeth's heart beat rapidly. The shape was something from her childhood, an appearance, a vision, a dream. She had seen something like it before, and it had spoken to her. When? Where?

"Fear not, I am Michael," the moving image said.

Elizabeth looked at Gregory and Catherine. "Did you hear that?" She tried to stand, to reach out to the image, but her legs folded again and she sat back down.

"Hear what?" Catherine wrapped her arm around Elizabeth's shoulder.

"I didn't hear anything," Gregory said, studying her face. "You look like you've seen a ghost."

"No—wait. Quiet!" Elizabeth focused on Michael, and slowly he took the form of an angel, or at least what she thought might be an angel—white robe, heavenly face and hair, an Adonis of sorts, tall, but no wings that she could see. She guessed that only she could see and hear him.

"Fear not. I bring you glad tidings! Abram's body has gone home, through this portal between Heaven and Earth."

"How can this be?" Elizabeth asked.

"It happens between our worlds. Others have done so, journeyed to Heaven through our portals—our doors. Be not afraid. Your brother is happy. He is by the river. He is in the presence of God Almighty, the King of Glory and Lord of Hosts, the Alpha and Omega, in our world without end."

"But—"

"He is an Elijah. This is a tiding of great joy! This is a moment of grace, one of many that our dear Lord showers upon those filled with his love. It is a sign unto you that Heaven is real, Christ is risen, and you need not be afraid."

"What do you mean? The cave is a portal?" Elizabeth asked, intent on understanding these events, intent on any answers the angelic vision could give her.

"There are doors to Heaven in many tabernacles, in many sanctuaries. There are doors in mountains, in lakes, in streams, in other sacred places that have been deemed good and righteous and necessary for mankind's salvation."

"But—"

"I must go. This is for you—from him." Michael handed her a scroll bound with a golden ribbon. "Remember, all is grace, all is joy. Be not afraid. And . . . Elizabeth, caring Elizabeth, tell the others."

Elizabeth watched the form return to a shimmering image and merge into the wall of icons (or so it seemed to her). Then she studied the parchment scroll she held in her hands.

"An angel spoke to me," she said to Gregory and Catherine, who watched her silently. "He gave me this scroll. From Abram. The angel Michael really did speak to me. I am not making this up. I am not crazy."

Gregory nodded. "I believe you. And you have the scroll."

"I believe you, too," Catherine said.

"I will look at this later." She slipped the scroll into her bag carefully, to be read privately, with her full attention. She turned to Gregory and Catherine. "Michael spoke from the icons. He left through the icons," she said in nearly a whisper, trying to understand what she herself was saying.

"Icons are said to be doors to Heaven," Gregory said, drawing closer to the gilded images. "It appears some might be literal doors to Heaven. We too can be icons, Father Brubaker often says, and now I think I know what he means. We are passages through which God's love, our Lord himself, can move. In this way our lives become sacraments."

Elizabeth nodded. "Perhaps." She stepped slowly to the stone slab that had been Abram's bed. The golden cloth remained, folded neatly. She lifted it and buried her face in the soft woven fabric, feathery light. "Oh, Abram," she said, "let me come too. Do not leave me behind," she whispered.

Just as Elizabeth thought her heart would break, joy rushed through her. She looked at the icons and smiled slowly. "I must write down what the angel said. It was so beautiful . . . but it is already fading." Elizabeth tried to hold on to the image and the words.

She turned to Gregory and Catherine. A phrase came to mind. "Michael said that Abram is another Elijah. And there are other portals or doors—this cave is a portal." She looked up at the dome-like ceiling. "Abram has gone home, you see."

"A portal?" Catherine asked.

Gregory nodded, his eyes wide, clearly trying to process what all this meant, if true. "Elijah was bodily carried to Heaven in a fiery chariot, witnessed by Elisha. And the Virgin Mary is said to have been *assumed*—raised bodily to Heaven. The best evidence for the truth of the Assumption of the Blessed Virgin Mary is that no one, no church, has ever claimed her body for the purpose of holy relics."

"And there are others," Elizabeth explained. "Michael said there are others we do not know about."

"We need to report that his body is no longer here," Gregory said.

"To the park rangers?" Catherine asked. "The police?"

"To Father Brubaker," Gregory said. "He will know what to do."

Catherine put her arm around Elizabeth. "Would you be up to visiting Father Brubaker this morning at the chapel? The Sunday service won't begin for another hour. I'm going to check on my Berkeley apartment and pack some fresh clothes. That is, if you want me to stay with you a little longer?"

Elizabeth nodded. "Please do stay with me at Tilifos if you can. I have intruded on your time already, but maybe one more day? Have I been terribly selfish?"

"I'd be happy to stay as long as you need me," Catherine said, her eyes full of concern.

"Thank you." Elizabeth wavered between grief and happiness. The joy she felt was all-consuming and she was not sure what she was to do with it, this massive delight, comforting her, gladdening her. She was not at all sure what to do about Abram either, his taking his body to Heaven like this. And then there was the scroll. If it was from Abram, she wanted to read it privately, to be strengthened by each word. "You go to the chapel and tell Father Brubaker. But could you drop me off at home? I need some time alone—to read this. Father Brubaker can call if he has any questions."

"Steven and Caleb can guard the cave for now," Gregory said. "It needs guarding, even if it's empty." His gaze rested on the stone bed and the glimmering folded blanket.

"It is not empty," Elizabeth said quickly. "It is not empty." She glanced at the icons shimmering on the wall. "It is not empty," she repeated a third time.

Chapter 56

Sunday afternoon Catherine and Gregory walked up the Angel Mountain trail above the sandstone caves, having returned to check on Caleb and Steven.

Catherine had visited her apartment after the morning service at Saint Joseph's Chapel. She picked up her mail, packed a bag, and changed into jeans, a green tee, a pullover sweatshirt, a tan anorak, and her lace-up walking shoes. She had pulled her hair back to the nape of her neck with a tortoiseshell barrette. Gregory had exchanged his blazer for a hoodie.

They fell into a comfortable silence, stepping quietly along the path, roaming in their own thoughts. The only sound she heard was the caw of a bird and the padding of their feet on the dirt trail.

Saint Joseph's morning liturgy lingered in Catherine's memory. The booming organ, the procession with candles and incense, the robed clergy and acolytes—all these things—merged into her sense of being in another world for that hour. Her memories of visiting the chapel along with her mother enriched the experience. Doors seemed to be opening to new ways of thought and feeling. She would try and welcome these open doors, in spite of years of doubt.

Gregory had stood beside her, but she was not yet ready to evaluate what he meant to her. Too much had happened in too short a time, and on this Sunday morning she had observed and absorbed the rituals dancing through the sacred space as if an answer would eventually be apparent.

Father Brubaker's sermon struck a painful note of recognition, as he spoke about the national holiday of Thanksgiving, coming up on Thursday. What was the opposite of giving thanks, he asked. Complaints and grievances, he answered. Entitlements. He went on to explain that since folks had stopped giving thanks, depression and suicide rates had soared. He said that selfishness leads to ingratitude, which leads to depression. Counting blessings without ceasing leads to thanksgiving, which leads to happiness.

Was it that simple? Simply being thankful? Being less selfish? Yet from every source, it seemed, the world told her to do the opposite, to find herself, to pamper herself, to express herself, to take care of herself . . . the list of self-centered activities demanded by the world was endless. Me, me, me. Today's culture said to consider others as objects, means to an end, to judge others according to how they affected me, me, me. Trigger warnings were needed when others or other ideas caused discomfort. Today the culture advised to *use* others for self-gratification.

Perhaps her father would still be around if he had given thanks when he was told of her diagnosis. Perhaps then her life would have been different, with a father who cared, a father she knew. Yet even thinking along these lines sounded like complaining on her part.

They reached the vista point where they had stopped on Thursday's walk and looked out to the rolling hills. A breeze had somewhat cleared the earlier haze and they could see a low fog in the far distance. Gregory stood silently alongside her, as though he simply wanted to be near.

She turned to him. "The sun is low this time of year, even in midday."

He nodded. "Earth is orbiting at a different angle in winter. We don't get that direct sun overhead. Gives us those short days and long nights."

"The chapel was beautiful," she said.

"Yes, it was."

She moved to the wooden bench and sat down. He joined her.

"The fires are still blowing haze our way," she said. "We can't see very far."

"We need a good rain, especially in the north."

"Then there was the fire on the summit, and now the summit's closed."

"Someday we should hike to the summit," he said.

"Is there a trail all the way to the top?" She hoped she had the stamina for something like that.

"There are several trails that go to the summit. Best time is winter, actually, for the air has greater clarity, at least when it's clear." He laughed. "You know what I mean?"

"I think so. Summer has its own haze that shortens the viewing distance. Is that it?"

"Exactly."

"Do they know who set the fire at the summit? Why would anyone do that?" It seemed so peaceful out here, but violence and hate could erupt anywhere, she realized.

"Some kind of grievance or deep anger. The earthquake left a crevice in the top of the mountain. They need to explore it when it's safe. Any evidence could then be DNA tested."

Catherine recalled the news bulletins on Friday. "They put the fire out pretty quickly."

"That same night. It appears it didn't go far beyond the summit area, almost like there was a firebreak running in a circle around the peak. They said if the wind had come up there would have been way more damage, but the flames burned straight and up."

"Some called it a freaky occurrence. Some called it a miracle."

"It can happen," Gregory said. "I was staying in the Russian River area north of San Francisco when a kitchen fire destroyed a cabin. The surrounding forest and nearby cottages were untouched by the fire, because there was no wind. The fire burned straight up, and the only damage was that one cabin. At the time, some called it a miracle."

She gestured to the summit. "Maybe this was a miracle."

"They are beginning to speculate on any connection with Abram and his death, which happened around the same time, at least the same night."

Catherine nodded. "Abram! I wonder if there *is* a connection between Abram and the fire. The reporters seemed more interested in the pilgrimage yesterday and now they will conjecture about the body. There must be lots of people to interview."

"Yes," Gregory agreed. "There are many stories within the one story: Abram's gatherings, his preaching, his mysterious death, the pilgrims in procession to the cave to see his body. And there were the earthquakes, last Sunday and again on Thursday, coinciding with the beginning and end of Abram's preaching, the evening of his death. And now his disappearance on the following Sunday. The summit fire will be one of many stories told and retold."

"We are to sign statements as to what we saw or didn't see. Elizabeth too."

They fell silent, as Catherine reflected on the glowing body of Abram on Saturday and the absence of his body on Sunday, leaving the shimmering folded blanket and the indentation in the stone bed. The icons remained on their wall trellis, their light fading. She would never forget.

Chapter 57

They sat on the side of Angel Mountain, in quiet companionship.

Thinking about Abram and his glimmering cave, Catherine watched the shimmering light in the valleys below. On Thursday the tule fog from the east had obscured the lowlands, but today's haze was beginning to clear. A cold breeze had halted the coastal fog from the west and cleared the haze from the north. The November sun—a weaker winter sun, a white orb with less time in their sky—did its best to light up the world with autumn color. Patches of reds, golds, and greens emerged on the pale hillsides.

A hawk soared and a jay cawed. Something rustled in the bushes. Catherine was again acutely aware of the power of silence to amplify and enshrine the slightest sound.

"Father Brubaker is notifying the police," Gregory said, zipping his jacket against the chill. "They'll seal off the cave as a scene of investigation, if not a crime scene, at least for a time. We can check on Caleb and Steven on the way back. Hopefully the police will be there to relieve them soon. The brothers may need to make statements. The rangers can close off the sandstone tunnels and any access to the ledge."

"I wish I had seen Abram preaching."

"He spoke with authority and yet he spoke as though he—Abram—wasn't there. He sounded like he loved us so much that he completely forgot himself."

Catherine nodded. "Like the Thanksgiving sermon this morning?"

"Indeed, like the sermon. Loving others can be joyful. It's not what we do naturally—we're naturally selfish, being animals who have survived millennia, looking after ourselves first—but we can *learn* to love sacrificially. When we do, we find joy. It grows easier with practice."

"Like being rewarded?"

"In a way. Loving others—respecting and honoring each individual as a person made in God's image—is its own reward. The action and the blessing are one and the same, just as the sin is often its own punishment. We learn to obey God's law because the law is intended by our loving Creator to lead us to happiness.

"So we are selfish because of evolution?"

"Certainly survival encourages a kind of selfishness, self-regarding. But survival of the fittest and natural selection would also involve social patterns, choosing mates, raising families, getting along in tribes, communities, nations. The ones who get along are those who survive. Certainly within a species these natural selections occur. Cultures that devalue having children will die out sooner than those who value them, simply because of demographics, population.

"What about Adam and Eve disobeying God?"

"Eating of the fruit of the tree of knowledge was a kind of evolution, a selfish and disobedient choice."

Catherine could see pieces of the puzzle fitting into place. "In that sense, the Genesis story supports evolution, and vice versa."

Gregory nodded, thoughtful. "You may have something there. It needs careful wording, since God wants us to use our intelligence. Knowledge—when sought rightly and used rightly—is a good and holy thing. It's the disobedience that's the problem. It's the incorrect use of knowledge, without moral parameters, that becomes the challenge."

Catherine grew silent for a moment, then said quietly, "I received my Ancestors.com results. The report came through this morning via an email link to their site."

"Any surprises?"

"My percentages were mostly northern European. My mother said she was Irish, French, and Norwegian. Seems I'm similar."

"Mostly European?"

"A little Asian, Native American, and Caribbean as well."

"Like many of us. Each one of us is a melting pot, as they say, going back to Adam and Eve. What are you going to do with the information?"

"If I share the information online, a match might come up, and I might find out who my father is."

"Is that really important to you?"

"I always wanted to know. More from anger than love, I'm afraid."

"What difference would it make who he is? It's not who you are."

Catherine searched his eyes. They were thoughtful. "It's not who I am? You said something earlier about our choices being who we are?"

"Choices define us. But we are also unique combinations of many genes from many ancestors, which I admit your DNA test will identify to a degree. But we need to remember to add our choices since birth, the choices others have made for us, our environment—in your case, your father abandoning you balanced against your mother's love for you. They say we should even count our prayer life and church attendance, which, studies show, make people happier and less depressed."

"But you don't know the reason my father left," Catherine said abruptly, then regretted her tone. She rarely mentioned her mistaken diagnosis. Abortions happened all the time for reasons of abnormalities, including Down's, as well as reasons of convenience. No one would sympathize, she had assumed, and might even be hostile. Yet she had told Elizabeth, she recalled, but that was in the context of her job interview, relating the reason she had resigned. She felt she had to explain the personal aspect of the issue.

"No, I don't know why he left," Gregory said quietly.

In the ensuing silence Catherine tried to calm her beating heart. She inhaled deeply and looked out over the valleys and rolling hills spread out toward the west, toward the great Pacific Ocean, which couldn't be seen.

"I don't know why he left," Gregory repeated, "and you don't have to tell me."

"It's okay. I was diagnosed with Down's syndrome."

Gregory turned to her. "They misdiagnosed."

"And my father wanted me aborted. That's why he left. Actually my mother left him, she was so hurt. At least that's what she told me. She did her best for me, being two parents instead of one."

"Did she have family support?"

"None that I knew of. We were alone, the two of us, except for a few friends."

"Well, I'd like to add myself to the inner circle," he said, smiling. "I'm an orphan, you know."

She laughed. He did have a beautiful smile. "You mentioned you were raised by your aunt?"

"My parents were killed in a drive-by shooting in Denver. They happened to be in the wrong place at the wrong time."

"But you knew who they were, in terms of genetics."

"They died before the technology was available, as did Aunt Jane. But I never saw a need to understand their genetic makeup to find my own identity. I was driven to become a doctor to cure Parkinson's. That became my identity."

"And you became involved in genetic research."

He raised his brows and nodded, folding his hands. "Curing disease seemed a noble use of such powerful information."

"Leave the genetics to the scientists rather than the genealogists? Cures rather than family trees?"

"And the theologians perhaps, or ethicists, if you will. We should use genetics for good, not for ill. We need to consider the implications of such knowledge. Secrets kept a lifetime could go viral. I read recently where a family was nearly destroyed when the adult children discovered through genetic matches that they had half-siblings they never knew. Each of their parents had had affairs."

Catherine nodded, growing overwhelmed by the implications. "Genetic searches could have huge ramifications. Might encourage abortions."

"Might discourage adultery or casual relationships."

"The #MeToo movement—and sexual harassment of all kinds—could make use of such DNA evidence."

He shook his head with obvious concern. "I'd really like to see more parameters defining the use of this information, if possible. Perhaps that will be my mission. There are many sides to the genetic question, many facets to such knowledge, many repercussions, rather like an ever-branching tree of knowledge: the Garden of Eden all over again. Knowledge is a great responsibility. Gene editing is the new frontier, and many are worried we will be making permanent changes to the human race, for good or ill. But who decides?"

"Seems like Pandora's box at this point—beyond control."

"Forensic testing is worthy. As an example, we might learn who set the bonfire." He glanced toward the summit.

"How does that work, exactly?"

"It would depend on what they find, of course. If the DNA is degraded the odds of a complete profile are decreased. Bones often survive fires, and DNA samples can be taken from the marrow of teeth. Then the profile must be compared with others, either in a data bank or from hair samples, etc."

"In that case you would have to guess who the arsonist was," Catherine said, thinking back on the gatherings in the meadow.

"If they find anything, it will be part of a complete police investigation. 'Did anyone see someone suspicious that day?' they'll ask. That reminds me, I did see someone suspicious in the crowd during the week. I need to give the police the few photos I took."

"Really?"

"He appeared to be leading the antifa protest."

"There might be videos and you could pick him out." Catherine recalled the news reports and social media photos and filmings.

"If they find something on the mountain, it might help. Otherwise, probably not. The books burned were library books—UC library books. Didn't you work for the UC library?"

As Catherine recounted her time at the library and the terrible shooting of students from the fifth floor, she wondered aloud if the man might be the same.

"Could be. They may have DNA from that site."

"We should get back," she said, noticing the fading light.

"We should. The gates will close soon."

They stepped onto the path, and as they walked slowly down the hill, he reached for her hand. She didn't mind her hand in his, his hand in hers.

THURSDAY

Thanksgiving Day

Chapter 58

Elizabeth awoke on Thanksgiving Day to the sound of rain. Laddie had crept under the covers as winds howled and skies opened, deluging the parched Earth.

She pulled aside the damask panels and looked into the storm. The rain poured, obscuring the mountain and the cross, caressing and watering the Earth. She hoped the northern fires were out finally, that those who lost so much could now begin to rebuild their lives. She knew what devastation meant. She knew what rebuilding cost. She hoped there were not too many more fatalities, that the list would not continue to grow as rubble was sifted. She hoped the flooding that usually came with rains after fires would not be too severe.

She looked at the gray sky and marveled at the change in weather, so longed for. Mankind would always be at the mercy of nature, always seeking to tame it, finding shelter from its storms, food to eat, water to drink, air to breathe.

Thanksgiving. It was a day indeed to give thanks. She opened her gratitude journal. She was thankful for freedom, especially on this national holiday. She was thankful for her escape from the tyranny that threatened Greece—and the world—so long ago. She was thankful for the families that sheltered her in that terrible time. She was thankful for her brother, his life, and the time she shared with him. She was thankful for her husband, who had sheltered her in America and had taken Abram in as his own brother. She was thankful for Catherine, who had stayed with her this last week. She was thankful for Maria, who was already cooking downstairs. She was thankful for the aromas that drifted up the stairs and into her bedroom. Turkey. Gravy. Sweet potatoes. Stuffing. Cornbread. Maria's Thanksgiving tamales.

Elizabeth gave Laddie his insulin shot and soon joined Maria and Catherine in the kitchen. It appeared Maria had taught Catherine how to make French toast. Elizabeth sat at the pine table and listened to the sound of the rain tapping the windows and the espresso machine rumbling hot water through coffee pods. Catherine set a bowl of fruit salad in front of Elizabeth and smiled. "Good morning. It's raining!"

A timer rang, and Maria pulled the turkey from the oven, hissing in the deep roasting pan.

"Good morning, and thank you. Thank you for all you are doing to help me through this."

"It is for me to thank you," Catherine said as she returned to the kitchen to help Maria butter-baste the turkey and slide it back into the oven.

Elizabeth surveyed her table of guests.

These were the ones who accepted her invitation: Father Brubaker and his sister; Tony Mitchell and his wife; the brothers Caleb and Steven; Maria and her husband, her mother, and her elder son; Gregory; Catherine; Aunt Pat; and Annie. Laddie was hiding upstairs, far under the bed, in the deepest darkest corner.

They had all known Abram, or were closely connected to those who had known him, and Abram had said in his letter to invite any who had known him. These were the ones who had accepted the invitation to the Thanksgiving feast.

They had joined hands around the table as Father Brubaker said grace. Gregory carved the turkey. Maria passed the side dishes. Catherine poured the wine.

Elizabeth was thankful for them all, but the loss of Abram so recently, and the mourning of Samuel, which seemed never to end, still formed a gaping wound in her heart. How could she go on?

She rose from her chair, the scroll in hand. "Thank you all for coming. Abram left me this letter and asked that I read it to you today. It is his way of being here, sharing his love for you, and his thankfulness that you were a part of his life here on Earth."

Elizabeth read from the parchment scroll:

> Heaven, by the River
> Eternity
>
> My dear Elizabeth,

I am in Heaven now, but you are still on Earth. I am in the presence of God. I am happy.

Some have said I was so full of Heaven that I was no earthly good. But I learned on Earth that the only way to be of earthly good is to be full of Heaven.

Know that I experienced Heaven on Earth before my crossing into eternity. Know that Heaven can be found easily enough, if you seek it.

"Ha!" the priest cried, grinning and clapping his hands. Elizabeth continued:

Know that we have guardian angels who guide us to the Kingdom of Heaven. Mine appeared to me many times in the last days of my time on Earth. My good Angel Michael wrote these words down for me and kept them safe for you to read. All is grace!

There is a personal Judgment. I have repented my own failings and been forgiven. There will be a final and general Judgment when Christ returns to Earth and judges the living and the dead, and makes all things new. He will return to Earth in the same manner he ascended to Heaven. Keep watch.

As for these Judgments—and Heaven and Hell—the justice of God is to give man what he wants. In the end there are only two choices: to have God and in him everything, which we call Heaven, or to have nothing but yourself, which we call Hell.

Yet at every Eucharist we are judged as well, so in this sense we are already on the road to the kingdom. We confess, repent, and are forgiven. We ascend with the mystical presence of Christ, to this Heaven on Earth. With every Eucharist we are made new, renewed, reborn. With every Eucharist a new Heaven and Earth forms in our souls.

We are told to lift up our hearts unto the Lord. And we lift them up to the Lord of Heaven. We are told to give thanks unto our Lord God. And we give thanks unceasingly.

We are created to love one another, and we are created to be citizens of the Kingdom of Heaven. We pray thy kingdom come, and it will come and has come and is everywhere around us.

Learn the will of God and do it, for only those who do will enter the Kingdom of Heaven.

Enter the kingdom today and do not wait. The King is returning!

With the love of God that passeth all understanding (and it really does),

Abram Levin+

P.S. Elizabeth: Mama and Papa and Samuel are here and send
their love. So is Catherine's mother, Ellen, Gregory's parents,
and his Aunt Jane. The bishop is here too! There are many, many
other friends and family. All is grace!

Elizabeth handed the scroll to Catherine for safekeeping in a drawer
in the dining sideboard. Through the window, Elizabeth saw that the rain
had stopped for a time. Billowing clouds opened to a patch of blue outlining
Angel Mountain. The white cross glimmered in the grass in the sudden sun.
Elizabeth raised her glass. "To Abram, with thanksgiving!"

They raised their glasses, echoing, "To Abram, with thanksgiving!"

Other toasts followed: to America, to pilgrims, to family, to faith, to
friends, to our many blessings beyond counting!

Elizabeth noticed that Gregory and Catherine sat opposite one another
and at this moment their gaze met. For the time, Elizabeth lived inside their
gaze, thankful.

And beyond Catherine and Gregory, through the window, a rainbow
arced over Angel Mountain, a prism holding the colors of creation, a crown
of Heaven over Earth.

And they lived happily ever after, in a world without end.

Epilogue

Within a year, Abram's Cave became a shrine, some giving Abram the title Saint, others calling him Prophet. Numerous healings were reported by those baptized. Pilgrims continued to pray at the waters, the cross, and the cave. Abram's body was not found, at least not on Earth, and rumors abounded as to what actually happened.

Catherine and Gregory took charge of a foundation to oversee the cave, the pond, the cross, and the meadow. The foundation purchased the necessary access for pilgrims. To this end, Catherine was given Villa Tilifos to run as a retreat house for pilgrims.

Father Brubaker baptized and counseled. Others joined him, seeking hope, seeking happiness, seeking God.

Elizabeth passed away at home on Christmas Eve, as the pilgrims wound their way to the cave, carrying candles to a Christmas creche in the sandstone sanctuary. She saw a ladder to Heaven and began to climb, for Abram and Samuel beckoned her from the top. Laddie followed. Elizabeth climbed, one rung at a time, her joy growing with each step. She was grateful, so very grateful, to finally join her brother and husband, and with Laddie along too. When she arrived at the top, she entered a wood, and Abram and Samuel led her (and Laddie) through the woods to the river. She was delighted when she arrived at the river, for she discovered that Laddie could talk! He had a great deal to tell her, mostly good memories, but mainly he wanted her to know how thankful he was that she took such good care of him during his time on Earth.

Elizabeth's journals were published, alongside a biography of Abram (there was talk of a movie) so that the world would never forget to cherish the dignity of each and every person on this good Earth.

The cave was a portal (as mentioned by Michael), one of many doors from Earth to Heaven and from Heaven to Earth.

Catherine and Gregory became engaged in the spring, in the meadow near the pond, the cross, and the waterfall. They married in the late summer, in a simple ceremony in Saint Joseph's Chapel, presided over by Father Brubaker. Aunt Pat and Caleb were witnesses. In the fullness of time, Catherine and Gregory had many children who enjoyed hiking Angel Mountain and running through the sandstone tunnels. They acted out the story of the holy hermit who renamed—and reclaimed—the mountain, and who once lived in the sandstone caves, preached from the promontory, and baptized from the pool. They called him Uncle Abram.

The Worthingtons supported the local animal shelters. Their home, Villa Tilifos, was never without cats and dogs, no longer unwanted and unloved. Catherine opened a library devoted to Western civilization at Villa Tilifos, so that others could benefit from Elizabeth's remarkable collection.

From time to time Catherine dreamed Elizabeth visited her, or was it a vision? In the dream Elizabeth had found her mother, Ellen. They were best friends in Heaven.

Gregory finished his memoir, appeared on several talk shows marketing the book, then joined a family medical practice associated with Walnut Creek Hospital. He submitted articles occasionally to science journals, hoping to influence responsible use of genetic research. Gene editing had moved into gene building, and bioterrorism was an additional threat. He supported the new Stanford Center for Biomedical Ethics and spoke at their conferences regularly.

Catherine and Gregory attended Saint Joseph's Chapel, always bringing fresh roses for the Lady Altar. There they pondered the holy light that beamed through the high windows onto the crucifix, the tabernacle, and the altar. Caleb and Steven served Mass at the chapel during their years at the university. Caleb wanted to go to seminary but Father Brubaker made him wait until he finished his undergraduate degree in history. Steven learned to play the organ and was considering a career in biochemistry.

The bomb that Malcolm sent in the mail didn't go off as planned, but provided fingerprints and DNA for the police, which they added to the open case. They never found Malcolm's remains, for the crevice closed up within the next few days. The DNA samples retrieved were not human and unidentifiable. Malcolm's father sued the university and the state of California to overturn the student privacy laws regarding grades and enrollment—he felt he and other parents had the right to see such grades, given they were footing the bill—but most legal professionals thought his case was slim. He wondered what happened to his son, and eventually accepted his strange disappearance.

Father Albert Brubaker repeated over and over, "All is grace, all is grace. God is love, God is love," as he introduced more seekers to Christ, always keeping the red tabernacle candle lit and flaming brightly.

Endnotes

1   The *Te Deum laudamus*, in *The Book of Common Prayer* (BCP), 1928, 10–11. Tradition has it that Saint Ambrose (fourth century) sang this prayer as he baptized Saint Augustine of Hippo in the Milan cathedral. The prayer is often sung and follows the outline of the Apostles' Creed.
2   The *Venite*, Psalm 95, in *BCP*, 9.
3   The Beatitudes, Matthew 5:3–12.
4   "Great Is Thy Faithfulness," Thomas Chisholm, 1923, based on Lamentations 3:23.
5   The story of Abraham and Sarah, Genesis 18.
6   The *Jubilate Deo*, Psalm 100, in *BCP*, 15.
7   "All flesh is grass . . . ," Isaiah 40:6–8.
8   The Kingdom of Heaven parables, Matthew 13.
9   The descriptions of Heaven are taken from Francis J. Hall, *Eschatology* (New York: American Church Union, 1972), 156, 157, 158; and from 1 Corinthians 15:42–43, 52–53, Psalm 17:15, 1 John 3:2.
10 The *Laudate Dominum*, Psalm 148, in *BCP*, 524.
11 The *Angelus*, ancient noon prayers based on the Annunciation, Luke 1.
12 "What Wondrous Love Is This?," American folk hymn, 1811, Second Great Awakening.
13 "This Is My Father's World," Maltbie Davenport Babcock, 1901.
14 Numbers 6:24–26.
15 Isaiah 40:3–5.
16 "Jesus saith unto him, I am the way, the truth, and the life: no man cometh unto the Father, but by me." John 14:6.
17 "All Creatures of Our God and King," William Henry Draper, 1919, based on "Canticle of the Sun" by Saint Francis of Assisi, 1225, based on Psalm 148.
18 The Ministration of Holy Baptism, *BCP*, 280.
19 Aleksandr I. Solzhenitsyn, *The Gulag Archipelago* (New York: Harper and Row, 1974).
20 Psalm 19:1–5, in *BCP*, 363.
21 "Crown Him with Many Crowns," Matthew Bridges and Godfrey Thring, 1851, based on Revelation 19:12.
22 2 Corinthians 3:18.
23 Dante Alighieri, *Paradisio*, 1320.
24 Augustine of Hippo, *City of God*, bk. 22, ch. 30.
25 "Holy, Holy, Holy," Reginald Heber, 1827, based on Revelation 4:1–11.

Author's Notes

HEAVEN

We speak of Heaven with images and metaphors, for we have no other way to describe its glory and delight. These images reflect Holy Scripture (both Old and New Testaments) and the writings of theologians for over two thousand years.

Thus I have pulled together a number of sources that consistently reflect scriptural references to Heaven and eternal life.

In Heaven, Christ is seated at the right hand of God (Eph 1:20).

Heaven is the tabernacle (Rev 21:1–18), reflecting fellowship with God and the seat of Christ as the sacrificial Lamb and High Priest who intercedes.

As the holy city of Jerusalem, Heaven is full of splendor, protected by high walls of jasper and foundations of precious stones, with golden streets and pearl gates, protecting the redeemed, named in Christ's Book of Life (Rev 21:10–27).

God's glory provides all necessary light. God and the Lamb are the temple, so there is no need for temples (Rev 21:9–27).

The throne is in the middle of the city, and a pure river runs from the throne. The tree of life on the riverbank bears twelve fruits and healing leaves for the nations. In this way, Heaven is seen as a garden (Rev 22:1–5).

In Heaven we shall see God's face, and his name will be on our foreheads, anticipated by the ashen cross drawn on our foreheads on Ash Wednesday (Rev 22:4).

Christ is worshiped by heavenly hosts of angels and by the redeemed, men and women from all races and nations, "the spirits of just men made perfect" (Heb 12:23).

Saint Paul speaks of the third Heaven (2 Cor 12:1ff.), but other New Testament references are to one Heaven.

The names of those redeemed are recorded in Heaven (Heb 12:23).

Heaven is a fulfillment of our life on Earth, a unique and individual completion of who we were and are created to be.

In the Nicene Creed, Heaven is referenced:

"I believe in one God the Father Almighty, Maker of heaven and earth, And of all things visible and invisible: And in one Lord Jesus Christ . . . Who for us men and for our salvation came down from heaven, And was incarnate by the Holy Ghost of the Virgin Mary, And was made man: And was crucified also for us under Pontius Pilate; He suffered and was buried: And the third day he rose again according to the Scriptures: And ascended into heaven, And sitteth on the right hand of the Father: And he shall come again, with glory, to judge both the quick and the dead; Whose kingdom shall have no end" (*BCP*, 71).

And in the Holy Eucharist, the Mass, the *Sanctus* refers to the ongoing praise of the heavenly hosts:

"Therefore with Angels and Archangels, and with all the company of heaven, we laud and magnify thy glorious Name; evermore praising thee, and saying, Holy, Holy, Holy, Lord God of hosts, Heaven and earth are full of thy glory: Glory be to thee, O Lord Most High" (Isa 6:3; Rev 4:1–11; *BCP*, 77).

The image of the woods of the cross is my own, as is the use of Jacob's ladder. The image of the cross as living and life-giving is often portrayed in the tradition of flowering a white Easter cross, turning a cross of death into a cross of life.

Many hymns sing of Heaven, reflecting Holy Scripture.

And who knows? These images may be literal. To what degree, it matters little, since their essence of joy has been promised to us by Christ.

LOCATIONS

The campus library is not meant to be a specific location on the UC campus. None of the UC libraries overlook Sproul Plaza.

Mount Diablo, the sandstone caves, and the neighboring towns of Lafayette, Walnut Creek, and Danville do exist, as does the Queen of Heaven Cemetery to the north of Lafayette. The layout of the trails in this story is fictional.

Saint Joseph of Arimathea Anglican Chapel (traditional Episcopal) exists and is situated one block from campus on the corner of Durant and Bowditch, built in 1974. A parish, formed from the Berkeley community as well as students, worships there regularly. The chapel is known for its excellent acoustics, and the pipe organ, on loan from the university, is tuned to early music tonality.